THE SHAMEFUL SUICIDE OF WINSTON CHURCHILL

PETER MILLAR is a British journalist, critic and author, named Foreign Correspondent of the Year 1989 for his reporting of the later days of the Cold War and the fall of the Berlin Wall for *The Sunday Times*. He is the author of *All Gone to Look for America, 1989 The Berlin Wall: My Part in Its Downfall*, *The Black Madonna* and the translator of several German-language books into English including the best-selling *White Masai* by Corinne Hofmann, and *Deal With the Devil* by Martin Suter.

THE SHAMEFUL SUICIDE

of

WINSTON CHURCHILL

PETER MILLAR

ARCADIA BOOKS

Arcadia Books Ltd
15–16 Nassau Street
London W1W 7AB

www.arcadiabooks.com

First published in Great Britain by Arcadia Books 2011

Copyright Peter Millar © 2011

ISBN 978-1-906413-85-9

Typeset in Minion by MacGuru Ltd
Printed and bound in Finland by Bookwell

Arcadia Books supports PEN, the fellowship of writers who work together to promote literature and its understanding. English PEN upholds writers' freedoms in Britain and around the world, challenging political and cultural limits on free expression.
To find out more, visit www.englishpen.org or contact English PEN, Free Word Centre, 60 Farringdon Road, London EC1R 3GA

Arcadia Books distributors are as follows:

in the UK and elsewhere in Europe:
Turnaround Publishers Services
Unit 3, Olympia Trading Estate
Coburg Road
London N22 6TZ

in the USA and Canada:
Dufour Editions
PO Box 7
Chester Springs
PA, 19425

in Australia/New Zealand:
The GHR Press
PO Box 7109
McMahons Point
Sydney 2060

in South Africa:
Jacana Media (Pty) Ltd
PO Box 291784,
Melville 2109
Johannesburg

'Should the German people lay down their arms ... over all this territory, which, with the Soviet Union included, would be of enormous extent, an Iron Curtain would descend.'

Joseph Goebbels
Das Reich **newspaper, 23 February 1945**

'I must tell you that a socialist policy is abhorrent to British ideas on freedom. There is to be one State, to which all are to be obedient in every act of their lives. This State, once in power, will prescribe for everyone: where they are to work, what they are to work at, where they may go and what they may say, what views they are to hold, where their wives are to queue up for the State ration, and what education their children are to receive. A socialist state could not afford to suffer opposition – no socialist system can be established without a political police. They would have to fall back on some form of Gestapo.'

Winston Churchill
Election address, 1945

'History will be kind to me, because I intend to write it.'

Winston Churchill, 1948

'... though God cannot alter the past, historians can; it is perhaps because they can be useful to Him in this respect that He tolerates their existence.'

Samuel Butler
Erewhon Revisited, **1901**

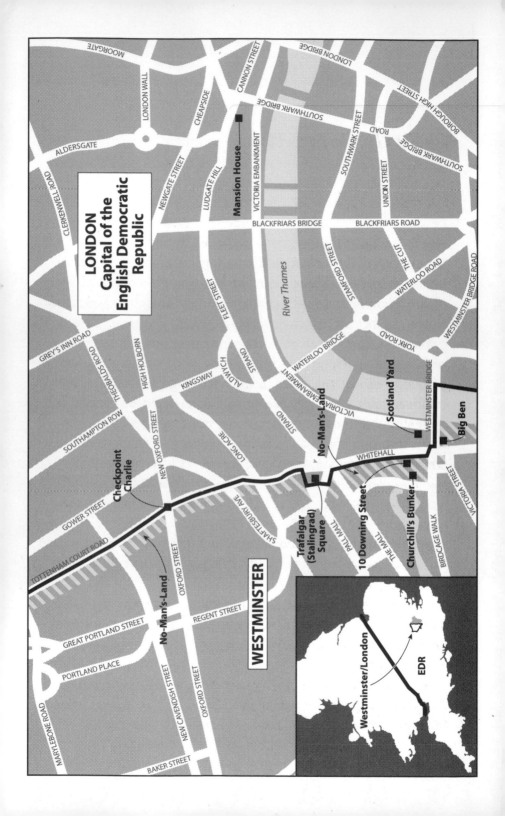

OVERTURE: *Zero Hour*

Downing Street, London, September 1949

The house that sat at the heart of the world had no name, just a number like any other. And had long since been reduced to rubble. Like every other. War was the real great leveller. But even in destruction the semblance of similarity between this house and any other was false.

From the centre of a global web of countless colonies, domains and dependencies, a local filigree network spread beneath the ground. Beneath the fallen masonry, the eighteenth-century brickwork that had crumbled into dust, the shards of marble from staircases and fireplaces, emerging from what once had been cellars for wine and coal, a labyrinth of debris-littered tunnels still survived, leading like a choked artery to the crippled body politic's residual nerve centre, which stubbornly still functioned even though its life support system was slowly, surely, failing.

Even here the dust permeated; the last tangible traces of grandeur ground to grit stuck to the skin and irritated the eyes. Dust to dust. The old man closed his eyes to shut out reality. But he could not shut out the noise, though it was more felt than heard: a dull, persistent rumbling, broken by intermittent juddering thuds. As if the earth was shaking. As well it might.

All eyes were on him, if only surreptitiously. In the specially designed, one-piece, grey pinstriped 'siren suit' that he referred to as his 'rompers', he had so long resembled a big, bumptious, cigar-puffing baby. But not any more. He looked shrunken, wizened, as though he had surrendered at last, if only to his years. He no longer paced, not even with the aid of his stick, but emerged from his sleeping quarters to stalk the Map Room sombrely, oblivious to the flickering light from the caged safety light that with every advancing shock wave swayed above his head like on the deck of a ship in a storm.

The telephone lines were silent now, the red, white and black on the centre table no longer linked their attendant lieutenant colonels to distant command centres that had long since collapsed. In the radio room pretty girls with drawn faces and tremblingly rigid upper lips, eavesdropped on the end of the world: a high-pitched, scratchy, chimpanzee chatter of distant voices interspersed with crackle and the soaring, dipping banshee howl as they chased up and down the frequencies for the ghosts on the airwaves. In an ever more alien ether. Tortuously twisted hairclips beside the mugs of half-drunk, cold, weak tea testified to the terrible tension that gnawed at their innards.

Occasionally, increasingly rarely, contact would be made. And held. Sometimes, only sometimes, the voices in the ether asked for orders. The answer they were given was always the same. The same as it had been for days now: 'Hold on as long as you can.' No one dared address the follow-up: 'And then?' Just as no one dared approach the old man. The rule had, in any case, always been 'speak when you're spoken to'. And he hadn't spoken now for more than twenty-four hours. The man famed for holding forth for hours on end, with no more audience than a pet dog, had been reduced to a sinister silence. At least in what passed for public.

In recent days he had retired only rarely to the little bed in his cramped quarters off the Map Room, armed as ever with whisky, though even that was now in short supply. The champagne had long gone, the empty magnums of Pol Roger a mocking memory of better times. He slept, if at all, for no more than an hour or two at a time, emerging, glass in hand, to stare at the 'big board', watching bleakly as one piece after another was removed. Like a giant chess game. An endgame.

Except that while the enemy had been playing chess, he had been playing poker. Bluffing to the end. He had taken the big gamble, and seen the cards fall against him, just as they had done more than thirty years ago at Gallipoli, on the Turkish coast. In another war. Another lifetime. Lady Luck favoured those who dared, he had believed. But Lady Luck was just another tart. All he had got was the quick fuck. And now it was his back against the wall. He almost smiled at the coarse metaphor, but the time for smiles was past. As was the time for metaphors.

Fine phrases had not been enough. The blood had run dry. The sweat had been wasted, the toil in vain. There was nothing left but the tears. He had been defeated on the beaches, defeated on the landing grounds, defeated in the fields and in the streets. He, and those who had put their trust in him.

On the wall next to his bed the great map of the British Isles, with its shoreline, cliffs and beaches colour-coded according to their defensiblity, was defaced with the string and pins that charted the inevitable encroachment of the red tide.

In the Map Room itself the great geophysical charts that had once allowed him to watch his erstwhile allies' expansion from the depths of the steppes to Berlin and beyond had been torn down long before they became his enemies and reached the English Channel. The scale had changed by then; the global had become personal. The map now was one with which he had been familiar all his life – the map of London – one on which he had hoped he would never have to play the terrible game of war, let alone see his playing chips reduced to this. The markers with the familiar emblems of proud regiments represented little more than remnants, huddled together like sheep in a pen.

He could barely bring himself to think of the reality they represented, the reality above his head: London's familiar streets transformed into a battleground with bus shelters turned into barricades, taxi ranks become tank traps, the last ditch defenders – little more than boys some of them – crouching with bazookas behind Regency balustrades and East End dustbins, from Peckham to Piccadilly, in burnt-out pubs and the smoking remains of Pall Mall clubs. All equal at last, in their final hours.

With a brusque, angry gesture he swept the markers away.

The old man took the smouldering stub of his fat Havana cigar reluctantly from his mouth and ground it out on the fine-tooled leatherwork of his desk. Then he stood for a moment transfixed by the sight of the crumbling ash. Ashes to ashes. Like the taste in his mouth. His heart was heavy as he took down the Sam Browne belt and the holstered semi-automatic Colt that had served him so well. He knew what he had to do. There was only one way out now.

The girls on the silent switchboard peeked out silently as he pulled on his khaki greatcoat and his peaked cap. Then, leaning heavily on his stick, he made for the door that he had not used for nearly three weeks. The door that led upstairs, to the world above, to Armageddon.

One of the girls made to go and help him, but her colleague held her back with a restraining arm and tears in her eyes. No, her look said, though like the rest of them she said nothing. If words failed even him, what could anyone else say? Let him *go, her eyes said. To do what he has to do. It's over. For all of us. Nonetheless, the girl got up to go and wash her face, to dry her tears.*

Behind the eyes that held back tears, there was, for the first time, also fear. They had heard the stories, of the butchery, the wanton savagery and the wholesale rape. Of the women in Dover, Hastings and Brighton who had blackened their faces with coal dust, dressed in drab overcoats and pulled their grandfathers' darned woollen socks over their legs. And still had not been spared.

As the old man passed them, those he was leaving to their own fate, he wondered if he ought to make a gesture, to say goodbye. But he no longer knew how to face them. He prayed they would escape the worst, though he doubted it.

Disguises would do him no good. His face was familiar the world over. Even in the benighted ranks of the ignorant enemy. He let his hand reach inside the greatcoat, settle on the familiar pistol grip. Then he turned the handle on the reinforced steel door and took the first step on the staircase that led up to what was left of the world, and to his own appointment with destiny.

And those that watched him go, or for form's sake pretended not to notice, knew that what they were witnessing was a death. Not the death of a man – what was one more amid so many? – but of an empire. And an era. From now on there would be a new world order.

Already the world above looked changed beyond recognitions, a world turned on its head. His tired, bloodshot eyes blinked beneath the weary wrinkled lids and smarted from the cordite in the acrid air. A cacophony assaulted his ears, of screaming sirens, howling aircraft engines, the staccato chatter of distant machine-gun fire and the dull oppressive persistent percussion of artillery. Closer to hand, he could hear the mechanical screech of cogs and cranks that hauled heavy armour across the fallen brickwork and shattered Portland stone facades, the T-34s and the new, monstrous Stalin tanks, remorselessly grinding their way over the ruins. Coming closer by the moment.

Stumbling, frightened – he admitted it to himself as he would have done to no one else – he peered through the dust-choked air past the remnants of Downing Street to the ruins of Whitehall, then turned his gaze in the other direction.

Winston Spencer Churchill, First Lord of the Treasury, 41st Prime Minister of the United Kingdom, Commander-in-Chief of imperial forces drawn from five continents, the man who had once boasted that the British empire and its Common-wealth might last a thousand years, wiped a tear from his eye. As he stumbled towards what had once been the green oasis of St James's Park, its trees long since felled for firewood, he hefted the weighty revolver in his hand. He knew he no longer had a choice.

Behind the plinth of the Clive statue, peering over the toppled bronze statue of the empire's first great hero, the insignificant little figure, with her woolly hat and tear-streaked cheeks could not believe her eyes but the image remained imprinted on her retinae forever.

Chapter 1

Bermondsey, East London, 1989

Fog makes fools of us all. You see shapes in the shadows, where there are no shadows, no shapes. In a fog, without noticing it, you can bump into reality. Or worse.

His heart was pounding, his pulse loud in his ears. He breathed, when he dared, in short, wheezing gasps. The fog was already deep in his lungs. At his back the brick wall was cold, damp, slimy with mould, the broken paving slabs beneath his feet wet, slippery and treacherous. A wrong step risked a fall. If he fell they would be on him in a heartbeat.

He sniffed the fetid night air, a hare seeking the scent of the fox. How far away were they? These were their streets. Their city. Their goddamn fog. It was in streets like these, just across the river, that Jack the Ripper had eviscerated a dozen young women. Was this how they had felt as the predator closed in?

Footsteps sounded in the opaque yellow-grey emptiness behind him. Uneven. Hesitant. Those who made them were as aware as he was of the slightest noise in a world without vision. They were near. Nearer than he had thought possible. He didn't know for sure how many there were. Three. Maybe four. Maybe more. More than enough to take him down.

He had to move. But the sound of running feet would be like a homing beacon. Even if he knew which direction to take. He strained his hearing, moving his head slowly from side to side as if his small, tightly pinned-back ears were radar scanners. But there was nothing. Just the fine rain falling invisibly on wet streets. A sinister susurrus that seeped from the smog might have been guarded whispering. Or distant car tyres in the drizzle. It faded away.

Hugging the slimy wall behind him, he slid his foot silently along the pavement, holding his breath, his fingers creeping along the damp brickwork, until they reached a window, a cold glass pane of unthreatening darkness. There would be no muted glimmer to betray his passage.

Beyond the window, a door, old wood with peeling paint, fronting right onto the street. Then another window, also in darkness. Then another door. Even in bright daylight he could get lost in these alleyways that ran between ancient warehouses, punctuated here and there by a rubble-filled gap, like the remains of a rotted tooth: the lingering legacy of the Blitz. Or the Liberation. Whatever they called it. Whatever.

He could hide amidst the rubble. But not forever. There were hours before dawn. He imagined himself crouching in frozen numbness behind some toppled chimney stack until the weak grey daylight revealed his pursuers sitting there watching him with sardonic smiles.

He paused. And caught the ghost of other footsteps stopping too. Almost an echo, but not quite. Too close for that. Involuntarily he caught his breath. With the chilling casualness of an old friend putting a hand on his shoulder to soften the blow of bad news, someone, in terrifying proximity, said his name aloud.

He ran then. As he knew they meant him to. Feet slapping on the wet pavement, his feet and theirs, loud after so much studied silence. The distance that separated them rapidly shrinking. Straight ahead. A wall loomed. Faceless brick. Too high to scale. Right, then left. How regular was the street pattern? How well did they know it? Was he running nowhere? In circles? Into a trap? Into the river?

The river. A fool's gamble. But the leanest odds were better than none. A mouthful of polluted water could be fatal, but less certainly than a bullet in the brain. Which way? The Thames here twisted in giant loops permeated by the docks. And in any case he had lost all sense of direction.

He took a left. There was a distinct slope away from him. Fuzzy dark angular shapes of iron pulleys and winches protruded overhead. If he could find a way into one of the ancient Victorian structures they might never find him. But the iron doors would be locked, with steel bars on the few accessible windows.

The street was cobbled here, treacherously slippery. The long line of warehouses curved around towards the left, broken by tiny alleyways, some barely the width of a man's shoulders. Some, he knew, were dead ends, giving access only to locked side doors and cellars. Somewhere around here was the area known as Jacob's Island, which Charles Dickens had called the 'most pestilential part of the metropolis'. The villainous Bill Sykes had lost his footing here and been sucked under by the Thames mud.

Cold sweat poured down the inside of his shirt. Too damn old for this game. But then he hadn't expected to be playing it. Somewhere along here there was an old public house that backed onto the river. If only he could find it. From his left came a low, eerie groan of metal on metal that could have been an inn sign creaking on its chains. He stopped and held his breath and in that instant realised that he could no longer hear the sound of his pursuers.

Was it possible? Did he dare believe, even for a second, that he might have evaded them? They would have expected him, after all, to head west. He knew, of course, only too well the temptation of the desperate man to clutch at any straw of hope and was determined not to yield to it. Even so, the emotion that flooded through him – along with sheer unbridled terror as something rough and hairy descended over his head and constricted his windpipe in a brutal choking grip – was acute disappointment.

'Ssshh!' said the voice in the darkness, strangely, terrifyingly familiar. 'Ssshh!'

Chapter 2

The most sinister thing about portraits of the dead, Detective Inspector Harry Stark had always been told, was the way their eyes followed you. He had heard how in old castles there used to be peepholes concealed behind the eyes of ancestral images on the walls, and that those who were spied upon could not tell the difference. It was not a rule that applied to the two dead men whose photographs hung on the wall behind his desk in New Scotland Yard: Vladimir Ilyich Lenin and Clement Richard Attlee.

Every time Stark turned to glance up at the two photographs looking over his shoulder what struck him first of all was indeed their eyes. Far from following you, the eyes of both men stared straight ahead, full of certainty, seeing nothing. There could be no peepholes hidden behind those dead eyes. But then who needed peepholes when the walls had ears?

Stark had not been born when Attlee had 'seen the light', as the history books had it, and trampled on the old ogre's fresh grave. But he did not question the presence of the two portraits on his wall, any more than he questioned that of their latter-day incarnation, the portly, grey-haired Arthur Harkness, in the trades union and city council offices, national railway stations or in the shabby surgeries of the National Health Service.

Stark looked around at the walls of his own office and let out a soft sigh. There were times when he wished the Metropolitan People's Police would splash out on a bit more colour. Nothing gaudy or extravagant, just an alternative to the ubiquitous government magnolia emulsion. Even just a fresh lick. It must have been a fine room once, back in the 1890s when the great Gothic palace of New Scotland Yard with its high gables, mansard windows, tall Tudoresque chimneys and fairytale turrets in red-and-white-striped brick had soared above the recently laid out Embankment, then named for Queen Victoria rather than the 'Victory of Socialism'. He would have looked down on the river across a sea of pale green leaves on the young lime trees that lined the pavement as the horse-drawn carriages of the gentry trotted by.

Hard to imagine now. The trees were chopped down in the winter of 1949–50 to provide fuel for the freezing population in the bombed and blasted ruins. The building itself bore the usual pockmark shrapnel scars from the last-ditch defence put up by those who had failed to recognise their impending liberation. Not to mention the great hole carved in the Portland stone of the main entrance, *prima facie* evidence of a direct hit from a T-34 tank shell.

It was widely believed that the shell had been fired by the selfsame T-34 that now stood a hundred metres or so away on a plinth by the river, where once an ancient Egyptian obelisk had stood, as a permanent memorial to the Liberation. On any ordinary day, when the long hours of the afternoon ticked away with nothing more challenging on his desk than another mound of perennial paperwork, Stark would look down on the old tank, before involuntarily letting his eyes drift along the Embankment to that other memorial of the dark days of 1949, the blackened stump of the great Victorian tower that had once housed a bell called Big Ben. And in front of it, closer, more familiar, the long, barrel-topped, three-metre-high concrete symbol of the post-war order: the Anti-Capitalist Protection Barrier. Or as most people called it, on either side, the Wall.

Was it really that different, he wondered sometimes, late at night, on the other side of the Wall, in the other London, 'Westminster', the anomalous enclave left behind by the sweeping red tide of the Liberation? An occupied colonial outpost under American imperialist control, the official press called it; a consumer paradise of free speech according to the radio and television broadcasts that found their way into the ether. But then they were paid for and run by the Americans. And the Yanks would say anything. Wouldn't they? 'The American dream is the workers' nightmare' the slogans said. 'Not so much free men as wage slaves!' Stark knew them as well as everyone else. But 'wage slave' was only a label, Stark mused to himself as he fed another triple carbon-flimsied form for recording the grievous crime of 'Misappropriation of the People's Property' – party jargon for someone nicking a jar of pickled eggs from the People's Own Pickled Eggs production line – into his ancient Hermes typewriter.

The paperwork was nothing new. His father had told him that. His father was why he had joined the police in the first place. Following in the old man's footsteps. There were those, both in the force and outside it, who respected him simply because he was 'Comrade Stark's Boy'. Not that he had been 'comrade' Stark when he first entered the 'old Met' back in the mid-1930s. The old man had been a staunch trades unionist but also a believer in the rule of law. He had joined the army on the outbreak of war in 1939, believing strongly in the need to fight the Hitler-fascists, but had not taken long to express his doubts after the 1945 'continuation' when Churchill and the Yanks had enlisted the remnants of the post-Hitler *Wehrmacht* in their crusade to stop the spread of communism into the heart of Europe. They were 'fighting history', old man Stark had muttered privately to trusted friends. And so it had turned out. He had been one of the first to sign up enthusiastically for his old job in the rechristened Metropolitan People's Police.

Adding a single word to the force's title hadn't changed the essence of what they did, he had told his son, and that was catching crooks, street-robbers, wife-beaters, rapists and conmen, making the world a decent place for decent folk. Solid working-class values. English values. Those were the words still ringing in young Harry's ears when he signed up on his eighteenth birthday in 1975, barely eleven months after the old man's all-too-early death. He had either never heard or forgotten the stuff about endless forms detailing snaffled jars of pickled eggs.

The late afternoon sky was rapidly darkening over the Thames, rain spattering on the windows. Stark was sitting over a fifth mug of barely drinkable tea, literally twiddling his thumbs, when the telephone rang. The co-occupant of his office, a rotund, middle-aged, rosy-cheeked man with flat estuary vowels picked it up, listened for a few minutes, then turned to Stark with a mixture of astonishment and anxious excitement showing on his owlish face:

'We've got a murder, sir,' he said. 'Border police have found a body. Hanging underneath Blackfriars Bridge.'

Chapter 3

Stark felt sick. Sick to his stomach. Sick in his soul. It was partly a hangover from too many after-work pints with Lavery in the Red Lion the night before, but mostly the foul stench from the sludge of effluence called the River Thames, its repetitive heaving motion beneath him and the reek of diesel from the smoke-belching engine of the chugging little cutter belonging to the border patrol. But there was also something deeper, underlying, an intangible lingering melancholy of depression and disillusion.

Black smoke belched out of the rear end of the little grey-painted boat as it puttered through the murky river water. Up ahead the great black sooty dome of St Paul's loomed against a morbid yellow sky, still fractured after all these years like the cracked open shell of a bad boiled egg. It was as if the war had ended yesterday rather than forty years ago. The struggle for socialism, it seemed, was never ending.

The lumpen object hanging from the underside of Blackfriars Bridge, seeping already congealing blood. The cutter heaved to almost immediately beneath it and a crewman dropped anchor. Stark looked up reluctantly. Blood oozed through rough sacking like the pectin his mother squeezed through muslin at jam-making time, and dripped in slow, heavy globules to form a viscous puddle on the rusty deck: reddish brown and slimy, adding its own rich copper and iron aroma to the fetid cocktail of the ambient atmosphere. There was also the unmistakable smell of human faeces.

Stark took two swift paces to the port rail and threw up over the side.

'You all right, sir?' called an insufferably cheery voice behind him. 'Yes,' Stark lied. 'Fine. Just fine. Carry on, sergeant. You've got enough on your hands,' and he waved Lavery forward towards the abomination dripping onto the deck.

The bulky, thickset Kentishman grinned and called forward two uniformed constables to take the weight of the obscene object, while the border patrol crewman used a hooked blade on a long pole, used for God only knew what obscure riverine purpose, to saw through the thick rope that held the thing dangling there like some rotted Christmas decoration.

Stark let a few dangling threads of bitter bile fall into the stinking murk of the river, wiped his mouth and turned to watch them, a grim rictus on his normally placid face. He tried and failed to derive a note of optimism from the first signs of spring greenery on the vegetation growing from within the cracked eggshell of St Paul's. Opposite, the great monolithic chimney of Sir Giles Gilbert Scott's Bankside power station kicked out its own contribution to the spring smog as it struggled to provide the power for a city plagued by brownouts. Somewhere downriver, from one of the hulking Comecon freighters drifting out on the ebb tide from the Russia or East India docks, a ship's horn sounded, like the cry of some plaintive primeval dinosaur.

'Easy does it, lads,' called Lavery as the last remaining strands of rope parted and the two constables on the slippery deck took the full strain of the dead weight fallen into their hands. For a second one of them, caught out by the sudden change in equilibrium, lost his footing and slipped to one side. Stark thought that the whole caboodle was going to come crashing down on deck transforming tragedy into farce. But the man righted himself at the last minute, losing only his helmet, which Stark grabbed even as it rolled towards the edge of the deck.

He picked it up and held it in both hands. It occurred to him that if he had had it earlier, its bulbous shape might have been a tempting receptacle for the meagre contents of his bilious stomach.

Lavery awkwardly helped the two uniformed men lay the body horizontal on the deck. Stark turned the helmet around in his hands, instinctively giving a quick polish to the familiar enamel badge – the red-on-white cross of St George with the party's superimposed red rose that marked its owner as an officer of the Metropolitan People's Police. Once upon a time, when he started out in the force as a lowly beat bobby, he had worn one himself. He handed it back to the constable, who thanked him with just the ghost of embarrassment and put it back on, adjusting the strap around his chin. Propriety restored. We're still English after all, thought Stark.

'All right, all right,' called Lavery. 'Let's have a look then, shall we?'

Stark nodded, though the question had been rhetorical and directed to the two constables. Lavery was already grappling with the rope, trying to loosen its grip around what they assumed to be a human neck. The blood oozed on either side of it, in crimson bubbles. Stark looked away.

'No good, sir. I shall have to cut through the sacking.'

'Whatever you have to, sergeant. Whatever.'

They both knew there was no point. Whatever – whoever, Stark corrected himself – this gruesome parcel contained was already dead. The real work would be for the pathologist. But they had to be sure. If there was any chance …

'There we go. Oh, bloody hell …'

Lavery had used one of the constables' standard police-issue Red Army knives to slice through the sacking and reveal a human face. Or something that had once resembled one. Of the facial features themselves there was almost nothing left: just a mass of seared and torn tissue where eyes and nose should have been, as if it had exploded from within.

Even from where he stood, Harry Stark knew he had never seen anything like it in his life. But only because he had been lucky. This was the face of a man who had been executed, and not by hanging. That had been as gratuitous as it was grotesque. This was the unmistakable remains of someone shot in the back of the head. At close quarters. With the muzzle placed at the soft spot behind the base of the skull.

The two constables stood back, as did Lavery, waiting for the detective inspector to approach. But Stark was in no hurry. There was something deeply wrong about this.

When Lavery had first mentioned the scene in his telephone call, before the circumstances had been described, Stark had assumed it was a suicide; that was what a 'body at Blackfriars' usually meant. Over the years the bridge had become a favourite spot for suicides, most of them old men, sad derelicts who had once been bankers and stockbrokers, regarded in the bad old days of pre-war capitalism as masters of the universe but since the Liberation scorned by the party as usurers and leeches. Eventually more than a few of them decided they could take no more and had come to end it all in sight of 'the City', the little square mile of ancient

London from where their finance houses had once dominated the planet.

There was, of course, always the other alternative. Blackfriars Bridge was the frequent scene of another kind of foolishness: failed attempts to commit what the state considered treason. Every now and then some deluded soul – fewer over the years – would throw him- or herself onto a passing upriver barge, usually under cover of night, in the futile hope that they would go unspotted by the vigilance of the river border control, the frontier guards at Westminster Pier, or their canine companions. None succeeded. At least none that Harry Stark had ever heard of.

This was something at the same time simpler and much more complicated. Murder was not exactly unknown in the English Democratic Republic, although it was rarely publicised. Humanity, even under developed socialism, was not yet wholly free of its baser side. The party admitted that. Ordinary people killed for many reasons: out of blind, irrational fury, out of drunkenness, out of passion, for love, for sex. Even for money.

But most murders were committed out of sight, down dark alleyways, in crumbling tenement blocks, the bodies disposed of in shallow woodland graves, on bombsites or abandoned wasteland, at worst dismembered and hidden amongst the household trash. Murder was a crime the criminal tried to hide. This was different. That was what worried Harry most: this open flaunting of an atrocity, this obscene two fingers in the face of authority was something unheard of. It was a gesture.

More than that, it was a challenge, and not only to the police. This had all the trappings of a crime much more dangerous than mere murder: subversion. Subversion was a crime that could be dangerous not only to the victim, but also to the perpetrator and – what worried Harry Stark most right at this moment – even the investigator.

He told the helmsman to turn the wheel and steer the grimy little boat with its unwholesome burden towards the north bank of the Thames.

On the Victory Embankment the ambulance stood waiting, dirty white, spattered with rainwater from the gutters, defacing the red cross and red rose that on the battered vehicle looked less impressive than they did on the policeman's helmet. The emergency equipment inside, Harry knew, would be of a similar standard: old, worn-out, over-used. Amongst all the drains on the state's resources, the National Health Service, much trumpeted as the pride and joy of the English Democratic Republic, always seemed to trail near the bottom of the list. Just above repairing St Paul's.

Not that it mattered in this case. The ambulance was merely a mode of transport. To the morgue, via the forensic pathology department at St Bartholemew's hospital and the tender loving scalpel of Dr Ruth Kemp. Stark wondered if the good doctor would be with the ambulance, already waiting for her charge. He knew Kemp well, liked her, but found her enthusiasm for fresh corpses disconcerting at the least. He wondered what she would make of this one. He wondered how many she had seen before in this condition. But that was the sort of question Harry Stark knew better than to ask.

The cutter pulled up at the rusting iron pier where two burly medical orderlies in soiled green hospital fatigues were already waiting with a trolley. Stark nodded to them and with the constables' help they manhandled their unwieldy burden onto the trolley, and rattled it up and down the gangplanks onto the pavement. Kemp was indeed there. Stark made a brief gesture of acknowledgement to the small, stout figure in a thick coat stamping her feet and pulling on a cigarette next to the open rear doors of the ambulance. She nodded back. But her attention was elsewhere.

Stark followed the line of her gaze and spotted it almost immediately; the long low black Bevan saloon that could have been a hearse but wasn't, although some of his fellow citizens considered the sight of one as ominous an omen. The black tinted windows were supposed to add to its aura of anonymity but in fact only shouted all the louder the identity of its occupants, the sober-suited, quiet spoken men who prided themselves on being the 'sword and shield of the party': the Department of Social Security. Stark swore under his breath.

Chapter 4

'Trouble?' said Stark to the small dumpy figure of Ruth Kemp who continued to stare at the stationary black Bevan as he sidled over to her.

'Maybe, maybe not. But I'd go with maybe,' she replied, turning to look up at the policeman who towered over her. 'Depends what they make of that,' and she nodded in the opposite direction to where a line of uniformed People's Police had blocked the road to both vehicles and pedestrians.

Most of their fellow citizens gave a wide berth to any incident that attracted police presence, but in this case a small group was arguing with the uniformed officers. One of them, a woman, loudly.

Stark sighed and wandered over towards them, his heart sinking rapidly as he did so. He recognised the voice, or not so much the voice as the accent: Mancunian. Even though they weren't officially supposed to, policemen listened to news 'from the other side' as much as anyone. And there was no mistaking the strident Northern tones of Sian Morris, roving reporter for that delusional relic of a vanished world order, the so-called British Broadcasting Corporation. And self-styled 'scourge of the Stalinists'.

As Stark approached, the man behind her thrust a television camera forward and the long grey furry zeppelin of a microphone boom appeared over the helmet of one of the uniformed policemen.

'Can you put that away, please,' Stark said in his sternest voice, extending a hand at the same time to block the lens that swung automatically in his direction.

'Excuse me, sir, we just want to know what's going on. We're only doing our job.' The woman's voice was like a cheese grater on a blackboard.

'I'm sorry, this is a police matter. You have no authorisation.'

'We're a news team, BBC. We have a permit. Is that a dead body you've found?'

Stark sniffed and shook his head. 'I'm sorry. You have to leave.' He was polite but firm, the way he had been trained to behave should such an eventuality ever arise.

'We have every right ...' the woman said. 'Is this an escape attempt? What don't you want us to see?' Morris looked younger in person than she did on the box, Stark noted, quite pretty really if it wasn't for that awful voice. And her attitude. He shook his head.

'Move these people back, please,' he said quietly. The constables, five abreast, advanced at a steady pace. The BBC team retreated, the cameraman still trying to film through the thicket of police gloves raised in front of his lens.

'Who are you then?' the woman was yelling, as she was forced along the Embankment. 'Secret police, are you? One o'them Dossers? Or just an ordinary old PeePee in a suit?'

Stark clenched his fists involuntarily, then, realising that provocation was exactly what the woman had in mind, with a determined effort closed his eyes and his ears, turned his back and walked away.

'What did they want?' asked Kemp, briefly removing the glowing stub of cigarette from her plump pale lips.

'The usual. News. Bad news.'

'Is there any other sort?'

'I heard on the radio this morning industrial production figures were up again.'

Kemp smiled at the irony: 'Onwards and upwards for the

people's economy then. Not everyone seems to be cheered up though,' she gestured towards the grim figure of the corpse on the trolley. 'What do you think of that one?'

'I don't think. There's no future in it.'

'Nice line, I must remember that one.' Kemp gave him a thin smile. They walked back towards the ambulance together. The black Bevan by the far kerb remained inscrutable as ever. Its occupants, if there were any, showed no sign of emerging.

Kemp's two hefty helpers had manoeuvred the corpse, still wrapped in its damp and bloody sacking, into the back of the ambulance and were standing along with Lavery by the open doors, wiping their hands on their overalls and lighting up.

'Charming. All your lot smoke? I thought they'd discovered it was bad for the health.'

Kemp dropped her own cigarette butt and stamped it out beneath a surprisingly elegant shoe that looked as if it might be real leather. Stark had never noticed before that she wore heels at work. Particularly her work. Kemp moved across to the ambulance and clambered in. Stark noticed her attempt to conceal an involuntary intake of breath.

'There's a lot of things bad for the health, DI Stark, as I'm sure you know. Not least what happened to him.'

Stark raised his eyebrows but kept his distance. 'That's for sure.'

Kemp had pulled on a pair of rubber gloves, prised back a bit more of the sacking and was prodding at what remained of the corpse's jaw. Stark turned away as he watched her dip a finger into the bloody mess.

'Gelling nicely. Rigor started already. Probably been dead a couple of hours at least. Any idea who he is?'

Stark shrugged and called: 'Lavery.'

'Sir?' The sergeant left off his desultory conversation with the ambulance men.

'See what you can find, will you.'

With a face that showed how much he appreciated the high-end tasks entrusted to him, the heavy sergeant clambered into the back of the vehicle next to the pathologist and used his knife to enlarge the rent he had made in the sackcloth. Stark kept his distance. He still wasn't sure his stomach was up to it. Ruth Kemp had no such qualms.

Stark turned around, looking back up towards the bridge. Traffic had resumed. Lines of chugging red buses filled with early morning commuters heading for work in the ministries, torn between brooding frustration at yet another traffic hold-up and relief at a few more minutes saved from the stultifying boredom of the workplace.

'No ID, sir.'

Lavery's head sticking out of the rear of the ambulance. Stark went across to him. The body bag – which was, after all, what it was, he reflected – had been cut open from head to toe, revealing, beneath the bloody ruin of its face, the remains of a tall, stocky man in what appeared to have been smart casual clothing: jeans, an open-necked check shirt and a reddish-brown jacket, although it was hard to be certain about the original colours given the quantity of blood and other bodily fluids. The stench was overpowering. Stark found himself gagging again.

'What do you mean, no ID?' Everyone carried something. It was illegal not to. Citizens were obliged to carry their state-issued ID cards at all times. Even visiting foreigners, including those from 'up North' were supposed to carry their passports and valid visas.

'Just that, sir: no ID. No wallet. Not even any money. Not in his jacket pockets, or in his trousers. And I've looked as close as I can. In the circumstances.'

'Nothing at all?'

'Nothing to identify him. Only this.'

Lavery was holding a square of unfolded paper. 'It was in the side pocket of his jacket. I thought it might be a document of some sort. But it's not.' He turned it over in his hands as if doing so might encourage some strange metamorphosis.

'It looks like one of those whatchamacallits, you know, "winkies".'

Stark frowned. He knew the term of course, he had always assumed it was some form of rhyming slang he wasn't quite familiar with, like saying 'dog' for phone, because it was short for 'dog and bone'. 'Winkies' was what people called books or poetry or pamphlets frowned on by the state and printed on illegal presses. They existed in Moscow too, where they called them *samizdat*, 'self-published'. Stark had considered them more or less an urban myth: the only one he had ever seen had been a scrappily printed version of a Northern television schedule.

'What does it say?'

Lavery gave him a wry grin. 'I think it's Shakespeare. Unless of course, it's a message for you, guv.'

Stark snatched the paper from his hand. It was the same, poor quality greenish paper the television schedule had been printed on. But there was only a date, 23 April, the national holiday in four days' time, printed large, and beneath it a single line capitalised in a similar huge typeface: AND ENG-LISHMEN AT HOME NOW ABED SHALL THINK THEMSELVES ACCURSED THEY WERE NOT WITH US AT THIS HOUR.

Stark sniffed at the irony, turned it over and felt his heart stop. The image was unmistakable, in socialist red of all colours, the great ogre himself, the bogeyman used to scare children to sleep at night, sporting the twin symbols of capitalism – fat cigar and bowler hat – leering, his hand raised in that trademark gesture that summed up what he thought of the world. Two raised fingers: Fuck You!

Chapter 5

Col Charles Marchmain of the Department of Social Security steepled his fingers as his black Bevan saloon pulled away from the pavement. Through the indigo-tinted side windows, which obscured vision into the vehicle but not from it, he watched the little tableau as its participants – the two lumpen ambulance orderlies apart – affected to ignore the big black car accelerating past them.

He noticed, and appreciated, their studied lack of interest. It was something he was used to, expected even. The more anyone assumed the DoSS was interested in them, the more they affected not to be aware of their existence. It was often a useful indicator of guilt. Not in this case of course, at least not as far as he knew – Marchmain was not a man to take anything for granted – but it was extremely unlikely. Extremely. He had encountered this sort of attitude before too: a deliberate attempt to feign total indifference on the part of those who feared their own competence was being questioned, or in danger of being usurped. They too hoped, in their own way, that if they ignored the men from the DoSS, they would simply go away. Of course, they never did.

Marchmain had taken particular care to arrive on the scene just after the detective inspector, his sergeant and two constables had climbed aboard the police river boat. He had ordered his driver to wait in a side street until he was sure the little party had embarked, then pulled out. The cordon of uniformed officers that closed off the Embankment to other traffic parted as soon as they saw the Bevan approach, the marque alone being enough identification. Nonetheless Marchmain had told the driver to stop and show his badge. Respect was one thing, but sloppiness another.

Then he had done what he did best: sat, and watched and waited. He was an excellent observer, not so much trained as impassioned. There was much more to be learned, he resolutely believed, by careful observation than from most direct questioning, even when physical or psychological incentives were involved. Getting the right answer, after all, wasn't always the point. In this current little matter, for example, he was absorbed more by the questions posed than by any possible answers.

He watched as the boat came to the pier, the trolley was wheeled up by the ambulance apes, the body loaded and unloaded, noticed how the senior man hung back, as far as possible from the gore, how he greeted the portly little pathologist with her passé fashion pretensions.

He had watched as the policeman went to deal with the irritating Northern news team, and was impressed with the calm and level-headed manner with which he removed them, despite the woman's taunts. Marchmain wondered if he would have been quite so level-headed himself at that age, and decided on balance probably not. People like that were an aggravation that in the old days did not have to be shown quite such exaggerated tolerance.

He noticed however, that the policeman's sangfroid seemed to evaporate somewhat however when his tubby little sergeant set about searching the corpse for identity papers and found nothing. Yes, he thought, that would unsettle anybody. He watched as the detective took the piece of paper his sergeant proffered to him and noticed the expressions of puzzlement and then shock on his face as he turned it over.

Interesting, Marchmain thought as he gave the man in the front seat the curt order to drive off. It would be more interesting still to see what the policeman made of this case. In particular given that the policeman in charge was Detective Inspector Harry Stark. John Stark's son.

He was young for the job. But perhaps, under the circumstances, that was not wholly surprising. Marchmain had known Stark senior well. He had been a remarkable man. In many ways. One of the best party cadres of his generation. He had played a key role in the early post-war years, when there was still a degree of demoralised uncertainty, not just among older members of the force, but amongst the much-needed new recruits, many of whom had served in the army, and fought against those they were now told to regard as their liberators. Those had been difficult times, and John Stark, an experienced trades unionist, had blossomed amidst the rubble; he had been a realist, a rationaliser and an optimist. And he could inspire those qualities in others. He had been a leader of men. What had happened to him was a genuine tragedy.

Marchmain wondered which, if any, of the father's qualities his son had inherited. In particular he wondered if they included the one that in his experience was simultaneously most dangerous and most useful: an independent mind.

Yes indeed, he would watch developments closely.

This had the potential for being interesting. 'May you live in interesting times' was said to be an old Chinese curse. Col Charles Marchmain considered it his personal motto. And what was more interesting still was that Stark had found something: a piece of paper from the dead man's pocket that he was now thrusting towards the dowdy middle-aged pathologist with a look of incredulity on his face. Very interesting indeed.

'What the hell am I supposed to make of this?'

Ruth Kemp glanced down at the sheet of unfolded paper in the detective's hand then recoiled in horror as her hand automatically pulled back from accepting it. She stared at the image, then looked up, not so much at Stark as beyond him, through the still open ambulance door.

As if on cue, the black saloon had slid away from the kerb, pulled out slowly into the middle of the empty road and moved forward towards them. Only as it drew level did it accelerate and disappear, heading east, under the bridge, into the bowels of the City.

'Maybe you should ask them,' she said.

Chapter 6

Clement Attlee was not amused. The stern dead eyes on his portrait made that perfectly clear. But then Harry Stark wasn't exactly having the time of his life either. A murder investigation did not land on his desk often. The trouble with this one was that it didn't want to land at all. The lack of an identity not only hampered the investigation, it buggered up the paperwork.

There were forms to be filled in. Almost as many for a suspected murder, it turned out, as for stolen jars of pickled eggs. But pickled eggs were a known quantity. Unidentified corpses were not. And a name was what the mutilated body now enjoying the careful attention of Dr Kemp and her assistants on a slab at Bart's mortuary signally lacked.

Lavery had gone through the missing persons list. There were no more than a dozen adult males unaccounted for in the whole of the city. A countrywide request would take longer, at least another day or two. Neither would account for those who had gone missing voluntarily in a, usually futile, attempt to commit the treasonous act of emigration.

Theft of ID papers was almost unheard of, even in rare cases of aggravated robbery. Or at least the ordinary ID papers of the average citizen, which unlike those of the party *nomenklatura* conferred no benefits of access to special shops or travel privileges, and those were so tightly controlled that anyone attempting to use stolen documents ran a risk many times greater than the potential advantages.

Stark fed his first form and accompanying flimsies into

the rollers of the old Hermes and began typing. In the box which required 'complainant's' name he typed out the usual sobriquet for anonymity: 'Joe Bloggs'. There was almost nothing else to add: no address, no next of kin, no national identity card number, no National Health Service number, no trade union affiliation, no party membership, nor reason for refusal of membership. Most significantly of all, no Social Security number. Nothing to identify him to the omniscient 'Department'. There was another possibility, one that Stark was reluctantly coming to consider.

It had been an afternoon of blank walls and dead ends. Like the dead ends and blank walls all over the great map which covered the far wall of Stark's office. Unlike most maps available to ordinary citizens of the English Democratic Republic, that which covered the detective inspector's wall did not have blank space in the area marked 'Westminster'. It had a black-and-white tracery of streets with names, half of the city reflected in a ghostly mirror. The Wall had gone up in 1961, when Harry was little more than a toddler. He had no memory of the 'other side', the part of London his mother still occasionally, politically incorrectly, referred to as 'up West'.

As far as Harry and anyone under forty was concerned, what Northerners called 'West London' was effectively another city, one the party referred to as 'Westminster', purposely making the point – valid in theory – that it had been a separate city, the royal residence. For centuries the two might have been fused together. The party insisted it had merely performed a life-saving operation by severing a Siamese twin, wracked with the contagious disease of capitalism.

The Wall – the 'state frontier', Harry corrected himself, as

27

he traced out the scale of the barrier that cut not just through the city but surrounded the western enclave – in the north separated Barnet from Enfield, Hampstead from Highgate, Kentish Town from Camden Town, Marylebone Station from Euston, and in the south Lambeth from Southwark, Clapham from Dulwich, Croydon from Bromley. But it was in the heart of the old metropolis that the scar still proved most visible, where it ran concurrent with the boarded-up facades of former shops along Tottenham Court Road and Charing Cross Road down into Stalingrad Square, once named for another battle between other empires, then the flattened western side of Whitehall before crossing the river over Westminster Bridge and turning south along the Albert Embankment from where the Thames was suddenly an alien waterway.

The phone rang. Stark picked it up with something bordering on relief.

'Stark here,' he said.

'Yes, though if you weren't so absurdly squeamish about the Technicolor wonders of the human anatomy, you should really be here.' Stark recognised the gruff tones of Ruth Kemp. 'I've done the autopsy.'

For all his frustration at their lack of leads, Stark had not quite been able to bring himself to spend the afternoon in the formaldehyde-scented atmosphere of St Bart's forensic lab while the good doctor performed her grisly rituals upon the corpse. He had tried before and been evicted after emptying the contents of his stomach into a kidney dish for the second time.

'What have you got for me?' he said, ignoring the barb and lifting his pen to take notes, to go through the ritual motions that would give him something at least to fill a few of the empty spaces.

'The deceased was a well-built, relatively fit male, one metre ninety in height, aged somewhere between forty-five and sixty-five.'

'Well, that narrows it down.'

'Cut the sarcasm, DI Stark. You might recall the condition the body was in.'

Harry tried not to. 'Do we have a time of death?'

'We do. That too, however, is approximate, I'm afraid. As ever.'

'As ever.'

'It's particularly difficult because of the peculiar circumstances. Because he was hanging, the post-mortem lividity, caused by the red blood cells settling, in this case towards the feet, is less of a guide than usual while the fact that he was left over the river in the middle of the night means that the core body temperature would have dropped faster than usual ...'

'Yes, yes, yes.' There were always circumstances.

'But judging primarily from the onset of rigor mortis, and more specifically the level of potassium in the vitreous fluid of the eye ...' Stark squirmed; why was it that people like Kemp took such delight in the detail? '... it would appear that death occurred sometime between 2 a.m. and 5 a.m., some two and a half hours before the body was discovered.'

It had been a river border patrol boat, doing a routine sweep that had come across the body, much later than they should have done. The corporal in charge had blamed the fog, which had rendered their searchlight almost useless. And the fact, of course, that they normally scanned the water, not the air. Stark suspected he would probably face an inquiry nonetheless.

'The cause of death ...'

'... was pretty obvious' Harry interjected.

Kemp ignored him: '... was probably a bullet fired at point blank range from the nape of the neck, upwards and forwards, the trajectory effectively destroying all facial features. The subsequent hanging was incidental.'

Stark snorted. 'Incidental?'

'Under the circumstances,' Kemp continued, 'only the survival intact of the bulk of the occipital and parietal skull bones and the lower jaw ensured that there was enough structure to support the rest of the body.'

He hadn't thought of that. Had the killer deliberately not blown his victim's brains out because he needed the skull bone to hang him by? Had the obliteration of the facial features therefore been incidental or quite deliberately no accident. No papers, no name, no face ...?

'Nothing that might give any clue as to identity?' he asked, more in hope than anticipation. 'What about fingerprints?'

'Intact, as far as I can tell. But I'm no expert. Think there's a chance you've got him on file?'

It was a possibility. If it was a gangland killing – a few old East End mobs still operated – then there was a chance he'd have form and his prints would be on a database somewhere. The problem would be finding them. Scotland Yard's antiquated records system was nowhere near as comprehensive or as efficient as those who alleged they lived in a 'police state' believed. And anyway, the gangs did their killing in their own 'manors', like dogs marking their territory with urine. They did not advertise in public.

'I'll send someone round,' he said. It was still worth trying. 'In the meantime, I guess it's still Joe Bloggs. I don't suppose there'd even be any point looking for dental records.'

There was a silence on the other end of the line. Longer than he was used to in dealings with Kemp.

'Why do you ask?'

'I was just thinking things through. I mean there can't be anything left of the guy's mouth. Can there?'

A second's hestiation again. 'Actually, as I said, although the upper jawbone is fragmented and the palate totally missing, the lower half is relatively intact. In fact ...'

'Go on.'

'The thing is, Harry ...' It wasn't often she called him that. 'I don't often admit it but I'm not as well versed as I should be on dental aspects, but there's bridgework there, on the rear molars, and it looks to me to be of particularly good quality ...'

Stark lifted his eyes and found himself staring at the big white mirror-image on the map. He knew what she was going to say.

'There's something else. A couple of things actually. Not necessarily anything on their own ...'

'Come on, Ruth, if you're onto something, spit it out.'

He thought he heard the ghost of a chuckle, quickly suppressed. 'An unfortunate choice of words, it's the contents of his stomach.'

Stark made a face. He had too much imagination for details like this.

'... and his skin ...' Kemp continued.

'His skin?'

'Yes. Whoever he was, he had an interesting lifestyle. Within the last twenty-four hours he had consumed not just a small portion of standard street-corner fish and chips, but sometime before that a substantial good quality steak, blue cheese and a not insignificant amount of red wine. Also on the upper back were a number of small lesions, almost certainly early-stage BCCs ...'

'B … what?'

'Basal Cell Carcinomas.'

'Cancer?'

Was that what she was trying to tell him, that the man was dying anyway? But somehow he knew it wasn't.

'Yes, a form of skin cancer, but not the most serious. They're often harmless unless the disease spreads. More disfiguring than anything else. But they are consistent with having spent long periods in the sun, in hot climates …'

'What are you trying to tell me here, Ruth?'

'I'm not trying to tell you anything. You're the detective. It's just that, if you add it all together …'

Stark let the silence hang, let her lead him down the path he didn't want to tread.

' … if you asked me to hazard a guess …'

'Yes?'

'Then I'd say that, whoever Joe Bloggs is …'

The silence resumed briefly. Then Ruth Kemp seemed to decide the game was no longer worth the candle: 'He isn't one of us.'

Chapter 7

The overhead lights flickered, the yellow glow dimming until the filaments themselves could be seen burning red through the worn patches of the frosted-glass housings. They flashed unusually bright an instant, then oscillated in intensity between red and yellow before restoring the familiar low-level light that cast the carriages and their passengers in an oil-lamp ochre.

At Lambeth North the doors scraped open and the shuffling masses rearranged themselves, those within the train compacting tighter together as more pushed in than pushed out. A woman with a pallid face and a hairy upper lip sneezed loudly into Stark's face, then sniffed the residue back, turning away rapidly to avoid the embarrassment of an apology. For at least the fifth time that day, Stark felt physically sick.

He pulled the hand that was not hanging on to the overhead strap free of the throng and wiped his face. Those packed around him turned their faces down or away, watching only out of the corner of an eye to make sure he did not wipe it on them. He plunged the spittle-damp hand into his pocket and closed his eyes. So much for the National Health Service exhortation on the panel above the window: 'Coughs and Sneezes Spread Diseases: Catch your germs in a handkerchief.' It might have been funny; but nobody was laughing.

The train lurched forward in alternating spasms as if in coordination with the flickering lighting, a distinct possibility given that electricity for both lights and motion came from the ageing Bankside power station. Finally, carriages jolting and shuddering on century-old rails, the train turned a subterranean corner and with a screech of brakes rattled into Elephant and Castle station. Normally it made more sense for Stark to change here onto the Bank section of the Northern Line to get out at Borough, but in the circumstances he felt he needed fresh air. It was only one stop.

He resisted the temptation to elbow the woman with the moustache in the ribs as he joined the communal push towards the opening doors. The platform was as crowded as the train, rendering the carriage's attempt to void itself as hopeless as a drowning man trying to vomit under water. There was a certain, almost military, order to it, like a mock battle performed in deadly earnest on a daily basis by cohorts of some conscript mediaeval army. Only occasionally did an individual unused to the drill risk being trampled by failing to follow the flow. Stark noticed one such now: a tall, sturdy man, with a tanned weathered face, a hop grower maybe from the collective farms of Kent, battling against the flow towards the 'Way Out' signs at the far end of the platform. Stark as usual let himself be swept along in the opposite direction. The sign saying 'No Exit' was blatantly ignored because it clearly was an exit and was closer. As he turned the corner he noticed the big man, looking lost and confused, squeezed up against a peeling poster for the Transport and General Workers' Union holiday homes at Whitstable. Meanwhile the flow carried Stark to the foot of the wooden-treaded escalators that clankingly brought him up into the only relatively fresh air of the part of London that still bore the seemingly incongruous name of Elephant and Castle.

34

The fact that it did, his mother had told him proudly, in the days when they still talked much, was down to his father. Extreme elements in the local party back in the fifties had been keen to change the name of the busy roundabout that was the hub of South London to Clement-Attlee-Circus, an attempt to reinforce their politically correct anti-royalist credentials. When young Stark had looked puzzled she had explained it was widely believed the name was derived from 'Infanta de Castilla', for one of the Spanish princesses who had married English kings.

In fact, Harry's father had pointed out at a local party meeting, it was simply the name of a long-vanished pub whose sign had portrayed an elephant with a howdah on its back, symbol of the Worshipful Guild of Cutlers, in reference to the ivory used in their knife handles. As impeccably working class as the junction a mile down the road known as the Bricklayers' Arms.

It was one thing to play down people's religion, re-evaluate their history, redefine their nationality, but take away all atavistic identification with their home neighbourhood and you ran the risk of having nothing left. That's what his father had argued with the party bosses, his mother told him. And there was truth in that, Stark had realised. He had been impressed.

The streets around the 'Elephant' bore no resemblance to the busy hub Harry Stark's father had known in his pre-war youth, yet they had changed little in all the years his son had known them. The Elephant of today was a mixture of ugly concrete tower blocks thrown up on the wasteland left by the Luftwaffe Blitz in 1941, followed by the 'historic misunderstanding' of the working class who had been fooled into siding with the armies of capitalism at the Liberation of 1949.

The Stark family was lucky. It was almost certainly down to his father's influence among the housing cadres of the local party that they still had a house to themselves. A real house, in one of the little streets of Victorian terraces that had somehow survived both bombs and bulldozers. It was only a small house, two-up and two-down, but it allowed them the luxury, at the expense of what would once have been called the downstairs sitting room, of a bedroom each for himself, his mother and his sister.

Would Kate be in, Stark wondered, by the time he got home. He was worried about her. Though not as worried as their mother was. She'd got 'in with the wrong crowd, always out late, drinking and I don't know what, not dressing properly, not keeping herself tidy like a decent young girl should'. Stark had tried to reassure her, tell her it was just natural, the way young people were these days. Kate would grow out of it. After all she was still in her teens, just about. Just about, his mother had echoed. The girl would be twenty years old in a few weeks' time. By that age she was already married, to a respectable man, and pregnant too, carrying you, Harry Stark, much good did it do me. At times like that, Stark just smiled and kissed the old lady on the forehead which brought a tear to her eye. Too much discussion of the family history was never an easy topic.

Kate had been a late birth. His father had been fifty-six years old, his mother just over forty. A bit of an accident, people said. The same ones in general who had tittle-tattled back when they first got married. His mother was just turned twenty and Lieutenant Stark, as he already was, nearly fifteen years older. Back then the gossip hadn't been about cradle-snatching, more the opposite: that young Violet Easton was 'on the make', picking a party member on purpose, and a policeman to boot. There was also the fact that she was six months' pregnant with Harry at the time.

Stark only found out the 'word on the street' about his parents when Katy was born shortly after his tenth birthday, and the same tongues started wagging again, saying this time that accidents only happened to them what didn't take precautions. The inference was clear – that Harry's father wasn't Katy's – but no one said it in so many words, not in Harry's hearing. And they would never have dared to the old man's face. One way or another, he had never said a word, had given every appearance of rejoicing in the new arrival, despite the extra strain on the family's resources. But when he died a year later, from a heart attack, there were more than a few who said it was the shock that had killed him.

Stark didn't believe a word of it. He could see more than a fair reflection of the old man in the dogged, single-minded way his 'kid' sister took up causes and clung stubbornly to ideas, even if they weren't ideas the father she had never known would have approved of. Harry didn't really care what the backstreet gossips said. Any more than he really cared, in the depth of his soul, who had killed the poor bastard whose mutilated remains were lying on Ruth Kemp's dissecting table. The difference was that finding out the answer to that question was his duty. At least until someone told him otherwise and took it off his hands. That was a development he was half expecting, and more than half hoping for. If the DoSS wanted to do the dirty work, Harry Stark was not going to stop them. And he didn't care either if they knew it. Maybe that was why he felt as if there were eyes boring into the back of his head.

An unseasonably cold wind was blowing scraps of newspaper along the gutters. The crowds that had poured out of the Tube melted away into the backstreets, bus queues and the few remaining pubs. There had been more once, many more. In his childhood, pubs had still been the hub of the community. Everyone had a local and everyone in it knew everyone else. There had been more shops too. But when rationing had continued far longer than anyone expected, and the new regulations made it harder to remain as owner of a small business rather than an employee of the state, the corner shops disappeared and the pubs began to dry up.

Before the war, old people said, the Elephant had been awash with small shops, ironmongers, greengrocers, butchers and tobacconists, with a cinema and a variety theatre. Today there was a giant shopping centre built in to the ground floor of the concrete tower blocks, except that half the shops had never been opened and the others were so short on goods they may as well have been empty. One week there would be an excess of plastic Polish potties, the next maybe garden products or unseasonal wooden Christmas decorations that were about all the decimated German economy was allowed to produce.

There were butchers still but it was pot luck what you found in them. Sausages were a staple, as long as you didn't analyse the meat content. Harry's walk home from the Tube took him past one. The crude stencilled signboard out front which would once have proudly declared the owner's name read simply 'Meat and Sausages', as if somehow accepting that there was at best a slight correlation between the two, although the sign above the shop next door read 'Flowers' but was empty. It opened only occasionally, usually in late spring when a grey lorry would pull up and unload a riot of incongruous colours from the Dutch tulip growers' collectives. Its neighbour boasted 'Fruit and Vegetables', which was an exaggeration, certainly in the winter months, when there would be little on sale but cabbages, onions and knobbly grey potatoes.

Stark hurried past and slowed only briefly when he passed the one real attraction the Elephant still retained. At least the generic sign hung outside here had tradition behind it, even if 'Fish and Chips' was also something of a euphemism. The chips could be relied on, and weren't that bad usually, but fish was rare and fresh fish all but unheard of. He had heard a rumour that the cod and haddock trawled in industrial quantities from the waters of the North Sea were in sharp decline. Perhaps one bleak day in the near future the sign-writers would come along with their brushes and paint over the word 'Fish' and another staple would be gone forever. But not just yet. The smell of frying oil and vinegar drifted into the street. An old man in a flat cap and thick glasses was staring hungrily into the window; Stark pressed a sixpence into his hand. The old man flinched. Begging was banned. But Stark gave him a reassuring smile.

He was tempted himself. Lunch had been a curling sand-wich of dried-up ham from Mavis the tea-lady's trolley, snatched at his desk and washed down with yet another mug of the vile brew that flowed, ready sugared and milk-powdered from her mobile urn. But what he needed right now was refreshment of a different sort: alcohol. Preferably lots of it.

A pint after office hours was something of a Yard ritual. He and Lavery, like most of the rest of CID, would nip around the corner to a run-down pub on the corner of the wasteland that was Whitehall. The Red Lion had once been a favourite with members from the Houses of Parliament, in the days when there had still been a parliament housed in the ruin that now lay on the other side of the Wall. Today it was a tawdry little inn on the edge of nowhere maintained only as a watering hole for flatfooted policemen. Stark believed it had been kept deliberately tacky to discourage any foreign visitors who ventured down in the hope of snapping a rare photo of Big Ben's blackened stump from 'the other side'. It was strictly forbidden to take photographs of the 'state frontier', and there was a guard on regular duty to make sure the rules were obeyed. The brave few who still came were rarely tempted to linger over a refreshing pint in such a 'historic' setting once they had seen the dour-faced men who sat over their warm beers in the 'Lion'.

There was a more salubrious establishment not far away, just off Northumberland Avenue, a relatively well-preserved old Victorian pub with leaded windows and plush, if slightly faded, velour upholstery, that rejoiced in the name The Sherlock Holmes. Stark suspected the name pre-dated the war and was an attempt by some long-dead publican to cash in on his famous near-neighbours at Scotland Yard. It was maintained as a sort of showpiece by Inside England, the state tourism authority, to impress on Northerners or 'other foreigners' who wandered down from Stalingrad Square, that they were now in 'real London', not the glitzy phoney Yankee showcase of 'Westminster'.

In any case The Sherlock Holmes had been taken over by another sort of 'detective', the ones who looked down their noses at the men of the Yard every bit as much as the fictional sleuth had done. There were always representatives of the Department in The Holmes, as there were anywhere 'foreigners' were to be found in number. There was probably always at least one incognito in the Red Lion too, just to keep an eye on the 'colleagues'. That was one reason why tonight Stark wanted to drink somewhere else, where he wouldn't have Lavery pressing him volubly for his thoughts on a case that by rights should never have been theirs. And might not be for much longer. Stark had thoughts all right, but none he felt like uttering aloud. At least not in 'mixed' company.

He was headed for his local. A local was a rare thing these days, but all the more to be treasured for that: as close as you could get nowadays to a pub in the old style – a home from home, where people said what they thought without worrying who was listening. That, Stark thought wryly, was real social security.

The cold nip in the air only sharpened the thin sour smell of stale urine that rose from the gutters as Stark turned the corner of Gaitskell Street and saw the welcoming lights of the pub. Like everything else in this world, it had seen better days but Del, who ran the place, did his best. He had even got hold of a can or two of paint and spruced up the outside with a lick of cream gloss on the brickwork and a splash of dark vermillion on two welcoming words above the door, 'The Rose'.

He had taken care not to disguise the ostentatiously empty space left when they had covered up 'and Crown'.

Chapter 8

Even as the lights began to wink out in the government offices opposite, as Harry Stark flicked upwards the brown Bakelite switch that extinguished the naked bulbs hanging from the ceiling of his corner turret, the figure crouched on the muddy shore of the Thames stretched out a hand and began to climb.

Mudlarks were extinct. The all-caring state had created housing and jobs that deliberately eliminated that subspecies of London humanity who had for centuries eked an existence foraging for washed-up flotsam from freighters, groats from the days of Elizabeth or sesterces slipped from the leather purses of Roman merchants come to buy slaves at the markets of Londinium. The past was another country. It could not be visited without a visa.

The real reason the mudlarks had been swept away, most folk said, was that the river presented an easier frontier. Banning foraging meant there was no excuse for anyone who might hope to slip on board an upstream freight barge, even though these days they too were inspected by the sniffer-dog teams at Westminster Bridge.

But when the mists came in from the North Sea and mingled with the output of the metropolis's myriad smoking chimneys to form what was famous worldwide as a 'London peculiar', there was precious little even the strongest search-light could do to penetrate it. Which was what the figure crouched in the mud by the bottom rung of the ladder below the embankment had been counting on.

It was not easy, especially with a burden to bear. But it was because of that unusual unwieldy cargo that to approach from any other direction would have attracted unwelcome attention. Had anyone been watching, which thankfully on such an evening with the fog building, squeezing the breath from the lungs and replacing it with foul air clogged with soot and colly, there was not, they might have seen a slight, nimble figure clamber over the embankment wall like some lithe-limbed river serpent and scurry for the darkness.

Of the darkness, there was more than enough. A mountain of shadow smothering the already impenetrable fog. A mountain of colossal, geometric proportions. A vast behemoth of dirty brown brick, an oblong devoid of other form or design save for the great tower that topped it, a huge ugly square-sided chimney that rose forever into the opaque hell of the heavens, belching from its uppermost orifice great toxic clouds of black fumes that the ambient atmosphere recognised as kin and embraced.

Close up, almost touching the brickwork, a sinister low hum could be heard emanating from the depths of its bulk, as if the great edifice itself were somehow alive. In reality the hum was nowhere near as loud as most east Londoners would have liked, nor as constant. Starved of the plentiful supplies of coal from the mines of Lancashire and North Wales for which it had been intended, and forced to operate on irregular deliveries aboard freighters from Stettin and Gdansk, the great turbines within provided less than adequate electricity for their half of the city. Bankside Power Station was a crippled giant.

But one hell of a blank canvas. With speed born of practice, and no little trepidation, the agile figure, invisible at the base of the brickwork, unpacked and unfolded the

43

semi-rigid card sheets from inside a large flatpack folder. From the backpack came a small, light aluminium ladder. The soft clunk it made when it hit the wall caused the figure to freeze an instant. Out in the fog, on the river, red and white lights glowed faint and a dull amorphous yellow glow moved in the murk swinging now this way, now that, like the single eye of a blind Cyclops. Then it passed.

Quick now. There was little time. But this was also no time to rush. The job required exactitude. No room for sloppiness. The pieces held in place, the outline only just visible now. A ghostly shape waiting to be given body. Adjust the facemask. Make sure the plastic welders' goggles are sealed against the face. An accident could cause partial blindness. Another noise, a soft patter. Footsteps in the fog. Multiple. Drunks reeling home from the pub? Stopped. Muted voices. Too quiet for drunks. Silent now. A pair of lovers with nowhere to go seeking the solace of the flesh in the anonymity of the filthy night? Or a conscientious pair of beat policeman marking their territory rather than toasting their toes by the station paraffin heater? The last was most dangerous. But also least likely. The footsteps resumed. Approaching? No, retreating. Fading softly away.

Back to work. Time for the spray, Shake the can gently, wrapped in rags to mute the sound of the weight within stirring the paint. Spray. Not too close. Not too far. Even. Consistency was the key. Keep it even. Not too much, no drips, not even on the card. Then wait before peeling away. A few minutes, that was all. A few minutes standing there in the dark. Not daring to breathe in. Solvent fumes mixing with the murk, adding to the chemical cocktail in the air. They had thought long and hard about the methodology: the stencil. Quick, accurate and in theory, once the design was made, the cut-outs completed, so easy anyone could do it.

Then quick again, easy does it, dismantling as important as assembling. Packing away. Eyes a-twinkle, heart-thumping, adrenalin pumping. Then slip away, out of the shadow and over the wall, bags slung over shoulder, the cargo as precious as ever but its job done for now. One last look before dropping down the ladder, gazing through the dismal dark up at a spectre of the past, once more incarnate in the present, two-dimensional in paint on brickwork, four-dimensional in the minds of men, and women. A challenge to history. Giving it the V-sign.

V for Victory.

V made by two fingers.

IN YOUR FACE.

Chapter 9

In the public bar of the Rose there was a warm fug and the usual smattering of folk either standing at the counter or seated around the little tables with their heavy cast-iron legs that had been there since the pub opened two days short of Queen Victoria's Golden Jubilee. On another planet, in another universe.

Stark nodded to a few regulars he knew by sight but not by name: the bloke with the wall eye and the frozen cheek, the result of some industrial accident; the little fellow in his eighties whose face was as crumpled as yesterday's newspaper, eyes screwed up tight into what looked like ecstasy and might have been despair but was almost certainly just old age and apathy; the one with the lank hair and the permanently black eye who talked to no one but was never silent, muttering incessantly into his beer. At the far end of the bar were the little coterie Stark styled 'the intellectuals': a trades union official, a retired schoolteacher and a bit-part actor. And Del himself, robust, rotund, red-faced and profoundly devoted to a life with no more surprises.

Stark pulled up a bar stool and ordered a pint of Red Barrel. Del nodded to him as he pulled back the stiff hand-pump that forced the ale up from the cellar.

'Evening, Harry. Cold one, ain't it.'

'It is, Del. It is,' Stark replied and took a long slow pull on his pint, savouring the bitterness of the beer and the cosy familiarity of the surroundings, the same old faces, hard, craggy, factory faces mostly, save for 'the intellectuals' of course, the trades union man in his shiny Slovakian suit, the teacher in his worn cords and the actor in imported jeans.

Everyone who drank regularly in the Rose knew Harry was a policeman. The Westminster tabloids might call members of the Metropolitan People's Police 'PeePees', and the nickname had caught on among their own readers and folk 'up North', but amongst those who had – even before the Wall – always felt the 'East End' was proper London, as opposed to the cosmopolitan bit 'up West', politics had had no effect on tradition. Even those classes that were histori-cally not overly fond of the police, they still called them the names they always had: cops, rozzers, 'Peelers' even, though most just settled for 'the Old Bill'. The nickname for the grey men from 'the Department' however, was all theirs. DoSSers were just DoSSers. People knew the difference.

A tall man in an overcoat came in behind Stark and grunted rather than spoke the brief word 'beer', indicating dismissively with his hands that a half of anything would do. Del served him, watched as he carried it to a solitary seat in the corner, looked back at Stark hunched introspectively over his pint and sighed; he knew when people wanted to talk, and when they didn't. It was an essential part of the trade. He turned back to the intellectuals whose conversa-tion was growing unusually heated. Stark drew nearer, more out of idle curiosity than a desire to get involved.

'A blockbuster! That's what they're calling it. As if it was some other new-fangled bloody bomb. I call it a downright provocation. Absolutely disgusting.' Davy Hindsmith, a convener for the Tube drivers' union, old guard and nearing retirement, was never a man to pull his punches. He clearly did not agree with the opinions of the man opposite him, and at least two decades his junior. Ken Atkinson was in his

47

late twenties and intensely proud when anyone in the pub – or in the street – recognised him from the bit part he played in *Ups and Downs*, an ETV soap opera set on a Sussex collective farm.

'Come on, Davy old man. That's just advertising speech, the way the Yanks do it. They're always inventing new words. Just think of the challenge. For the actor. Playing a role like that.'

'Playing is bloody right. Playing bloody Mickey Mouse with history. It's a diabolical liberty.'

Stark had no idea what they were on about and wasn't about to ask. He had noticed Lizzie who worked behind the bar evenings Thursday through Saturday come in, trailing a cold draught in her wake. She rubbed her hands together, hung her thin raincoat on a hook, and with a nod to Del, slipped through the hatch in the bar counter and began arranging glasses.

Stark ventured a brief smile but she wasn't looking his way. He liked Lizzie Goldsmith. She was a pretty girl, with an air of vulnerability underneath the bluff exterior she put up as a defence against some of the more predatory customers. She had a trim figure, dark eyes and high cheekbones that in certain lights gave her face an exotic look, though in others could make it look frail and haunted. Once Stark had imagined he saw bruising there and wondered if someone was knocking her about, but even his most oblique attempts to hedge around the subject were greeted with a sarcastic comment that suggested he should mind his own business.

Since then their relationship had improved as a result. Having rearranged the ranks of upturned jug-handled pint glasses and filled the sink with water to rinse the used ones as they came back, Lizzie looked along the bar, and nodded to him. Del was too engrossed in the conversation of the pair at the end to pay attention to Stark's empty glass and with a smile Lizzie took it off him and refilled it.

'Cheers, love,' said Stark. 'A man could die of thirst around here.'

'At least they won't show it over here.'

'It'll end up on television though. Sooner or later.'

Hindsmith threw his eyes to ceiling. 'More's the pity.' Stark was waiting for him to say they should never have taken down the jamming masts that back in the fifties had tried in vain to block the broadcasts from the powerful BBC transmitters in West London's White City. He didn't.

Lizzie mouthed at Stark, to ask, 'What are they talking about?'

He shrugged. It took Del to join in, silently mouthing in his own right two words that had been on Harry Stark's mind all day but which he had not heard pronounced out loud on more than half a dozen occasions in his lifetime: 'Winston Churchill.'

Chapter 10

'Say the name out loud, why don't you?' said Hindsmith. 'You can now, you know. What with all this *glasnost* or whatever they call it this new bloke in the Kremlin wants to see. Revisionism, that's what I call it. Spreading rumours about old Uncle Joe, blackening a good man's name. Start down that road and see where it takes you.'

'Where might that be, precisely?' said Atkinson, the actor. Hindsmith spluttered into his beer.

'Here. Where we are now. Letting the bloody Americans rewrite history. Making a film. Called *Bulldog Breed*, about a dead rottweiler, singing the praises of one of the bloodiest old imperialists who ever sat in Downing Street. And that's saying something.'

'You can't be sure they're singing his praises. Nobody knows the plot yet. It doesn't come out for another month.'

'I'll bet you two of your fancy so-called "British" pounds it'll be a whitewash job. The Yanks reckon Moscow's blinked first. Try and put a pair of tarnished wings on the old devil and they reckon they can stir the shit with impunity. Before you know it they'll have their cowboy actor president grandstanding, calling for 'that Wall' to come down, so they can turn us all into capitalist wage slaves, consumer cannon fodder for the capitalist exploitation economy. Just you wait.'

Stark could hardly believe his ears. Del was looking distinctly unhappy. The other customers were conspicuously paying attention to their own business. A conversation like this in a public place was almost unheard of. Stark reckoned

Del would have put the mockers on it in a flash if the bloke holding forth hadn't been a card-carrying communist and redder than red-blooded member of the Socialist Labour Party elite.

'It's just a film,' said Atkinson.

'Just a film? There's no such thing as just a film. That's what that evil little cripple Goebbels said when he got Leni Riefenstahl to knock out a few reels for him. Ever seen *Triumph of the Will*?' Atkinson shook his head. The Nazi propaganda piece was infamous but not available for public viewing.

'Well I have. And let me tell you, it's dangerous. Just like this will be. You pretend to be an artist, man, for God's sake. You should know more than anyone how easy it is to get people on board. Half the country follows your daft soap opera. Let me tell you, this will be a serious attempt to turn black into white, to mislead people about the historical truth.'

'What is the truth?'

Stark had the feeling the young actor was trying to make a philosophical point, but Hindsmith just looked at him as if he'd just announced he had a fairy godmother.

'The truth is that Winston Bloody Churchill – and I mean bloody – was a two-faced bastard who did the dirty on his most important ally. The minute the Krauts got rid of their Charlie Chaplin lookalike in that bomb attack back in '44, the old son of the aristocracy thought he saw a chance to team up with the Prussian posh boys and take over the world. Put Uncle Joe back in his place, and a damper on the working man's aspirations once and for all.'

A deathly hush had descended over the rest of the crowd at the bar. Davy was reading from the history book, the way they had all learned it at school. Mark Holt, the retired teacher, was nodding sagely, though Stark noted he had his eyes firmly closed.

'Might have done it and all, the Yanks, the empire and the Junkers all pushing the profit motive right the way back to the Urals. Except Zhukov and his boys were on a roll, weren't they? Took Berlin and kept on rolling, all the way to the sea. And with popular support roaring them on. Half the German troops didn't know which way they were supposed to be facing.'

'Yes, well, up to a point.' Stark knew the point and part of him inwardly admired the young actor's bravery in making it. 'I mean it did take them the best part of another four years. The popular support wasn't quite overwhelming.'

Hindsmith stared at him as if he'd been slapped in the face. 'Load of bloody reactionaries trying to play the old nationalist card, particularly on this side of the channel. The communists in Italy and France stood up to be counted. Even under the old bowler-hatted bastard some of our lads were bold enough to go out on strike.'

Stark knew the continuation of the war, just when most people thought it was coming to an end, had been highly unpopular. His father had admitted as much. The way it was taught in school was that Churchill had ridden roughshod over popular sentiment.

'The Yanks couldn't take it, didn't have the balls. Zhukov and co. would have rolled right on up to Northumberland and beyond if they hadn't threatened to use their bloody weapon of mass destruction. They were like rats in a barrel trapped around that embassy of theirs in Grosvenor Square.'

'It ended the war, though, didn't it?'

'Only because we – the forces of progress and socialism, that is – had one too, and they didn't know it. Mutual

Assured Destruction, that's what gave us the ceasefire. And peace ever since.'

'MAD, I believe they call it,' said Stark. It was his first intervention in the discussion. He hadn't intended it, just couldn't resist reminding them of the extraordinarily apt acronym.

'Call it whatever you like,' said Hindsmith. 'That's history. And anyone who doesn't believe it is deluding themselves. Dangerously.'

Chapter 11

For a second Harry Stark almost thought he had misheard, that he had conjured up the words his own imagination had been haunted by all day. But in that same second he realised with an absolute certainty he had not.

What other subject was likely to cause as much automatic, awkward controversy or inspire Del to come straight in with the 'guvnor's sanction'? Shut it, he had said. No surprise there.

The real surprise, Stark realised, lay in hearing something like that discussed publicly at all. Okay, neither man had mentioned the WC words out loud, but everyone involved, including Del and the other couple of less voluble hangers-on who had simply stood there gaping, knew what they were talking about. It was not that long ago that a conversation of that kind other than among trusted long-time friends and close family would have been asking for trouble. Maybe it was something to do with the new mood in Moscow, all this talk of a new official 'transparency'. *Glasnost*!? Harry Stark would believe in that when he saw through it.

If any of the others in the bar had noticed the brief altercation, they showed little sign of it. The young couple at the table nearest were too engrossed in each other to notice anything short of an armed assault on the premises, while old Stan and Mary sat side by side on the green imitation-leather banquette near the door staring silently into their gins, as they had done every night for as long as he could remember, the contented quiet calm of an old and settled relationship, or perhaps just senile stultification, Stark had never quite been sure. The tall man in the corner had unfolded a copy of the *Morning Star* and sat with his nose deeply buried in it, as if he was the one individual who really cared what Comrade Harkness had told the fortieth anniversary Congress of the Essex Autoworkers' Union.

Without him even having to raise his glass or wave the customary pound note over the counter, Lizzie was there, the usual, almost wicked wry smile playing at the corners of her mouth. Stark gave her a questioning look to which she replied with a barely perceptible shrug of the shoulders. Stark went to open his mouth but realised he had no idea what to say. Lizzie mouthed 'another time' at him and said:

'Another one, Harry?'

'Not tonight. Tired. Time I went home for my tea.'

He wrapped his scarf around his neck, flicked a hand at Del by way of farewell and got a brusque nod in return as he pushed open the door into the blustery night,

What Harry Stark meant by tea at that moment, looming vividly in his mind's eye, was a fish and chip supper, just as he had promised himself half an hour earlier. There was no point in waiting until he got home. His mother was used to his unsocial hours and Katy was always out with her friends these days, which made Stark more of a regular at the fish and chip shop than was good for his waistline.

The smell of cheap cooking oil sharpened by the tang of rough vinegar evoked an almost Pavlovian reaction from his senses. Stark stopped abruptly in front of the familiar frosted-glass door of the chip shop, only obliquely aware as he did so of causing someone behind him to lurch out of his way, muttering what sounded like a curse before scurrying past. Stark paid no heed. What he wanted was a fat piece of cod in crispy batter and a packet of greasy chips to go with it. His humour had recovered to the extent that his usual pessimistic precognition failed to recognise the expression on the face behind the counter.

'Evening, Mr Stark,' said Johnny, a spotty boy of barely seventeen who had been taken on just before Christmas and seemed to always do the early evening shift now. The greeting was as pleasant as always; the look on his face, however, was apprehensive.

'If it's your usual, Mr Stark ...'

'It is indeed, Johnny. Cod and chips and don't stilt on the salt and vinegar.' Stark could feel a benign glow of satisfaction settling on him, the product of good beer and anticipation of familiar food.

'It's just that we're out of cod, sir.'

Stark blinked, as if he hadn't heard, but he had. 'Out of cod? Well, what ...' but the words faded away as he surveyed the empty top tray of the fryer where at least one or two pieces of ready-cooked fish usually sat in their batter waiting for the impatient customer.

'It's just temporary. Least, that's what the bloke on the truck said. Billingsgate market's rationing at the moment. Said it should be all right again in a couple of days.' The boy shrugged, as if to say it wasn't his fault, which it wasn't. But Stark's bubble of contentment had been deflated, his mood of peaceful resignation punctured by a sudden anger. He muttered an obscenity almost violently under his breath. The boy behind the counter looked alarmed.

'Chips then,' growled Stark. 'A bag of chips, please. I assume they're still delivering fucking potatoes.'

'Yes, Mr Stark. No problem.' Johnny bent his head and began shovelling chips generously into a greaseproof bag.

Stark closed his eyes and let the disappointment subside. Just another hitch in the supply chain. He pushed a ten-pence piece over the counter and took the warm reeking parcel, wrapped as usual in that day's copy of the *New Times*. Some traditions survived: the need to save on scarce resources meant the party stomached seeing its leaders' otherwise hallowed words and faces used as wrapping. Stark barely noticed the picture of Harkness, the elderly General Secretary, giving serried ranks of Dagenham car workers a foretaste of his speech on the forthcoming holiday.

Outside it was just starting to rain, a fine misty drizzle, the sort that was persistent rather than aggressive but sank into clothing, skin and hair almost by osmosis, the sort that could give you pneumonia before you knew it. The detective's fingers grubbed open the package and a rash of vinegar spread across Comrade Harkness's serious face.

The street was empty, quiet, save for the occasional swoosh of car tyres on wet tarmac. Stark dipped his fingers into the warm carbohydrate mush of his vinegar-sodden chips and tried to take what comfort he could in his fishless supper. He pulled his coat collar up, heedless of the grease marks left by his fingers, and quickened his pace. It was a good ten minutes' walk home, long enough for him to finish his chips and get comprehensively soaked.

He ducked into a doorway for a minute for the sake of enjoying a few mouthfuls unadulterated by rainwater, and noticed a shadow move in the insipid lamplight across the street, as if someone else had done the same thing. It was no night for anyone but an idiot to be tramping the street. Like the idiot who had almost tripped over his feet as he entered the chip shop. And was now sheltering in the doorway opposite? Waiting for Stark to emerge?

Stark watched the spot where he had seen the movement, but there was nothing apparent. He put another chip in his mouth and moved out into the rain. Four doorways on he stopped again, suddenly, and ducked once more into shelter, turning as he did so. Once again he caught a glimpse of movement, as if someone on the other side of the road, maybe forty metres back, was shadowing his steps. Could it really be that he was being followed? Policemen sometimes followed other people. No one followed policemen. Except – the thought crept up on him like a mugger in an alleyway – except for those who thought themselves above the law.

The sight of the black Bevan lurking on the Embankment had lingered with Stark all day. Not just its presence, but its peremptory disappearance, as if arrogantly dismissing them. Stark, like most ordinary CID men at the Yard had little love for 'the Department' and less for those who worked in it. It was nothing to do with politics, or so he told himself. More a matter of taste.

He knew also that in the scheme of things, in the world of *Realpolitik*, the DoSS carried the clout that counted. Even if he was not technically outranked by a DoSS officer of similar status, he was always outflanked. They were playing a different game: one in which only they knew the location of the goalposts. And even then they kept moving them.

And now they were playing tag in the rain, were they? Or was it Harry Stark getting paranoid just because some rain-soaked drunk on the other side of the road was ducking into doorways just like he was? Maybe, but somehow he doubted it. And the doubt irritated him immensely.

Stark moved out of the doorway and quickened his pace. From the corner of his eye he caught a flicker in the lamp-light, enough to convince him that the figure on the other side of the road had done the same. Instinctively he moved his left arm against his body to feel the reassuring bulk of his shoulder-holstered pistol. There was always the outside possibility that he had been spotted by some amateur footpad new to the district and unaware of the identity of his mark. If any would-be mugger really was targeting him, then he would be in for a very nasty surprise indeed. Stark doubted it. The streets were dark but generally safe. This was Bermondsey, not Soho where, according to 'Wicked Auntie' at least, muggings were a part of daily life. He laughed a silent, bitter laugh. It was a comparison he was unlikely ever to make in person.

No, the more he thought about it, putting one chip after another into his mouth, the more he was certain that his clumsy tail was wagged by the men who were ferried around in shiny black Bevans, and considered honest coppers like him lumps of pig iron to do with as they pleased. If that was the case Harry Stark would show this one what sort of metal he was made of.

He quickened his pace again, then stopped. Abruptly. Fumbling in his pocket as if he had forgotten something, he found a coin and let it slip through his fingers and rattle into the gutter. He bent down as if to pick it up, using the opportunity to glance between his legs and see the figure on the other side of the road moving with improbable slowness. Apart from the two of them, the road was deserted. A few cars were parked here and there, one still covered in its winter tarpaulin, waiting for the coming of spring. A solitary battered Fellow Traveller, trusty workhorse of the upmarket proletariat, splashed by in the opposite direction, taking some functionary home from his day at the bureaucratic coalface. There were no other pedestrians. The man stood out like the proverbial sore thumb. It was hard to believe they could be so incompetent. The idea that they were 'secret' police was a serious misnomer; sometimes they could hardly be more obvious. But then that was part of the arrogance.

The same arrogance that sent someone to follow him home, as if they didn't know where he lived. It was a culture not of surveillance but of intimidation that made you feel you had something to hide, even when you hadn't. Well, if they acted like backstreet muggers, Stark was willing to treat them as such.

He stood upright and walked on, maintaining a brisk but unhurried pace as far as the junction with Pankhurst Street, where he routinely took a right. The rain was heavier now, big full-sized drops that splashed on the kerbstones. The figure behind had lagged back, as if he knew that too. Pankhurst Street was long, straight with terrace houses on either side, easy to keep an eye on someone from a more discreet distance than this amateur had so far managed. But this was Harry's home turf.

The house on the corner had once had grander pretensions than its neighbours, exemplified by stucco pillars projecting from the yellow London brick. The impression of a porch, as well as the reality, had long since been shattered, probably by stray shellfire, but what remained was an alcove easily deep enough to conceal Harry Stark. Reluctantly jettisoning the few remaining chips in their vinegar-saturated newsprint, he folded himself into it, wiping the grease from his fingers on his coat sleeve before closing them around the grip of his handgun.

Within seconds he heard hurrying footsteps. His tail would have reached the corner only to find the long stretch of Pankhurst Street unexpectedly empty. A figure appeared in view almost directly in front of him, tall, angular. There was something in the hunch of the shoulders, a stance that appeared both timorous and unaccustomed, like a man playing an unusual role, that seemed obliquely familiar.

A mental picture came to him, of an awkward figure emerging from the Tube, head and shoulders above the crowd but pushed by it to one side. Had he been following him since then? In the pub? The solitary figure in the corner absorbed in his copy of the *Morning Star*? He might as well have been reading the *Guardian*, the DoSS house journal. He turned his head towards the ruined porch.

Stark launched himself from the doorway, bringing the butt of his revolver sharply down behind the man's ear as his left foot lashed out at the vulnerable back of his knee. The figure crumpled. Stark fell on him. His right knee pressed down on the small of the back, his left hand seized the man's hair and jerked his head back sharply, to feel the muzzle of Stark's revolver pressed against his temple.

'Armed police! Identify yourself.' Stark bellowed the words. Over the top, but according to the rulebook.

The response was a half-choked gurgle, then a gasped oath: 'Jesus fucking Christ! Okay, okay, don't kill me!'

Involuntarily Stark pulled back, instinctively relaxing his grip, almost foolishly releasing it. He let the muzzle of the revolver retreat to the point where it no longer made an indentation in the soft, painfully vulnerable flesh of the temple. It was not the old-fashioned obscenity that had shocked him, but the accent in which it was uttered. He craned his neck forward to get a look at the incalculably alien life form sprawled beneath him.

'You're an American?' he said.

Chapter 12

Stark stood in the rain, water streaming down his face and stared into the eyes of the man he had just pulled to his feet. Small rabbit-eyes, still in shock, lower lip visibly trembling as he replaced a pair of spectacles with hopelessly twisted frames on the bridge of his nose. Despite his size he looked lost, nervous, more a frightened gazelle than a hunting dog. A far cry from the trained hoods of the Department. But then his accent alone proved that.

'Who the hell are you?' Stark asked, authority rather than anger in his voice.

The reply bubbled up like a spring in flood: 'Fairweather, Ben, Benjamin Fairweather, *New York Times*. Pleased to meet you. I'm very sorry. I didn't mean … I'm sorry. I …' He wiped his nose with his sleeve.

'What? The New York …?'

'*Times*. I'm a reporter.' Rain was dripping in a steady stream of droplets from his lank hair. 'Can we …? I mean, you don't need that.'

Stark looked down and realised he was still pointing his pistol point blank at the man's heaving chest. Still watching him carefully, he put it away.

'Why were you following me?'

'I wasn't. I mean, that is, I wanted to see if you were being followed. And to be sure I wasn't.' He looked around, warily, at the empty street, as if to prove it.

'What?' Stark had heard tales of the way the foreign press, Americans and Northerners, worked: sitting in their offices making up stories about the imminent collapse of social-ism when all along it was their own societies that were on the brink of anarchy. Stark wasn't sure just how much all of that was true, but he did know that western newspapers printed stories alleged to have come from 'dissident sources behind the wall.' Stark knew some of these 'sources': drift-ers who grumbled because they were too incompetent or lazy to do a proper job, and only too happy to take convert-ible 'British' pounds as opposed to English ones, cultivat-ing malcontents and petty criminals, those who refused to accept proper jobs, and elevating them to the status of 'dis-sidents'. The sort of people who painted honest policemen as the devil's disciples and called them PeePees (though never to their faces).

Why an American journalist might be following Stark around the back streets of Bermondsey on a stinking April evening he had no idea and he could not imagine any he might approve of. This dripping youth did not exactly look like a shock trooper of capitalist imperialism but he still had one hell of a lot of explaining to do.

'ID.'

The American fumbled in his overcoat, produced a thick wallet and from it a yellow laminated card with a photo-graph of a smiling young man in thick-framed spectacles, with a tan that suggested he was more used to Florida beaches than English rain, and in Gothic lettering the words *New York Times*.

'I ... I've changed my glasses,' he stammered, answering the question Stark hadn't asked and fiddling with the thin wire wreckage on his nose.

'Passport.'

'Look, you have to listen to me.'

'Passport. Please.'

From the same pocket emerged a leather-bound US passport. Stark thumbed through it, scanning the stamps and the visas: *République Populaire Française* once in June the previous year and again in September, *Deutsche Volksrepublik* once, three years ago, and then a flurry of red and white, blurred crosses and roses for London, capital of the English Democratic Republic from Westminster, through the Oxford Street/Tottenham Court Road border checkpoint. A frequent visitor but not an overnighter. Today's stamp was no different; he had to be out by midnight.

'Detective Inspector Stark. I need to talk to you.'

Stark shook his head. How the hell did some American reporter know his name? The rain was pouring down, bouncing off the tarmac. Whatever Stark needed it wasn't this. Or double pneumonia.

'So talk.'

The American looked around him, every minute more like a drowning rat.

'Is there anywhere we could go. To get out of this.'

There was, just two minutes away, with a hot cup of tea waiting and a warm bed that Harry Stark was looking forward to climbing into. But he was damned if he was inviting some suspicious representative of the ideological family into the bosom of his dysfunctional family.

'If you want to talk to the police, make an appointment. Contact the Home Office press department. Don't follow policemen at night. It's dangerous. Now get out of here. It's time you went home.'

Stark pushed him aside, and walked past. Whatever idiocy he wanted could wait.

'You don't understand,' the voice was almost pleading.

And that's not the half of it, thought Stark, walking on, faster.

'It's about the body. The one they found hanging underneath the bridge.'

Stark slowed, but didn't quite stop. Why was it he had somehow known all along that this couldn't be coincidence.

'You haven't got an ID yet, have you?'

Stark slowed his pace but kept walking.

'I can tell you who he is.'

The detective stopped and turned around. The American was holding his wallet in his hand: 'I have a photograph.'

Chapter 13

In the rain the watcher waited, uncomplainingly. That was, after all, a substantial part of his job. And he was dry, if not warm, inside the anonymous little Sputnik car. That was the trade-off, the deal. If sometimes the job was dirty, you could wash your hands afterwards. In a flat of your own, with hot water, and a fridge full of food.

Coincidentally exactly the same thought was running through the head of his boss at that precise minute. Col Charles Marchmain gazed out from the high windows of the Department of Social Security's offices at the cosy curtained windows of the staff apartments in the surrounding tower blocks of the Barbican Estate and thought how fitting it was that he and his co-workers lived where they did.

The Barbican had been the name of a long-vanished gate to the ancient City of London, a tower from which the city watch ensured the security of its inhabitants, a job for which they were well rewarded. Less had changed, he mused, than some people thought. Today's inhabitants of the 1960s highrise Barbican development were the moral descendants of the men who manned the Barbican gate all those centuries ago, and they too were well rewarded, not least with a self-contained housing complex with shops, concert hall, cinema and underground parking, A city within a city.

You did your bit for the state, and the state saw you right. It was not a moral choice; it was an economic one. Marx had been right; economics was the basis of all human activity. It was, of course, just a fancy modern way of describing a law that had been known since before the dawn of human history; the law of survival. And often, in the cause of survival, compromises had to be made. Even in a socialist society everything had its price. And a job well done brought its own rewards.

Marchmain's reward, for example, was that it had been a long time since he had been required to spend an evening sitting in a Sputnik in the rain. The Soviet-made Sputnik was an unpleasant, uncomfortable little car, particularly in comparison with the big plush Bevans, but the incalculable advantage in the watcher's line of work was that they were the most common cars on the streets of the capital. They also came in very few colours. Although he had lately observed an irritating trend for 'sky blue' and 'apple green', undoubtedly the brainchild of ministries with more time on their hands than was good for them, most remained solidly beige. Beige was the colour the colonel preferred. The one he would have chosen if he had been designing camouflage for the streets of his city.

Marchmain's relatively lowly employee, parked only twenty metres from Detective Inspector Harry Stark's house was doing a job that was essential to maintaining the established order. Those who did not like the established order despised those who maintained it. But that was the way of things. The alternative was revolution. And the party was vehemently opposed to revolution.

If there was an irony in that, the colonel was oblivious to it. He understood the Marxist principle of dialectics: thesis, antithesis and synthesis. He understood it to mean you looked at both sides of the argument and adopted the solution that suited you best. That was what he liked about the philosophy: it seemed only common sense. He had heard there were other, more doctrinaire interpretations, but as that did not seem to make sense to him, he declined to explore them.

He was often impressed by how many ordinary citizens seemed to have come to the same conclusion. Like the boy in the fish shop, for example, who had spotted the clumsy tail, possibly even before Harry Stark. He had done well, calling in on spec to leave a message on the 'anonymous' citizen's advisory line, the tape recorders which were in reality monitored live twenty-four hours a day, just because he noticed something unusual about a Significant Person. Marchmain had been pleased.

Sometimes he wondered what they would do without their ready army of Fellow Travellers, that invisible army who chose, for small reward, to be of service to the Department. Just as he wondered how many of them knew that the phrase used to describe them was English for the Russian name of the first Earth satellite and the mundane little car to which most ordinary citizens aspired: Sputnik. Precious few, he imagined. The English had never been good at foreign languages and, despite compulsory lessons at school, Russian had proved no exception to that rule.

The human Fellow Travellers were as integral a part of the Department of Social Security as the four-wheeled variety was part of the socialist dream. It was yet another volunteer who had noted the suspicious stranger in the pub. The man who both arrived and left just after Stark, and within minutes one of the colonel's little friends had gone to the public phone to do the proper thing. Marchmain was impressed, in a curious sort of way.

But then he was a connoisseur of the common people. Watching them was what he did for a living, taking in the minutiae of their existence, collectively and individually, noting subtle changes, behaviour shifts, taking stock of new acquaintances and adding as required to the list of those observed. From a professional point of view, it was compelling, even obsessive work. But there again, it was just what he did for a living. For some, it seemed, it was a way of life.

There were times, only times, Marchmain told himself as he sank back into his swivel chair, when he almost envied the man on the spot, the man who followed orders without thinking. Not that he didn't follow orders himself, it was just that he was also obliged to do at least a minimal amount of thinking. And he was not a man who liked to define his life by the minimum.

The radio on his desk buzzed. Marchmain glanced at the flashing red light and flicked the switch next to it. The voice was the one he had been expecting, that of the man in the little nondescript car sitting in the rain in Bermondsey.

'Strongbow and Fisherman have entered property,' it said.

Marchmain nodded thoughtfully to himself. It seemed Detective Inspector Stark was bringing a visitor home to meet the family.

Chapter 14

The American perched on the edge of Harry Stark's single bedroom chair nursing a mug of scalding tea. Stark sat opposite him, on the bed, doing the same, like a pair of old-fashioned adulterers embarrassed by their first hotel room tryst.

The American took off his battered spectacles, rubbed the lenses on his tie, fiddled with the twisted frames and put them on again. They still looked ridiculous.

'I'm sorry about your glasses,' Stark said.

The American shrugged. 'It's okay. I have another pair.'

Stark nodded. Of course, he would have. It was the sort of thing Americans had. And here he was, a man who had a spare pair of glasses, sitting in the meagre surroundings of a southern English home. A policeman's home to boot. Some American reporters, he imagined, could make a story out of that alone. He envisaged the ticking off he would get from the Chief Constable if the Stark domestic household ended up the subject of a *New York Times* Sunday supplement feature.

Luckily Katy was out. She usually was these days. Out more often and later with the friends her mother didn't approve of. Kids who wore their Young Pioneer uniforms sloppily if at all, preferred jeans and sneakers, imports from 'up North', the sort of stuff you could only get if you had relatives in Leeds or Manchester who sent presents at Christmas. Or sent money so you could buy them in the hard currency shop in Cheapside where they only took 'British' pounds, not the everyday English ones ordinary folk had in their pockets. Mrs Stark didn't approve of any of that, just as she knew her late husband hadn't. Just another thing she held against her daughter's current lifestyle.

The minute Stark had put his key in the lock, she had stuck her head round the corner of the sitting room door, a hatchet look on her face to disguise the anxiety he knew it concealed: expecting it to be Katy, ready to tell her off, venting her concern as anger. Harry had told her a hundred times not to worry, that it was only a phase, that kids were like that these days. But he would have preferred her not to have been standing like an inquisitor in the hallway when he led Benjamin Fairweather into the house.

'Just someone from work, Mum,' he had said as nonchalantly as possible. 'Be a love and fetch us a couple of mugs of tea, would you,' he added, turning her around and shepherding her back through the hall door before she had a chance to ask questions, or Fairweather had a chance to open his mouth. The last thing Harry Stark wanted was for his unusual visitor to become a focus of conversation for neighbourhood tittle-tattle.

Mrs Stark knew more than to gossip as she queued at Smithfield for the meat stores to open. Careless talk costs lives, she had been taught as a girl and she had seen nothing in her adult life to believe things had changed. But that did nothing to stem her curiosity, honed already to razor's edge when she knocked on Harry's door to deliver the tea and the idiotically grinning Benjamin Fairweather had taken it from her hands with a 'Gee, thanks, Mrs Stark, sure is good of you.' He couldn't have shocked her more if he'd sung 'God Save the Queen'.

Stark had warded off her machete glances as he

manoeuvred her towards the door, closed it firmly, then opened and banged it shut again to be sure the old lady did not have her ear pressed to the other side. He glared at the American.

'Sorry about that,' said Fairweather, 'just being polite. I'm from Boston. New England. Most people in the US think we talk like the British – the English I mean … as well – but I guess it still sounds kind of different over here. Maybe I should keep my mouth shut.'

Stark nodded. 'As a rule of thumb. However, right now I'd prefer it if you did some talking. But keep it concise.'

'Sure thing. That's why I'm here. Oh, and call me Ben.'

There was less of the lost-dog look to him now, Harry thought, as if he had shrugged off the awkwardness and embarrassment with the rainwater. He stood up and took off his wet overcoat – 'If I may,' Harry nodded – sat back down and took a sip of tea like a junior Harvard professor about to deliver a tutorial. He put his hand inside his jacket pocket and asked, 'Do you mind if I smoke?'

Stark shook his head. The American produced a flip-top box, the sort you saw on BBC commercials. Marlboro. Stark knew the jingle as well as the national anthem. They played the latter at television closedown every night: 'There'll always be an England, while there's a country lane, Wherever there's a cottage small beside a field of grain' – the bucolic image the party peddled to its collective farmers and factory-worker high-rise dwellers. Most people preferred the illicit BBC diet of *LA Vice* laced with ads for 'the big taste from the big country.' The American flicked open the packet.

'Want one?'

Stark had been trying to give up. But it was a lot easier to abandon Bulgarian factory-floor sweepings than it was to turn down finest Virginia. He hesitated, but only for a moment. The American leaned towards him and with a silver Ronson that produced a clean clear flame at the first click lit up both of them.

'Thanks.' It was a word Stark had not anticipated using this evening. The American took a quick puff. Stark inhaled deeply, hunched forward and listened. It was the first lesson he had learned in detective training: don't always be in a rush to ask the questions.

'Go ahead,' he said.

'First of all, I had better show you this.'

The American opened a bulging wallet and from a zipped compartment produced a two-by-three centimetre pass- port-style photograph. Harry leaned forward to take it. The man in the photograph was middle-aged, early forties at a guess, thickset with dark, beetling eyebrows beneath a head of swept-back hair just beginning to turn to pepper and salt. He had wide, smiling, self-confident eyes and the sort of smooth suntanned complexion that suggested frequent exposure to a stronger sun than that of southern England. Or Northern England, come to that.

'Who is he?'

'That picture is at least five years old, probably more. His name is Martin Bloom. And I am almost totally certain that it was his body that your men found this morning hanging under Blackfriars Bridge.'

'Almost?'

'Detective Stark ... Harry, if I may ...'

Stark said nothing. Why Americans tried to force a phoney familiarity on complete strangers was beyond him.

Stark looked at the photograph. It was possible. But given the state of the bloody corpse he had dispatched to St Bart's morgue earlier that day, almost any photograph of a thick-set middle-aged man would have been a candidate. Apart from this improbable American's assertion that they were one and the same, Stark had no reason to believe it. On the other hand he was signally lacking in alternatives.

'Who is this man, and what makes you think someone would want to murder him?'

Fairweather smiled, a smug little self-confident smile.

'So you have ruled out suicide? It was a bit unlikely, wasn't it?'

Stark winced at his error. Yet somehow he didn't think he had given anything away. If this man really knew who the victim was, then he already knew far more than Harry Stark did.

'Like I said, his name is Martin Bloom. Born and brought up in San Antonio, Texas, but also a British citizen, courtesy of the fact that his mother was a Londoner. From your part of the city, I might add, although back in the day when there was no division. She was what they called back then a GI bride.'

Stark showed no expression. He still had no idea where this story was going any more than he had the faintest idea where Mr Benjamin Fairweather was coming from, in any sense other than the geographical.

'You still haven't told me what this Mr Bloom was doing in the capital of the English Democratic Republic.'

The American leaned back in Stark's little wickerwork bedroom chair causing it to creak.

'He was working for me.'

'What?'

'It's simple enough. Martin Bloom was a journalist, like myself. But a freelance, not a staffer. Because of his British passport it was easier for him to come over here. I'm sure you know there are fewer visa restrictions for visits from your former compatriots.'

Stark instinctively looked up in supposed offence.

'I'm sorry, citizens of the Federal Republic of Britain if that's what you prefer. We're both men of the world, detective. Whatever.' He shrugged his shoulders. 'The other thing was his accent. Unlike me, he could speak the English language as you guys speak it in England. He didn't walk around with a big sign above his head that said "Yank" in flashing neon every time he opened his mouth. He could pass as a native. People talked to him. Told him things.'

Stark gave him a quizzical look.

'That sounds suspiciously like deliberate deception to me, Mr Fairweather. Foreign journalists are supposed to go through the official channels.'

As far as Stark was concerned, the American had just confirmed that this was a case for the Department. Whatever Mr Bloom, if that really was his name, had been up to, it sounded no good. No good at all.

The American leaned back again, and sighed, and bent forward giving Stark the distinctly patronising impression he thought he was talking to a child.

'I know it's different over here. But you have to understand, at least try to understand. I'm not talking about some sort of espionage here, even if maybe that's how some people in your system might see it. Journalism in ...' – he struggled for the phrase – '... our world, it's, it's just different. It's not about reporting what the authorities want reported.'

Stark raised an eyebrow.

'I don't mean your authorities, I mean ours too. No matter what they tell you in the official press here, our press really is free. We ask questions. Uncomfortable ones. And there are some people over here who wish things worked the same here too.'

And there were some, thought Stark, who were determined to make damn sure they never did.

'You must have noticed the world is changing. I know it doesn't feel like that in London, but there are people thinking the unthinkable. Even in Moscow.'

Stark blinked. Twice. The trouble with what Fairweather was saying was that it was true. Sort of. Things were happening. Elsewhere. There was talk of a free trade union in Poland, not tied to the party. There had been economic reforms in Hungary, a move towards letting more people be self-employed. There had been student marches in Paris, although there again, there always had been. But most significantly of all there was a new man in the Kremlin. Talking a new language. Words like *perestroika* and *glasnost,* rebuilding, openness, unfamiliar words that had people across Europe dusting off their Russian dictionaries. Even Lavery had said the other day he'd heard *Pravda* was more interesting than *New Times* or the *Guardian* these days.

But that was elsewhere. London was London, and London didn't change. The old guard in the Mansion House had been there forever and showed no sign of moving out in the foreseeable future. Even old Harkness's heir apparent was older than the new man in Moscow, handpicked for a seamless handover, and not any time soon either. *Glasnost,* they joked in the Red Lion, was a foreign concept, and an abstract one at that. The English didn't deal in abstract concepts; they dealt in concrete ones. Summed up by a three-metre high concrete wall.

'What if I told you,' the American leaned forward conspiratorially, 'that there are people here, in this society, who feel it is time for a change. People who have a story to tell. A great story, one that could change your world and maybe mine too?'

Stark sat back. He felt like saying he sincerely hoped he was not going to be told anything of the sort.

'That's what Martin Bloom was doing, Harry. Trying to talk to people, trying to give people over here something they desperately lack – a voice.'

Stark could have replied that his father had always taught him it was all right having a voice as long as you knew the consequences of what you said. But deep down there was a part of him that understood what the American was saying, even if he could not quite believe it.

'It's not a crime, Harry. At least it shouldn't be. It's not subversion or starting a revolution. It's just letting people have a discussion. Is that really such a bad thing?'

'And for this, you're saying, this Mr Bloom was …'

'For this, Mr Bloom was killed.' For the first time, there was anger in the American's voice. 'For this he was hung like some piece of carrion underneath a bridge over the Thames. I'm not saying journalists are one hundred per cent on the side of the angels, here. Maybe he had no right to expect kid-glove treatment but he sure as hell didn't deserve to be murdered in cold blood and strung up like some piece of butcher's meat.'

'And who are you suggesting is responsible?'

The American drew on his Marlboro and exhaled a long grey plume of smoke towards the solitary low-wattage light bulb that dangled in its drab shade from the ceiling: 'Jesus Christ, Harry, don't give me that. You know who killed him as well as I do: your so-called Department of Social Security.

'The same people who killed your father.'

Chapter 15

High in his Barbican tower, Col Charles Marchmain opened the buff file on his desk and perused the details of the day's surveillance of the American whose passport and press card proclaimed him to be Benjamin Fairweather, special correspondent of the *New York Times*.

Such a status on its own marked him out as a PIN, a Person of Interest. The Department liked acronyms; it removed the inconvenience of thinking of human beings. Fellow Travellers were FTs. But a PIN was also a Potential Nuisance (or as Marchmain privately put it a Pain In the Arse), and Fairweather undoubtedly fell into that category. That was to say he belonged to a whole regiment of foreign journalists, Northerners or Americans, who made it their business, or at least the business of their press baron masters, to create the worst possible image of the Workers' and Farmers' State.

. Until his meeting with Detective Inspector Harry Stark, however, it had not been known just how much of a nuisance Fairweather in particular could be. Now it was. He had graduated to the higher category of CN, a Confirmed Nuisance, an acronym for which Marchmain also had his own private alternative.

Fairweather had entered the capital over the Oxford Street/ Tottenham Court Road crossing point at 2.27 p.m. Marchmain quietly applauded the admirably precise timings kept by the border guards. That was approximately two hours after the BBC midday television news had, inevitably but regrettably, carried the story of the body under the bridge.

Marchmain had made a point of watching the broadcast. It followed a familiar format – the party press referred to the BBC as the Bigoted Bourgeois Channel – making the most of blurred footage shot from a distance and backed up by the strident tones of that dreadful Mancunian woman with a chip the size of Mother England on her shoulder. The camera showed the police holding them back, a glimpse of Stark putting his hand over the camera, and there, in the background, an unfortunate glimpse of his own black Bevan saloon, number plate happily unreadable at that distance. Back to the female commentator for a few unsourced, contentious comments about the 'shady world on the other side of the Wall' and the obligatory closing shots of the cheap plywood crosses by the foot of 'Big Ben' – the tacky so-called 'memorials' erected by Westminster's propaganda department to make martyrs out of traitors. The insinuation was as insidious as it was contrived.

When the American journalist crossed the border little more than two hours later, a team of low-level Department minions latched onto him within 100 metres of the checkpoint as they usually did with visiting PINs. At that stage it was just routine. Nothing elaborate, just the day-to-day passing of target to target among the teams who usually worked the tourist trail from Stalingrad Square to St Paul's.

Fairweather had initially blended in with the sightseers, gawping at the Admiralty Arch as if he'd never seen it from the other side, where tourists and celebrities alike were taken to stare over the Wall. He took a few photographs of the fountains and the great bronze Landseer lions controversially rehabilitated from their exile as imperialist symbols, now nestling by the feet of the great Boudicca-like figure holding aloft a rose symbolising the English Motherland. The symbolism was not wasted on Marchmain: the imperial lions tamed by a replica of the towering Soviet colossus on the Volga.

Fairweather appeared to be a perfectly standard tourist, up to a point. Occasionally he lingered too long at one spot or another, took too few photographs. Significantly he never once had to be reprimanded by the uniformed beat bobbies used to gently informing visitors that what they called 'the Wall' was the state frontier, not a tourist attraction, and definitely not for posing against.

But there Fairweather had parted company with the usual tourist round. He had shown no interest in the National Gallery, or heading off towards the great damaged dome of St Paul's. Instead Fairweather had repaired for refreshment, to the Red Lion on Whitehall, the uninviting watering hole whose usual regular company of police regulars, notably taciturn towards outsiders, deterred all but the most determined drinker. He had sat near the window, as if keen not to miss a detail of the capital's passing pedestrian traffic, and scrutinised with eager anticipation every new arrival. It looked, the early afternoon shift reported at knocking-off time, as if he were waiting for someone.

Someone who never arrived. By five thirty as the evening shadows began to lengthen over the Embankment, genuine tourists started wondering whether to use up their remaining 'English pounds', the E£25 per diem they had been obliged to exchange at the official one-to-one exchange rate, on some of the uninspiring 'honest English fare' in one of the state-run Corner House restaurants. But instead of searching out an eating house without a queue or making for a cab back to the checkpoint, and the supposed culinary delights of Westminster, he ambled the hundred metres or so down to the Victory Embankment.

He looked like nothing so much as 'some poor bloke stood up by his bird', one of the more colloquial junior observers had reported. And indeed, it could have been a poignant spot for a lovers' tryst by the river as the daylight faded. But if Fairweather had come to gaze on the grimy Waterloo sunset he was doing so alone. No one came to meet him as the American stood and smoked his Marlboro on the waterfront, apparently rapt in admiration of the more exotic elements of Norman Shaw's architectural flourishes on the turrets of New Scotland Yard.

In fact he had shown a greater than usual interest in one monument on the banks of the Thames, the tank that sat on its pedestal outside New Scotland Yard. Indeed he had gone out of his way to take an artistic photograph of it, from an angle that would have included in the background the Gothic turret that housed the offices of CID. And one corner office in particular, that of Detective Inspector Harry Stark.

That was when, a little later perhaps the colonel would remark in caustic comments to his surveillance teams, the penny finally dropped. The call to the Barbican had quickly been routed to Marchmain's office and within seconds an unmarked car with siren sounding and lights flashing was pushing through traffic down Ludgate Hill, along Fleet Street and the Strand. Sirens and lights had been doused by the time it drew up to the faded splendour of the Savoy Hotel's main entrance, where it delivered four very ordinary-looking members of the public. The porters and receptionists took no notice of them whatsoever as they quickly passed through the down-at-heel grandeur of the public rooms, descending a level en route to the River Entrance, the grand name for the hotel's back door, where they left again to blend with the stream of nobodies jostling along the Embankment. These were professional nobodies, the crème de la crème.

They were already there, one buying cigarettes from the kiosk by Charing Cross Tube station, one buried deep in the bus queue on Northumberland Avenue and two shuffling arm-in-arm along the Embankment by the time DI Stark, the crime scene detective from the morning's incident, instantly recognisable in the same grubby trench coat in which he had made his reluctant cameo appearance on the BBC lunchtime news, emerged, head down like a man with the weight of the world on his shoulders, and plodded in the direction of Charing Cross Tube, with Benjamin T. Fairweather (PIN rapidly upgrading to CN) immediately in ill-concealed pursuit.

Nobody followed him; the sort of nobody who wore the drab brown suit that defined the lower-ranking apparatchik civil servants who formed the bulk of inner-city commuters, and kept his eyes as blank and unfocused as the rest of them. The second nobody was a youth in the universal jeans and trainers outfit worn by a southerner with good connections or a slightly dowdy Northern tourist kid, who clicked his fingers annoyingly and whistled a poor version of some Merseyside beat anthem. Stark, who might be presumed to have more of an eye for a tail if he were at all suspicious, which he had no obvious reason to be, could not help but notice the shabbily-dressed middle-aged woman who affected a virulent early spring cold. She was, as she put it later with a laugh, 'right in his face'; certain conspicuous behaviour, she was fond of saying, was even better than invisibility.

Nobody else was a wet-nosed myopic old man with thick glasses, a flat cap and a grubby scarf pulled right around his neck, who sat seemingly staring into past memories. In fact the only thought that ever distracted him from his duty was the occasional wistful reflection that if a different fate had caused his birth thirty-six years earlier to have occurred a few miles to the west of his Bethnal Green birthplace he might one day have won an Oscar. But there was no such thing as a different fate. Everyone knew that.

Only in the less crowded streets around the Elephant was there a risk of even the most competent team being too obvious. As they emerged from the Tube, the bronchitic woman duly disappeared into the night, the boy to the news stand, while the old man easily kept up with Stark's unhurried pace as far as the chip shop where he stopped to stare into the window, deciding it gave him a good opportunity to drop well behind. He was much amused when the detective pressed a coin into his palm but still managed to mutter an appreciative guttural, 'Thanks comrade'.

The boy in jeans had watched from a distance as the American followed the detective into The Rose, before walking on to the phone box on the corner. The man in the brown suit had followed Harry's normal routine, changing to the Northern Line and emerging at Borough he picked up the duty Sputnik and Marchmain's instructions from the Department branch office.

He had been on spot, parked within sight of the Rose exit before the boy, who had lit up and given every impression of settling in to ring a series of girlfriends, left the phone box.

When the policeman left, the watcher let him go. He was for the moment at least a secondary target. They knew where he lived. Fairweather came out of the pub only a few minutes later, at least a minute longer than he obviously felt comfortable with to judge from the pathetically furtive and clearly panicky way he scanned the streets before deciding which way Stark had gone.

The watcher watched, faintly amused at their pas-de-deux in the all but deserted dark wet streets. He waited until Fairweather had turned the corner before he started up the engine, then drove around the block doing a quick pass in the opposite direction, and parked at the distant end. Engine off, lights out.

He watched from afar the altercation in the doorway with a wry smile. DI Stark had behaved almost as exactly as he would have done himself. Obviously a man who favoured a 'hands-on' approach. Whatever was going down, it appeared, was not a pre-arranged rendezvous. He watched however with greater interest when Harry Stark picked up the man whose head he had threatened to blow off, and then, apparently, invited him to his home. On the colonel's express order, crackling over the radio, he waited until the pair had crossed the road and turned the corner. From the moment the two men had set off together their destination had been obvious. But just because something was obvious did not make it comprehensible. And it certainly did not make it acceptable.

He was unsurprised therefore when the order came through to position himself with a clear view of the front door and remain there, with instructions to report any development. By then he was envying his colleagues, imagining they might have been released from duty. Though he was not surprised the following day to be told that that had not been the case, that in fact another team had been called in to watch the streets around, the alleyways, back gardens and any other way in which someone could leave the little house in Pankhurst Street without being spotted.

Benjamin T. Fairweather had been given his rope, a lot of it, and now it remained only to be seen if he would hang himself with it, even if that was an unfortunate turn of phrase under the circumstances.

Chapter 16

'What the hell do you think you mean by that?'

One moment Harry Stark had been sitting with his head on one hand smoking the best cigarette he had tasted in years and listening to a man he should consider an enemy of the people pretend to solve a murder case for him. The next he was on his feet glaring down furiously at an arrogant liar he suddenly wished he'd gone ahead and shot dead when the bastard mugged him an hour ago.

'Hey, easy on,' said the American, just sitting there, his own cigarette glowing between the finger of his outstretched hand as if he had just said the most reasonable thing in the world rather than spat on scared ground.

Stark's memories of his father were complex, a mix of youthful hero-worship and posthumous disillusion in the old man's ideals. A cruel blow of fate had taken his father away from his family just when they needed him most. All that was left was his memory and his status as a hero in the society he had helped rebuild after the most devastating war in world history. And that was a private history that no jumped-up Yankee journo was going to rewrite to his own rule book.

'Come on, Harry,' the American continued, as if he hadn't noticed the seething expression on the face of the man whose world he had tried to shatter from within. 'I'm just trying to treat you like an equal human being.'

'Don't give me that crap!' Stark barked, more angry than he had expected. 'I don't know what your game is, or who your missing person is or was. And I don't need to listen to any more of this. You follow me in the streets, then lure me with some tease about something that in no way concerns you, spin me a yarn about espionage and then try to tie my private life into it. Whatever game you think you're playing, it's over. You're leaving. I should have arrested you for prowling.

'And,' he glanced theatrically at his watch, 'you're about to be in breach of your visa regulations.'

The afterthought sounded slightly ridiculous, Stark realised as he uttered it, though it was almost certainly true.

The American stayed where he was, but his eyes narrowed as he looked up through a swirl of smoke. For more than a second Stark was sorely tempted to smash his fist into the man's all-too complacent face. Instead, he gestured abruptly upwards with a single finger, little caring if the American misinterpreted it:

'Come on. Up. Out.'

Fairweather didn't move. He shook his head gently, almost imperceptibly from side to side, like someone comforting an ailing relative, and said in a calm, quiet voice:

'My God, Harry, you didn't know? I mean, you really don't know?'

'What I know is bullshit when I hear it. And I've heard just about enough of it …' He made to grab the American by the collar.

'Wait a minute, please, Harry, just a minute.' The tone had suddenly changed. 'Hear me out, just a second, please, then if you want, I'll go. I'm sorry, I really am. I thought … I thought you would have known; I thought everyone knew, and just pretended not to. It never occurred to me …'

'What?' Stark snapped.

'That …' Fairweather sighed, tired or exasperated, it was

hard to tell. 'Harry, please, sit down again. Give me just five minutes, please. And then, if you want, if you'll let me, I'll be gone and you'll never see me again.'

Stark sat down, wondering as he did, why he was doing what he was told in his own home. But there was something in the American's tone, something in the way the man's eyes behind his mangled spectacles searched for Stark's and then rapidly left them.

'Harry, how do you think your father died?'

'I don't think. I know …'

The American nodded rapidly in hasty acquiescence. 'Just tell me.'

Stark closed his eyes. 'A heart attack. Nearly nineteen years ago. On duty. I remember. You don't forget something like that, you know, losing your father as a teenage boy. I cut out the obituary, from *New Times*, for my mother. We made a scrapbook. He was a hero,' and then, as if the term needed elucidation, 'a socialist hero.'

Fairweather had extinguished his cigarette and was rolling the stub between his fingers at the corner of his mouth.

'He was a hero all right,' he said.

'I'm sorry but I don't think I need to listen to anything you can tell me about my father.'

'Don't you, Harry? Are you sure?' The American had reached into the depths of his overcoat and once again produced the bulging wallet, rooted in it for a second and produced a small square of paper that he handed across without a word.

Stark took it and turned it over in his hands. It appeared to be a newspaper cutting, but printed only on one side.

'It's a photocopy, but it's genuine. Not *New Times*, *New York Times*, September 1970.'

Stark looked at it. There were people he knew, who could identify a newspaper just from the type font, but he was not one of them. Not that it mattered. The words would have had the same impact in any newspaper:

EAST LONDON EXECUTION
Secret Police in East London have executed a senior policeman believed to be an important member of an anti-communist dissident group, New York Times *sources have confirmed. The man involved was named as Major John Stark, a high-profile officer in the Metropolitan People's Police. Intelligence sources said Stark was one of the most important among many regime figures disillusioned by the recent events in mainland Europe.*

He was executed after the sinister Department of Social Security discovered that for the past three years he had developed and maintained links to a group known as The Underground. It is believed Stark had been feeding them official information.

The Interior Ministry in the communist-occupied zone denied there had been an execution and said Major Stark was a 'respected police officer who recently died of a heart attack', a frequent euphemism on the other side of the London Wall for unexplained disappearances of public officials.

Stark handed it back, shaking his head incredulously. 'This is absurd. How do I know it's genuine? And even if it is, why should I believe anything in the *New York Times* rather than in our newspapers?'

'If you don't know the answer to that, Harry, I can't tell you. But I think you do. There again, you could always check out the facts. You are, I believe, supposed to be a detective.'

'My father was a dedicated member. Of the Socialist

Labour Party. This is some absurd form of disinformation. Some game you're playing. You or whoever you work for.'

Fairweather gave a mock laugh. 'If only my editors had that much imagination! It's disinformation, okay, but the other way around. The obituary you cut out and saved was an attempt to preserve a myth and cover up an inconvenient truth. It was honest enough, in a way, but only if he'd died four years earlier, before the events of '68.'

'What are you talking about?'

'Oh, come on, Harry, not even your historians try to cover up that, even if they do talk in a language all of their own. The events of 1968, the crushed liberalisation in Prague, the suppressed student riots in Paris and Amsterdam. What is it your press calls it? "The anarchist counter-revolution"? Call it that if you want, or "Paris in the Springtime" as the more romantically-inclined headline writers our side of the Wall did. But it still came to the same thing in the end. Tanks rolling down the Champs-Elysées and Dam Square, no talk about letting "a hundred flowers bloom" or "sewing the new seeds of socialism". The men in Moscow back then had their own idea about how to run a garden – prune early and often: they used the hammer and sickle to good effect and didn't bother to wipe the blood off either afterwards. How many do you think died?'

For the second time in as many minutes Stark felt wrong-footed. He knew – everyone knew – that the official version, which accounted for only a couple of dead Soviet soldiers, hailed as 'martyrs to the communist cause and universal brotherhood', was a travesty. It was one of those little abstract lies that people lived with, not on a par with the big first-hand lie this man was trying to tell him about his own father. But even so, it put him at a disadvantage and he knew it.

'A dozen. Maybe more. Maybe several dozen altogether. Okay, probably more than officially admitted. It was regrettable, but necessary … inevitable.' That was what they said, the 'they' who said things about stuff like that. Ordinary people didn't. Ordinary people didn't even like to think about it.

'Come on, Harry, you know better than that. Even in your benighted little offshore teapot republic everyone knows better than that. And was it really worth it? Three hundred dead in Paris alone, over two days. Another hundred and fifty in Amsterdam. The same in Prague. And those are only the round numbers.

'Dozens more, maybe even hundreds, over the weeks and months that followed, in the purges, thousands of arrests, the scouring of party membership lists, the rounding-up of "off-message" intellectuals, which meant just about all of them. It went too far for many people, Harry, even some loyal old comrades, your father included. They did nothing immediately – it would have been suicide in the situation – but they made resolutions, private and in small groups, that the same thing could not be allowed to happen again. Oh, yes, even here. "We are the people of England who have not spoken yet" – they knew their Chesterton quote, turned it on its head and made it their motto; one or two of them found a voice, but they kept it quiet, working in the underground. Until the worms found them.'

Harry Stark sat, silently, and looked at the man facing him, looked at his smart, expensive overcoat, with the fat wallet in the inside pocket, along with the Ronson lighter and the Marlboro cigarettes, and wondered if he was seeing surface or substance. None of it made sense, this absurd Alice-through-the-looking-glass version of events, of his own life. And yet somehow, at the same time, it did: the mood swings his father went through when Harry was in his early teens and his mother put down to the old man drinking too much. Then the calm after the storm, the period immediately before and after Katy's birth when he seemed to be at ease with himself and his family, as if life had taken a decision for him, despite the scurrilous rumours behind his back, when he no longer seemed endlessly burdened by the cares of 'the Yard'. At the same time he was working late regularly, even overnighting at the office, something his son in a dozen years there had never had occasion to do.

Was it possible? Even remotely? That his father had had some 'road to Damascus' conversion, that for his last few years he had been living a double life? Living a lie? A lie that had been found out, and for which he paid the ultimate penalty? It was inconceivable, wasn't it? Suddenly, Harry Stark was no longer as certain as he had thought.

'Your father saw through it all, Harry. Don't think it wasn't hard. All of a sudden he started to question everything he ever believed in, stopped seeing the world in black and white. That's when he realised he could make a difference. Just like you can …'

'What do you mean?'

'By finding out how and why they killed the man whose body you found this morning.'

'I'll do that anyway. That's my job.'

'Sure it is. You don't believe that any more than I do? How long will it be before the DoSSers close in and close it down. They hung him up there as a warning, a warning to the people he came over here to contact. The people who're still following the path your father took. The only way you're going to do that job, Harry, the only way you can be the man your father would have wanted you to be, is to get in touch with them.'

'Get in touch with who …?'

'With the Underground. Or whatever's left of them.'

Chapter 17

Pankhurst Street was busy for the time of night. Two cars. One after the other pulled out and passed Kate Stark as she turned the corner, the hood of her parka pulled up against the slanting rain. She hadn't intended to be out this late and was thoroughly soaked, quite apart from the mouthful she was about to cop from the old woman and no doubt Sherlock Holmes too.

She was at least partly right. Old Mrs Stark's head was once again poking out of her sitting room as soon as she heard the key in the lock.

'What sort of time do you call this, young lady? Nearly midnight and you turn up looking like something the cat's dragged in. You're soaked to the skin, child. Where on earth have you been to this time of night?'

'Just out, Mum. You know, with my friends. And don't call me a child. I'm an adult now. Remember.'

'You may be an adult by law but you're not one in my eyes until you start acting like one.'

'Jesus, Mum, give me a break. I'm nearly twenty years of age. I can smoke, go in a pub, have sex,' her mother recoiled visibly at that one, much to Kate's amusement. She had thrown it in deliberately, prepared to come all coy virgin afterwards if needed. If only the old lady knew! 'If you really have to know, I was just round a friend's house with a couple of other people, just drinking coffee and talking about stuff.'

'Stuff?'

'Yeah, stuff.'

'What sort of an answer is that?' Mrs Stark shook her head wearily, but her anger was abating. Most of all when Kate was out late she was just worried about her. For all her sassy demeanour, she was a slight little thing for her age.

At least there weren't drugs out there. Or she didn't think there were. Not like in Westminster, where if you believed everything you saw on Wicked Auntie, kids Kate's age were out of their heads on marijuana half the time, the ones that weren't already in the gutter with needles sticking out of their arms from shooting heroin. She knew they exaggerated sometimes, but those photographs, the video clips they showed, they were real enough. Anyhow you could tell just looking at the young ones who came over, flashing their 'British pounds'. And them with tattoos and pierced noses like tinker muck, lording it all high and mighty. It was a bad influence.

'Anyway, come in here and sit down and have a cup of tea. There's a pot made, for your brother and his friend.'

Kate gave her mother an inquisitive look and craned her neck to look round the door into the sitting room. The last thing she wanted was for Sherlock to perform a repeat of the Spanish Inquisition, especially in front of company. Another Plod no doubt.

Her mother shook her head. 'He's not here. You just missed him. Him and his friend. Sat up in his room they did anyway, weren't going to have their little chat in front of his old mum.'

Kate shrugged. Why on earth anyone would want to listen in on her dull as ditchwater brother (PC in every sense of the word, some of her friends joked) talking shop with one of his rozzer mates, she could not imagine.

'He'll be back soon enough, though, I imagine. What with the time it is.'

Kate gave her mother a sidelong look. She was the one who got stick if she wasn't home when expected, not super Sherlock, her big grown-up brother.

'He'll be taking his friend to the frontier, I expect. Probably missed the witching hour and all too,' the old lady said in response, which only earned her another look. More directly querying this time.

'That's got you now, hasn't it? Wish you'd got back a bit earlier after all, eh? Not often your brother brings visitors home. Visitors of any kind. Let alone an American.'

Mrs Stark could not disguise her small satisfaction at even a minor victory in their continuing war of attrition as she watched her obstreperous, usually unflappable daughter's jaw drop in a gape of astonishment.

Chapter 18

The great grey steel and Portland stone shell of what had once been the Dominion Theatre lurked like an abandoned cave on the corner of New Oxford Street and Tottenham Court Road, a hollow relic from the days when there had been an empire and dominions.

Stark glanced at his watch, all the while keeping one eye on the American as he theatrically weaved towards the floodlit concrete sheds of the border checkpoint. It was twenty minutes past midnight. Officially that meant he had overstayed his day-visa welcome in the English Democratic Republic.

Stark had insisted on driving him there. Dealing with Benjamin Fairweather's visa issues was one headache he did not need or want. But preparations for the upcoming parade had forced a detour.

'What will you tell them?' he had asked the American as they pulled up by the kerbside at the end of the semi-derelict strip of boarded-up buildings that was New Oxford Street, the old eastern continuation of what was once the world's premier shopping street.

'Who? Oh, the border guards? That I had one too many in one of your excellent traditional English hostelries and lost track of time. It's not 1 a.m. yet. They don't want me any more than you do. Worst they'll do is make me change another forty bucks at the official rate for being here an extra day, and then take it off me because we can't take your money out.'

You're probably right, Stark thought to himself as he watched the barrier lift and the American produce his passport to a stern-looking BoPo, as he would no doubt call the Republic's border police. The American was more familiar with the procedures involved in entering and leaving Harry Stark's country than he himself would ever be.

He found it hard to imagine what it must have been like. When you could drive straight through Admiralty Arch, from Trafalgar Square to Buckingham Palace, one huge city and the heart of an empire. Somewhere over there, only a few hundred metres had been Leicester Square, with rich folk from all around the world flooding in to its theatres and cinemas, and the notorious clubs of Soho, a hedonistic world they thought would never end.

A relic of it still existed, so they said, over there, on the other side, migrated west to King's Road, Chelsea, and Hammersmith, names that were at the same time both familiar and little more than legends to him. He supposed he could have asked the American what they were like. But it somehow didn't seem right. Harry Stark had not been born when the anti-capitalist protection barrier had been built, had never known anything but a city of dead-end streets and roads to nowhere.

He looked down at the pack of Marlboro sitting on the passenger seat. It had fallen out of the American's pocket as he was getting out of the car. Stark had called to him, but the American had merely glanced back for an instant and said, 'Keep the pack. It's as good a way to kill yourself as any other.'

That hadn't quite been his final word though, had it? He had given Stark one ironic last smile and added: 'Think about it Harry. I'll be in touch.'

Stark turned the key in the engine and shook his head. How could he not think about it? Just what he was supposed to think was another matter. Another matter altogether. Especially sitting here, behind the wheel of his father's ageing Oxford, the little saloon car that had defined the last, brief, best days of his childhood. To Stark it still had a bit of faded magic. The car was an antique but functional. His father had saved and waited years for it, only to have it arrive about the same time as Katy when he really could have the used the money in other ways. But he had hung onto it, because it would be nice, wouldn't it, with Harry growing up and a young baby in the family to be able to get out of town now and then. The seaside, Margate maybe.

And Margate it had been, for that strange, improbably blissful summer, and afterwards even at weekends, whenever the demands of the Yard allowed, for the remaining months of his father's life. They were some of Harry's happiest memories: kicking football with the old man on the long, wide, windswept beach while his mother dotingly fed Katy behind a windbreak or in the back seat of the car. He had considered them perfect, carefree days. Now he wondered.

His father had taken him to the amusement arcade, with its peeling paint and sour smell of grease, sweat and seawater, buying old pre-war pennies at the kiosk to insert in gruesome fairground entertainment machines that must even then have been nearly half a century old: the Olde English Execution with its doll dropped to dangle through a trapdoor, the American Execution (perhaps not such a surprising survival after all) with its doll that jerked dynamically side to side before flopping over in its 'electric' chair, and young Harry's favourite, the French Execution, with the dramatic drum roll before the blade crashed down and the doll's head dropped off to reveal a flaking smear of red paint. There wasn't a Russian Execution: no figure kneeling down in a courtyard to receive an economical single bullet in the back of the neck.

But it wasn't the model executions that had made Harry squirm. The only one of those strange, antique mechanical toys that Harry had found grotesque, almost frightening, to the painful scorn of his father, was the one aimed at the youngest children of all: Jolly Jack Tar, a rubicund sailor with pink cheeks and rolling eyes beneath bushy black brows who rocked backward and forward to a raucous belly laugh that issued from the bowels of the machine. Come on, lad, his father had said, it's just a bit of a giggle, that one. But for Harry there was something enduringly, inescapably sinister in the painted smile and the disembodied laughter. After his father died, he never went back.

Now, all of a sudden, that laughter came back to haunt him, as if all along he had known all his life that it one day would. Hollow laughter for a hollow life. Had it all, the legend he had swallowed every day of his life, been a cruel joke he hadn't understood? Had the real man seen through the hypocrisies of the system he pretended to support, the same hypocrisies that with every passing day Stark found more suffocating? For nearly two decades he had been trying to live up to what his father would have wanted, at the risk sometimes of alienating his little sister. Had he all along been worshiping a phantom? Had the father he thought he knew been someone else entirely?

He turned the radio on, partly instinctively, partly to hear if there was still traffic problems caused by the parade preparations. Stark's heart skipped a beat as he heard a voice no one of his generation had ever heard live but none could forget: 'Even if the British empire, and its Commonwealth, last for a thousand years, men will still say this was their finest hour.' The radio was tuned to a Westminster station. It was an actor, an advert for the film he had heard them discussing in the Rose. A film that no one would have believed would ever be made nor should ever be made.

But then the world was turning on his head. He put the clutch into first gear, his mind whirling, the thought the American had planted there growing like a cancer: 'Find them Harry, find the people who can tell you the truth about your father, about the world you live in. There's a man who can help you, a church warden at St Paul's Cathedral. His name is Michael McGuire. He trusted Bloom and talked to him. He won't talk to me but he might talk to you. You are your father's son, after all.'

Am I, thought Stark, as he pulled away from the kerb. Am I?

In the little Sputnik parked among half a dozen others in the shadow of the Dominion, the driver pressed a button on his car radio that was not normally found on production models, gave his report and asked for instructions.

'Do nothing,' the calm voice at the other end replied. 'He can find his own way home.' One way or another, he mused silently. One way or another.

Chapter 19

Detective Sergeant Dick Lavery leapt to his feet and all but sprang to attention when Harry Stark entered his corner turret office at New Scotland Yard.

Lavery had expected his boss to be early, possibly sitting at his desk since the crack of dawn, given that they had just been landed with one of the most sensational murders since he had graduated out of uniform and made detective. Stark could be a stickler for punctuality and Lavery had fretted when he found his normal walk along the South Bank from London Bridge station blocked by DoSS men who weren't prepared to make exception for his police pass. The riverside path was temporarily closed, they said and declined to give a reason. Even so, he was at the office before Stark.

In the event it was nearly nine thirty when the DI stumbled through the door, looking like he hadn't slept a wink all night, threw his coat over a filing cabinet and slumped at his desk without even greeting Lavery with his usual cheery, 'How's it going, Dick.' Which was a shame, because for once Lavery had an answer.

'Things are … going pretty well, boss,' he said hesitantly, in answer to the question that hadn't been asked. 'Under the circumstances.'

Stark gave him a wan smile that may have been meant to be encouraging but was anything but.

'I've done the usual trawl. No missing persons. At least none who're putting their hands up.' The attempt at a joke fell flat.

Stark simply nodded. It had been agreed the day before that Lavery and a couple of the DCs would spend the rest of the afternoon and following morning checking up on the 'regular villains' of Whitechapel and Tower Hamlets where gangs ran smuggling rackets in American cigarettes and Scotch whiskies. Open warfare between them was rare but not unheard of. The brutality of the death was certainly not a problem. But Lavery's lads had sources among the minor cogs in the Whitechapel 'machine' who took it in turns to 'grass' up members of any rival outfit that looked like muscling in on their 'manor'. If there was any sort of turf war brewing, it would not take long to get wind of it. Particularly if it involved a ritual execution.

'Which makes the other option the favourite,' said Lavery.

'It does?'

Stark had not yet decided how much of the previous night's events to share with his normally trusted deputy. How did he know the American was not spinning him a line? A line with bait on the hook intended for one particular fish.

Lavery looked at him sideways: 'You don't think it's "river traffic" then, sir? It's just there was DoSSers … colleagues from the Department, I mean …'

Stark gave him a mock frown of rebuke.

'… blocking part of the riverbank on the south side, east of Blackfriars on my way to work this morning. Said it was temporarily closed and wouldn't explain.'

'Really?' Stark did not want to dismiss his sergeant's efforts but could not repress the note of scepticism in his voice. Even without the events of the previous evening, he had discounted the obvious possibility of the murder being a would-be escaper, a political dissident trying to commit the crime of 'fleeing the Republic', who had turned to one of the people-smuggling gangs and then failed to come up with the fare. Kemp had been fairly certain the man was 'not one of us'.

Yet the more he thought about it, the more possible it seemed. A 'fare' who defaulted on one of the 'cabbie' gangs that specialised in getting their fellow citizens across the border would be likely to be made an example of. Safer than simply handing him over to the DoSS who might extract inconvenient answers to awkward questions in exchange for supposed leniency. Kemp's opinion was, after all, circumstantial. There were at least a few EDR citizens who had lived in hot climes, specialists working in the People's Republics in Africa for example. It was not inconceivable that one of them had become disillusioned. But then why not just defect while abroad, walk into a 'British' embassy and claim asylum. No, it didn't make sense

On the other hand Stark could see no reason why he shouldn't let Lavery pursue the 'cabbie connection'. If he took what the American had said at anything like face value, Stark would be sailing perilously close to the wind. Right at this moment he could see no advantage in having anyone else on board. There was also the small possibility that if Fairweather's so-called 'Underground' actually existed, Lavery might end up coming at it from a different direction. By accident.

Lavery turned on the little black-and-white Logie Baird television that sat in the corner of the office for the ten o'clock news, almost immediately – on hearing the headline about Comrade Harkness's speech in preparation for the national holiday – switching to BBC Westminster. The news from the other half of London might be politically incorrect but it had the advantage that it wasn't written two days earlier. The lead item was a visit by the US Secretary of State to the Federal Republic Prime Minister's residence in Durham. That was followed by a story about protests against a new nuclear power plant in Cumberland. It was only when they got to the very last item that the sergeant sat bolt upright in his seat and tugged Stark's sleeve to attract his attention.

'And finally, more mysterious goings-on across the London Wall today as secret police blocked off the area around Bankside power station to remove what appears to have been an unprecedented example of dissident graffiti. What can you tell us, Sian?'

The screen switched from the newscaster to the familiar face and grating tone of Sian Morris standing on the Victory Embankment with the great chimney of the power station in the background.

'It's all over now, but earlier this morning dozens of plain-clothes Social Security men cordoned off the area around Bankside power station, which you can see behind me, to remove a remarkable piece of graffiti. As luck would have it, one of our cameramen was passing on this side of the river at the time, and managed to capture this astonishing footage.'

The image that appeared on screen was blurred, clearly shot at long distance through a telephoto lens, but what it showed was remarkable enough: a group of men with brushes on poles actively scrubbing at a larger than life-size image in red paint. An image of which two details were plainly visible: a trilby hat and two fingers held up in a V-sign.

And then the camera jolted wildly up into the air before levelling out to reveal a pair of hands struggling to cover the lens and the sounds of a scuffle. Clearly somebody objected to his filming. No prizes for guessing who.

'Nobody over here is saying anything officially, of course,' Morris went on. 'In fact nobody will even admit there was anything there at all, but I think most people would agree that that looks remarkably like it was a picture of the one man people over here absolutely *never* mention: Winston Churchill. This is Sian Morris, reporting live from East London.'

The male anchor in the Westminster studio turned to his female colleague and said, 'Quite remarkable, that.'

'Absolutely,' she agreed with a winning smile. 'I don't suppose it could have been anything to do with the upcoming *Bulldog Breed* movie?'

'I doubt even the advertising boys from MGM have those sort of contacts,' he replied. And they both laughed.

Lavery looked at his boss in open-mouthed astonishment, a look Stark had to try his hardest not to reciprocate as his thoughts flicked from the piece of paper found in the pocket of the Blackfriars body and the conversation in the Rose last night.

Instead he dropped his head and stared at his desk for a few seconds, then got up and with a glance out the window towards the rain clouds coming in again, pulled on his coat and opened the door.

'Sir?'

'Carry on, Dick, you're doing a good job. I think it's time I paid a visit to the museum.'

Stark was already closing the door behind him without a second thought for the expression of blank perplexity on his sergeant's face.

Chapter 20

The architecture alone was intimidating, Harry Stark thought as he walked along Great Russell Street. Even in the slanting rain that slicked the uneven cobbles of the courtyard the great fluted Doric columns, black with decades of encrusted soot and grime, looked less than welcoming. Only the presumption of global imperialism could ever have given the name 'British' Museum to one of the greatest collections of antiquities plundered from across the entire planet.

Was it possible that this was where he would find evidence to support the American's outrageous challenge to everything he believed … in? He hesitated over the final preposition even as he asked himself the question. Was it really everything he believed *in*, or just everything he believed. Weren't they the same thing anyway? Or were they?

The last time Harry Stark had been inside the Museum of Humanity, as it had been renamed in 1950, was as a child when his father had taken him to see what the old man had called 'the mummies and the marbles'. Even then he could not believe such a sinister-looking building could contain such marvels: the graceful snow-white athletes with their rippling muscles and stretched tendons, the straining horses with flaring nostrils. The board next to the sculpture explained how this was one of the finest examples of socialist realism in art dating back to the ancient world and the first great popular democracy. The postscript read: 'Loaned in perpetuity from the Hellenic People's Republic.'

Young Harry had stared in wonder, impressed that all

his teacher had told him was true: that great art was indeed heroic like the official painters of the Republic whose depictions of sturdy Kentish farmers or Dagenham car workers adorned every public building. Rather than the decadent art from up North, the homosexual Hockney, with his endless swimming pools, and the pseudo-proletarian Lowry whose stick men were a calculated insult to the working class.

He had said as much to his father and the old man had simply smiled and patted him on the head. Now, crossing that bleak portal for the first time since, the adult Harry wondered what his father had really thought. Had he believed the official commentary or had he seditiously thought all along what Harry himself had only recently come to suspect: that there was not a direct line of artistic evolution from the Parthenon marbles to the Heroes of Dagenham. Could the old man have secretly thought the government-sponsored art to be as lifeless as the empty Egyptian sarcophagi?

But it was not in the museum itself that he intended to look for the answer to a question he had never imagined asking, but in the separate institution it contained, the fabled Reading Room housed in its heart. The Marx-Lenin Reading Room, named for the two great communist thinkers who had elaborated their theories in this very room, had rights to a copy of every book printed in what had once been the United Kingdom until 1949 and the English Democratic Republic since. Entrance was reserved for scholars only, and senior, politically reliable ones at that. But subsidiary regulations also allowed access by members of the state's security services.

Stark believed, although he had yet to test it, that that definition could be stretched to include the Criminal Investigation Department of Scotland Yard. He had thought about putting on uniform for the occasion but decided he was not going to let himself be browbeaten by the system into behaving like one of its petty peacocks. In any case, he no longer had one that fit.

'Next please.' A large gruff woman with dyed auburn hair beckoned Stark brusquely forward. The inevitable portraits of the two great thinkers glared down at him from the oak-panelled wall, with Clem Attlee, their honoured disciple, and Arthur Harkness, the EDR's current heir to their ideology.

Stark walked up to the desk, flipped open his warrant card with its imposing Scotland Yard crest and thumped it down in front of her.

'Detective Inspector Stark, Metropolitan People's Police CID. I'm here to research historical information relating to a current case.'

The woman harrumphed, but was visibly taken aback.

'What case?' she made a show of residual aggression. Stark was ready for her.

'I'm afraid you don't have the clearance to know that,' he snapped, closing his warrant card and lifting it from the table.

The woman stiffened, then noticeably relaxed, as if somewhere in her regimented hierarchical brainstem a nerve cell had saluted and a 'stand easy' order been given.

'I apologise, Detective Inspector. If I may …?'

Stark gave her another stern look.

'Your warrant card, sir.' The woman noticeably wilted. 'For the log.' She gestured towards a vast, black imitation leather-bound ledger.

'Ah, of course.' Stark produced the card again, laid it down on the desk and watched as the woman opened the heavy tome and made a careful entry in a vast grid of boxes. It was something he hadn't counted on. How often did anyone ever go through that list of names? Probably, he sighed internally, more often than he cared to imagine.

The woman looked at the clock between Marx and Lenin and entered the time, 10.32 a.m., next to his name.

'Please go ahead, Detective Inspector Stark. I am sure the desk clerk will be most pleased to assist the People's Police.'

Stark nodded with a brief smile, no more than minimally courteous – he did not want to give the impression that he had anything to be grateful for – and pushed open the heavy oak door that led into the Great Reading Room.

He had heard of it, of course, seen pictures probably, though he could not remember where. But nothing prepared him for the reality. Out of the dark, dingy antechamber with its wooden walls, utilitarian carpet and brown-painted ceiling he stepped into an expanse of soaring light and space, a huge circular amphitheatre of book-lined walls beneath a vast dome pierced by high vaulting windows through which even the pallid light of an indifferent English springtime poured like rays from heaven itself. For a moment Stark held his breath in pure wonderment. That the grim neoclassical museum with its austere black columns could have such a jewel of light and clarity at its heart was beyond belief, almost as if the architect of this magical rotunda had deliberately set out to conjure a metaphor in stone for the illumination held on its shelves. Providing, he reminded himself, that it had not been extinguished.

He walked up to the main enquiries desk, a circular structure, as befitted the building, with windows and counters behind which clerks busied themselves with card indexes, book request forms in pink, grey and green, and pile after pile of the volumes themselves, pre-ordered and awaiting collection. Nothing, of course, could be removed from the Reading Room. That was a rule that had pertained even in Marx's and Lenin's day. Books were stored in the kilometres of shelving that surrounded the great circular building, built from ground floor up to just below the level of the windows, filling every inch of what had once been an empty court-yard in the middle of the museum. Those of sufficient status to merit a coveted reader's card ordered their books at the enquiry desk, collected them there and returned them every evening until they were no longer required. Only reference books and non-fiction were actually stored on the premises, fiction resided in distant outhouses, from where it had to be ordered days in advance.

But Stark was not interested in either weighty works of non-fiction or the purest fantasy, he was interested in the library's other great collection: ephemera. Newspapers. Only papers of record, of course, were stored, but that included not just *New Times*, the *Guardian* and the *Morning Star* but also pre-war papers and, most jealously guarded of all, papers from the other side, the other England: such blatant purveyors of anti-socialist propaganda as the *Daily Mail*, the *Daily Express* and the *Yorkshire Post*. There were even, Stark was led to believe, copies of the *New York Times*.

He approached the desk. A clerk who might have been a caricature of the breed looked up at him with watery eyes behind thick spectacles and pushed back a lock of hair.

'Yes, can I help you?'

'I need copies of foreign newspapers, this morning's from Westminster. And some older ones too.'

Oh yes, the eyes seemed to say, you do, do you? The mouth said nothing. There was something about him that Stark instinctively disliked, a sort of subservience that hinted at a concealed sense of superiority.

'It's quite important,' Stark added, as if the man's expression challenged him to justify himself.

'I'm sure it is. Now, how old are we talking?'

'Quite some time. September 1970 to be precise.'

'Well, if you know what you are looking for, and the precise dates and publications, you can start by filling out one of these forms. One for each publication, that is, and for each date of publication, if you follow me. There are more over there if you need them.'

A flabby, age-spotted hand pushed a handful of pink and yellow forms with flimsies attached for the copies bureaucracy demanded, and gestured behind Stark to a row of benches, with wooden seats and cubbyholes filled with a host of other, similarly colour-coded forms.

Stark took a seat and set to work. He knew what he wanted: first of all to see if the copy of the *New York Times* the American had shown him was genuine, secondly to see if there were other, similar reports in the Northern or Westminster newspapers. Even if he found everything he was – hoping for or dreading? – that did not automatically mean everything the American had told him was true, but at the very least it meant there was another, secret side to his family history.

September 17, 1970 was the date that had been scrawled in the margin of the cutting the American had given him.

He filled out a form for the first time in his life to gain access to the organs of the ideological enemy: the *New York Times*, the *Daily Mail*, the *Daily Express* and the *Telegraph*. In his mind he already envisaged the carbon copy of his request making its way that very evening in a sealed envelope to the Department of Social Security's Barbican headquarters, his file being called for, amended. And marked 'for action'? He wondered how long it would take before the inevitable interview followed. Not long.

For balance, or a semblance of it, he ordered *New Times* for the same date, and also for 23 September, the day after his father's funeral and the date of publication of the obituary he had tearfully cut out for the special memorial scrapbook he had made for his mother, for all of them. Then for safety, he bracketed the 17th for the *New York Times* and applied for the 18th and 19th too in the Northern papers. For today's papers he restricted himself to the main Westminster rags. Even so, altogether it made nineteen forms. He passed them over the counter to the flabby-handed clerk who took them without a word.

For the next forty minutes, Stark sat at one of the tables and studiously ignored the day's copy of *New Times* that he had brought with him to pass the anticipated time waiting for the papers he really wanted to read. Instead, he leaned back and let his eyes drink in the splendour of the great dome, its windowed segments meeting like those of an orange in the circular skylight at the apex. It was like looking at a formalised, manmade recreation of the sky itself, with the pastel blue highlighted by the lines of gold that marked the segments.

What must it have been like when it was new nearly a century and a half ago, the Victorian gold leaf still glinting in the sun? Karl Marx would have been one of the first to use it. Had he too been tempted to lean back and look at this magnificent display of bourgeois opulence in the service of learning, or had he just kept his head down and got on with *Das Kapital*? The idea that Lenin should have studied there too was one of those coincidences that inspire belief in fate. But then so had Oscar Wilde and Rudyard Kipling, the heroic-sentimental bard of empire.

Stark was still lost in his historical daydream when the surly clerk called him over.

'I'm afraid there's a bit of a problem with your requests.'

'What sort of a problem?'

'They're missing.'

'Missing? I thought you had a copy of every … Are you telling me someone has lost part of your archive.'

'I didn't say lost. I said missing. All of them.'

'I don't understand.'

The clerk shrugged and gave Stark a distinctly sceptical look. 'Really? I thought someone in your position would understand. Things don't get lost here. But that doesn't mean they are available.'

Stark stared hard at the man, as if reluctant to take in what he was telling him. What was rapidly becoming painfully obvious.

'If something from the archive is missing. Unavailable.' The man was talking to him as if to a particularly dim child. 'It usually means someone else has requisitioned it. On the orders of one or other government department.'

The emphasis on the last word made it clear that there was only one 'department' under consideration.

Chapter 21

Benjamin T. Fairweather crossed his legs and leaned back in the elegant Regency armchair, rocking the antique dangerously on its spindly rear legs. One of the things he liked about staying at the Dorchester was the *olde worlde* atmosphere, the feeling of being in Europe but a Europe that worked, rather than the grey and dreary inefficiency that communism had spread across the mainland.

He smiled as he picked up his early edition of the London *Evening Standard*. A hovering waiter replenished his tea, the line reached by the hot, dark liquid clearly visible through the fine bone china of the cup. Fairweather smiled and nodded. He knew when a man was angling for a tip. Even at the Dorchester.

He liked London, this bit of it anyhow. He liked that unique mix of old world style and conspicuous consumption. He admired the sheer chutzpah of the place, the way West Londoners carried on as if they were still the heart of an empire instead of an isolated enclave in an occupied country. He admired the way they threw money about like there was no tomorrow, even if it was American money. One way or another. This was Uncle Sam's showcase in Europe. That meant big bucks and big Buicks. Parked alongside the Bentleys and the Rolls Royces, impudent signs of affluence ready to be compared with the crappy little Sputniks on the other side of the Wall. Tanks on the enemy's lawn.

The locals knew how to milk it for all it was worth, saved from the fate of their fellow citizens by a last-ditch armistice

– when the Red Army had already swallowed half their country, south of a line from the Avon to the Wash, save for that isolated enclave around the US Embassy in Grosvenor Square, defended by US troops under orders to fight to the death. The history books recorded that the nuclear stand-off, implemented overnight when the Russians successfully tested their own atomic device, had sealed the status quo. A snapshot of a war in its closing stages, frozen in time forever. Or for at least the past four decades. Appropriately enough nicknamed the 'Cold War'.

From his table in the elegant, dining room of the Dorchester with its great bowed bay windows at treetop level Fairweather could watch the smart cars jostle with the panoramic tourist buses in the rush-hour traffic build-up along Park Lane. To the sharp-eyed observer, there was another side of London on show too, the side the com-munist propaganda machine tried to play up as exploita-tion whereas anyone with a brain knew it was just the free market in action. Sex was a commodity like any other. He had no doubt that worked the same on the other side too: except over there access was a question of status rather than price. One way or another, those who toed the line and played the game reaped the rewards. Though Fairweather had no doubt which side of his bread he preferred buttered.

From his current, ostentatiously impeccable position he was ideally situated to observe one of West London's less salubrious evening rituals: the dusk shift-change of the whores in Hyde Park. The chic, high-heeled ladies of the night with their fox furs and thigh-slit Burberry trenchcoats, were coming on duty, replacing the day shift's motley crew now strutting blank-faced and surprisingly straight-legged towards the Tube and their suburban child-minders. The

Burberries were almost an item of uniform, mostly worn with nothing underneath.

He wondered, fleetingly, what the 'day-girls' earned, dropping their drawers behind bushes or on the back seats of Jeeps for GIs as famously oversexed as the generation over here before them, and even more overpaid. The West London US garrison, with its inner-city Kensington barracks and the crowded airbase centred on the suburban Heathrow airstrip, was his country's biggest outpost in alien territory. West London – 'Westminster' as the commies called it, in their comic quaint pretence that it was and always had been a separate city – was the showpiece of how freedom, democracy and the capitalism that provided the riches which contrasted with the impoverished oppression of a supposedly egalitarian police state.

Fairweather turned his attention to the paper. The *Evening Standard*, like its stablemate the *Daily Express*, prided itself on being an institution. No, more than that, an institution with a mission. A mission from God. Both papers carried a stencilled image of a red crusader alongside the masthead, an indication that they were not just chronicles but ideological warriors. The owner of both papers, the late Lord Beaverbrook, had been a fervent admirer of the British empire, and one of the last to acknowledge – if indeed he ever had – that its days might be numbered. Or over. Since the outbreak of war in 1939 the crusader had been in chains, at first to symbolise the travail or conflict but for decades assumed – as intended – to represent the 'enslavement of our brothers' on the other side of the Wall. The Beaverbrook 'stable' unashamedly preached 'reunification of the United Kingdom', as if recent history had never happened, as if there was still a 'kingdom' or 'queendom' or whatever they wanted to call it, instead of the truncated, identity-challenged 'British Commonwealth', with its capital in Durham, and its fractious federation with the constituent elements of Northern England, Scotland, Wales and Northern Ireland.

The Beaverbrook paper never asked the nationality of the men who, under whatever coercion, had built the Wall, erected barbed wire and automatic weapons along the frontier and shot those of their fellow citizens who voted with their feet against the 'common good' of socialism. The *Express*, and those West Londoners who read it, thought – when they thought at all, Fairweather reflected – of the 'other side' in terms of occupation, rarely of collaboration. At most they preferred to think of a small communist elite who had sold out and 'kidnapped' their fellow citizens. It was a point of view, like any other. And Fairweather was more aware than most people that points of view could be what defined the world.

The waiter approached again and made for the silver teapot, but the American held up a hand. Tea made him pee.

'No thanks,' he said, and then added, as if an afterthought, considering that after all a little celebration might be in order: 'Do you know, what I really would like is a glass of champagne.'

The waiter, doing the habitual twenty per cent gratuity calculations in his head, beamed his approbation of transatlantic largesse: 'Certainly, sir. Napa or Sonoma?'

The American waved his hand expansively.

'Whatever. We're in London. You guys are in charge.'

The waiter gave him a thin-lipped smile in return. You had to hand it to them; waiters always knew the real odds. Then he dismissed the man from his thoughts and turned them back to Harry Stark. He wondered how he was getting on. After all, he expected a lot of him. A lot more than the detective knew.

Chapter 22

St Paul's Cathedral in the rain cut a desolate spectacle. Stark still retained an image of the great baroque dome, bigger than any in what once was Christendom save St Peter's in Rome, floating ethereally above the smoke and flame of the Blitz, a photograph he had found in his father's wardrobe, clipped from the front page of some wartime newspaper.

He had meant to ask the old man about it, but had never quite got around to it mainly because he could not think of an easy explanation for poking around in his father's things in the first place. Now he only wished he had done it more. The photograph had gone by the time he and his mother sorted out the old man's things after his sudden death.

The photograph, he knew, had to have been taken during the first phase of the war, when the capitalist government played up an imaginary image of such a national landmark's invulnerability. In reality the cathedral had been hit several times, though only by minor incendiary bombs that had been extinguished quickly by fire crews who had been ordered to ignore damage to people's homes to preserve this great symbol of empire and religion. To prove God was on their side. At least that was how Stark had been taught it in school.

The cathedral had not been so lucky the second time around when the Junkers and Heinkels had been replaced by MiGs and Antonovs. God had thrown in the towel. The apse had suffered a direct hit, the altar itself shattered by falling debris, the interior scorched by a fire that raged for nearly two days. That the great dome itself had survived was indeed something of a miracle, though due more to Wren's architecture than the will of God: a glancing blow from a Soviet howitzer shell had left a crack nearly ten metres long in which, thanks to some wind-blown or seagull-dropped seeds, a scrappy pine tree had managed to take root. Its straggly branches dipped disconsolately in the rain, like some frayed feather in a mad monk's headdress.

Stark looked instinctively up at the clock on the tower. The hands pointed to twenty past four, as they had, he realised with a bitter laugh, for the past forty years. Right twice a day, as they said. His own watch told him the right time was 1.45 p.m. He was late, but only just. After his tellingly futile search in the Reading Room, he had decided he had little choice but to follow the American's other lead. A quick call from the phone box on the corner of Great Russell Street to the cathedral offices had ascertained there was indeed a deputy churchwarden called Michael McGuire. It was he who answered the phone. The man seemed cagey, but then people often did when rung up out of the blue by a policeman. Stark said only that he wanted to have a face-to-face chat, gave no details. But when he gave his full name the man's tone changed, the latent hostility suddenly dissolving. He would be available during his lunch hour between one and two, he said, adding cryptically, 'Upstairs. Ignore the sign.'

Stark hurried the last few metres up Ludgate Hill past the statue of Lenin on the round pedestal before the cathedral steps. Once upon a time there had been a queen there. Victoria or Elizabeth, Stark had supposed, until Kate told him it had been Anne. Stark hadn't remembered an Anne. The great doors at the front, intended by Wren for use on royal occasions, were as ever closed. Stark had never seen them open. He walked round to the south side and pushed open the wicket gate set in the scarred wooden portal.

It was uncannily quiet. The cathedral nave was used as a practice or performance venue by music groups, playing anything from Shostakovich to Tchaikovsky. The party liked to boast of its sponsorship of culture, always providing, of course, that the culture in question had been previously approved. Although still in theory consecrated and available for religious use, St Paul's was in reality primarily used as a concert venue. Stark had vague memories of his father bringing him to hear a performance of the *Nutcracker Suite*, by the Woolwich Working Men's Symphonia. He remembered the architecture more than the music.

Even now the building impressed him, not just the scale but the relics it retained of a past otherwise consigned to oblivion. Around the walls, rain-streaked and soot-blackened, great sculpted chunks of marble statuary recreated in pseudo-classical heroic mode the last moments or noble poses of an entombed military aristocracy. It could have been Thebes or Karnak transported from the desert shores of the Nile to the soggy banks of the Thames. Even the names of these dead captains of empire interred around him had an eerie resonance as powerful as that of any pharaoh: Gordon of Khartoum, Nelson of the Nile, Wellington, the Iron Duke, his great black catafalque gathering dust and smeared with dirt. Ashes to ashes, dust to dust. Like his father. Like Martin Bloom. Like himself one day. One day all too soon if he was not careful.

Here and there a few tourists, whose accents and designer clothing suggested they came from up North, but also a tour party of French trades unionists, identifiable by the *Compagnie Touristique des Syndicats Socialistes* placard held aloft by their guide, wandered around talking amongst themselves and stopping for the occasional photograph. Unsurprisingly Wellington's tomb was the greatest draw for the Frenchmen. They wanted to make sure he was dead.

But of church personnel, secular or spiritual, there was little sign. A pool of water on the floor under the dome could have done with some attention, but there was no sign of a caretaker, or churchwarden, just a yellow plastic sign that said 'Wet Floor'. Stark needed someone to ask what constituted 'upstairs'. He assumed some sort of administration offices, though it seemed unlikely these would be anywhere but on the ground floor. The door marked Sacristy was locked. But there was a woman with thick glasses and a worn cardigan sitting reading a knitting magazine behind the desk of a dowdy little souvenir shop by the door. Stark approached her gingerly. She seemed unwilling to be distracted from her reading material. It was clearly a long time since anyone had purchased any of her wares, which was hardly surprising seeing as they extended only to a few black-and-white postcards showing the cathedral in the immediate aftermath of the war, with the red flag flying from the damaged dome, and a well-thumbed book on the works of Sir Christopher Wren.

'Excuse me,' he said. The woman paid him no attention. Stark was tempted to produce his warrant card but thought better of it. Under the circumstances. 'I'm looking for Michael McGuire.' No reaction, beyond a slightly dismissive glance over the top of her almost opaque spectacles. 'He said I'd find him "upstairs". Do you know where that might be.' The woman looked up, considered Stark as if he were some village idiot and then nodded, upwards towards the great concave expanse of Wren's dome, and pointed to a door in the wall opposite. As Stark turned towards it, she added, 'It's closed.' And went back to her reading.

Stark walked across to the door. It was open. But a sign placed centrally in the doorway said in large faded letters, 'Whispering Gallery. 259 steps. No lift.' Another sign, newer with more legible lettering, was hung over it, proclaiming: 'Strictly No Admittance. Loose Masonry.' Stark turned and looked back at the woman by the kiosk who despite her warning was showing no interest in him whatsoever, then up into the great void of the dome. And sure enough, there was someone up there. A figure just distinguishable beyond the balustrade. For a moment Stark was tempted to call out to him, to tell him to come down. Then he looked around at the milling dozen or so tourists and realised how ridiculous that was. The man was clearly mad, or paranoid, or both, but there was no alternative. He pushed past the sign and with a sigh he took in the '259 steps. No Lift.' Started up, instinctively reverting to a habit of his childhood, and counting: 'One, two, three ...'

Chapter 23

Harry Stark was panting heavily. He had not realised quite how unfit he was. He had started almost at a run but slowed to a veritable policeman's plod after the first 150 steps. They were low, to be sure, wooden, but dark and cluttered with bits of rubble and abandoned tools, here a brush, there a chisel. The restoration work on St Paul's had been going on for the best part of forty years and by the rate of progress it would be at least another forty before it was anywhere near finished.

The spiral had left him quite dizzy by the time he arrived at the corridors immediately beneath the dome. But it was only at the top of the last small flight of stairs that led into the gallery itself that the horror overcame him. In huge, sweeping, biliously nauseous waves. His eyes, which had rapidly become accustomed to the dark of the stairwell, suddenly reeled at the sudden glare of daylight pouring into the void of the dome through Wren's meticulously placed area of portholes, designed in an age without power. The sun had come out and celestial light was pouring into the house of God.

But it was not just the sudden eruption of light that sent Stark reeling. At the same time the world fell away beneath him like a giant bottomless well, sucking him towards it with a fatal seduction more powerful than gravity. Urging him, goading him, pulling him onwards, to throw himself over the narrow rail, to hurtle headlong to the welcoming embrace of infinity. Go on, it urged, go on, you know you want to! In a moment of sheer, unbridled, unanticipated terror Stark closed his eyes tight shut and turned to clutch the smooth unwelcoming plaster of the wall.

He had had attacks of vertigo before, but nothing like this, and he had not expected it *inside* a building. But the vast scale of the cathedral, the fact that the height above him was at least as great as that below, and with the all too visible crack that ran like a jagged lightning bolt down one side of it, all magnified the sensation unimaginably. His head was reeling, his heart pounding. Slowly, biting his lip, ashamed of the irrational fear and angrily aware that he was probably cutting a less than impressive spectacle for the man he had come to interview, he opened his eyes to the mouldy yellow stucco in front of them, and then more slowly still forced himself to turn around.

Michael McGuire, at least that is who he assumed it to be, was sitting calmly watching him from the other side of the dome. Stark managed a brief wave, still pressed against the wall. He had not expected this, in fact he had no idea how he was even going to edge his way around the circumference of the open maw that yawned in front of him. But the man opposite smiled and gestured with his hands to indicate Stark should sit down. He breathed a sigh of relief. Perhaps he was going to have mercy and come round to this side. But as soon as he sat down he realised that that was not what was going to happen. To his astonishment, stupidly when he thought about it, he immediately heard someone say his name. Quietly. Almost a whisper.

Of course, they were in the Whispering Gallery. His father had told him about it when he was a child, but never brought him here. He supposed it had been closed for safety reasons even then. Wren's architectural skill was such that the circumference was an almost perfect circle and words whispered against the wall were audible to anyone who leant their ear against it even on the far side. It was the perfect place, provided there was no one else in the gallery, to conduct a conversation in total secrecy.

'Sta-k, Harry Stark,' he heard as if a ghost was speaking from the wall itself. 'Welc-me'.

'You are Mi–' Stark began, then realised he was doing it wrong, speaking aloud as if trying to talk across the void to the man who had to be at least fifty metres away. The man frowned, looked down pointedly towards the floor of the cathedral, something Stark felt nauseous even considering, and then gestured towards the wall behind him.

'You are Michael McGuire,' Stark whispered to the wall.

The figure opposite nodded.

I'm here because I want to find out what you know about the murder of an unknown man I believe to have been an American by the name of Bloom. That was what Stark had planned to say to this mysterious churchwarden who might or might not be a link to a group of organised anti-socialist dissidents. What he actually said was: 'You knew my father.'

The man opposite nodded again, turned to the wall and whispered: 'Yes, I did. You- father, John, was a g--d man.' Stark was struggling to make out the words clearly. The gallery wasn't working as well as it should have done. Clearly the fracture in the great dome itself had had a detrimental effect on the acoustics. The light faded and a couple of drops of water fell in front of his eyes. He looked up. There were dark clouds overhead, rainwater coming through the crack.

'I need to find out more about him,' Stark whispered to the wall. 'I need to meet some people he knew. The same people an American came looking for a few days ago. A man called

Martin Bloom.' Stark was speaking slowly, quietly, but as clearly as he could. He wondered how much of what he was saying the man on the other side could actually hear and understand. He glanced across and thought for a moment he caught a glimpse of movement in the door that presumably led to the 'down' stairwell on the other side. McGuire had his ear pressed to the wall attentively and was nodding. He had obviously done this before. Stark wondered how many politically incorrect conversations had taken place in this way, far removed from the listening devices of the men from Social Security.

'I --ow what you a-- -alking about,' the wall whispered. 'But I -elieve Mr -loom is no longer -ith us.' That was saying the least of it, Stark thought. 'I can help you. But --is is not the -ight place.'

Stark was getting cross. He needed to ask the man some more direct questions. Sitting whispering against a wall was not the format he was used to for conducting police interviews. He looked across the vast empty space at the man with irritation, wishing he could pluck up the nerve to just march round there and collar him. And then he noticed it again, a flicker of movement in the stairwell entrance behind him. He went to call out, then turned to the wall to whisper but it was speaking to him.

Stark had missed his first words: '... -nderground,' he made out, but it was like weather conditions harming radio reception, perhaps the rain coming through the crack ruining the acoustics. 'You need -- talk to another man ... love ... the church ... bride ... Christ ...' and then suddenly the same word only this time not whispered, but shouted, 'CHRIST'. Stark spun round from the wall and jumped to his feet.

Opposite him the physical form of Michael McGuire was rising. And not just rising to his feet. He was lifting himself, or being lifted, up, up against the balustrade, almost to the point of no return when his own centre of gravity would take over and the laws of physics, irrespective of human insanity and irrational death wishes, would assume final fatal command.

And then he was gone. A split-second cry, lasting half an eternity, in truncated echo amidst the great marble columns and rising into the imperfect vault above, and then a horrible, dull, ineluctably final crunch from below.

Stark reeled as if he had been physically struck, and fell to the floor, his head hitting the wooden boards as he retched, clutching the cold stone of the balustrade with clenched knuckles. Jesus Christ, he told himself. Two murders in two days and each time you throw up. What kind of policeman are you? Against instinct he forced himself to look up, across the void that had swallowed McGuire. Disappearing into the stairwell opposite was a short, stocky, heavily built figure. Proof of what Stark already knew: McGuire hadn't jumped – he had been pushed! Taken by surprise, grabbed suddenly from behind before he knew what was happening and lifted bodily over the balustrade.

Swallowing down his terror with the taste of his vomit, Stark pushed himself to his feet, pulled his service Makarov pistol from his shoulder holster and did his best to run the half-circumference of the gallery, his eyes studiously fixed to the wall next to him, not daring to look up and least of all down, to the horrible sight he knew awaited him. It was easier than he thought. This was work, running for dear life in pursuit of a murderer.

Only when he gratefully dived through the doorway, into

the relative darkness, away from the gallery's deadly whirl-pool of light and space, did he realise his error. The doorway did not lead, as he had expected, to a separate stairwell, but into a corridor that led him back around the dome to the same stairwell he had come up. If he had simply turned around where he was and gone back, he would have been waiting for the killer. Now, instead, he could hear the feet receding rapidly into the distance down the wooden steps beneath him. Stark plunged after them, reckless of the danger of slipping on the worn treads.

He emerged into the nave of the great cathedral to the sound of a penetrating scream. It was the woman from the kiosk, her head darting back and forth between the crum-pled corpse and Stark standing there with a murderous expression on his face and a gun in his hand.

'Where did he go?' Stark shouted, only to be met by expressions of uncomprehending terror on the faces of the woman from the kiosk and the tourists, most of whom were clumped by the marble bases of the great memorials, while a few ducked down behind a pew. The wicket gate opposite flapped open in the rain. Michael McGuire's killer was gone, melted into the streets of the metropolis, beyond pursuit. Stark had no obvious way of finding him. No clear idea of what he looked like. No murder weapon to be found.

He turned his attention to the ruin of a human being that lay sprawled in an unnatural heap, a sinister pool of red spreading across the cold stone floor. The crowd of cowed onlookers retreated as he walked towards the body, holster-ing his weapon.

'It's all right,' he said. 'I'm a police officer.'

Not one of them looked reassured.

Chapter 24

They gathered together in the dark, faces lit only by candlelight, for they were, in the very real sense of the word, underground. About six metres underground by the roughest of reckonings.

There were eight of them in all. The tall man standing at the little square metal-legged table was speaking, addressing his comments primarily to a slight figure slouched against a wall in the corner with a hood pulled up, as if hugging the dark and shunning even the flickering candlelight.

'You've done well,' he said, his normally quiet voice resounding unfamiliarly in the echoing darkness. 'Put the cat among the pigeons and no mistake. Gave the buggers the shock of their lives, I shouldn't wonder, seeing old Winnie staring out at all and sundry across the Thames, large as life and twice as scary.'

There was a rumble of muted laughter at that. Although notably not from the figure in the corner.

'A true mark of brilliance, I reckon, using stencils and spray paint. Makes putting up a picture as easy as daubing a slogan. And they say a picture is as good as a thousand words. I bet there's been a damn sight more than a thousand words expended down the Mansion House and up the Barbican since this morning. Most of them not repeatable in polite company.'

He looked around at his audience as if anticipating another laugh, louder this time. He was disappointed. There was an edginess in the air, a sense that they'd somehow stepped off a cliff and there was no going back.

'I'm not kidding. I reckon we have a tool here that's not just a powerful weapon of protest, but a new art form. You watch – there'll be people talking about "the phantom of Bankside" before long.'

That did get a subdued rumble of amusement, including this time from the figure in the hood.

'That's if anyone ever sees them,' said the man seated at the table, his hands folded in front of them. He peeked briefly over the top of half-moon glasses at the elderly woman next to him and the tall man whose self-confidence he clearly didn't share.

'They had the area closed off and the paint erased within an hour or so. If it hadn't been for the BBC photographer passing by, with a camera and long lens, nobody would have noticed it.'

The big man shrugged. 'Maybe, but that was just a trial run, wasn't it. And it's hardly as if the photographer was there by chance now, was he?'

The bespectacled man looked up at him sceptically.

'Oh, come on, Malcolm, there are ways of doing things, you know. It's not that hard to tip off a foreign news organisation, you know. Especially in the current climate. An anonymous call from a phone box, saying nothing but a location and a time. Nothing incriminating in that. Yes, the DoSSers were probably listening in, but that doesn't do any harm either. Every time they interfere with the Northern press only increases the perception of this place as the police state it is.'

The man called Malcolm was shaking his head.

'It also increases the danger. To everyone involved.'

'We were never going to get anything done without exposing ourselves to danger. We all knew that. Have known it all along. But this is the best chance we'll get in a lifetime. You know it. There's a new mood in the air. Maybe not here, yet, but we'll never have a better chance. And time is against us.' The last phrase was said with a pointed if deliberately oblique sideways glance at the old lady who seemed almost to have dozed off.

'Bankside's one thing. This next step is a lot more risky.'

'We've got cover. You know that. Two lads on the detail. They're going to supply cover for the few minutes the job itself will take, then cover it up. Until we're ready.'

'There's a chance it'll be found beforehand. It's very risky. You know that. A site like that.' He looked over at the slight figure in the hood, but wasn't rewarded with so much as a glance in acknowledgement.

'Come on, that's what it's about in the end, isn't it. Publicity. Free speech. The truth?'

'Like the pictures they got of the body?'

There was a minute's silence, a tangible tension in the air.

'Yes,' the big man said at length, quietly as if by his very understatement he was emphasising his point. 'Like the pictures of the body.'

'It's just a bit unfortunate that the man they put on the case happens to be one Harry Stark.' He could not help but let his eyes fall on the figure in the corner, as if waiting for a reaction from that direction. A few seconds of silence passed first, and when there wasn't one, he added: 'Then again, maybe not. Maybe it was fated. For better or worse, eh?'

The figure in the corner shrugged, then as if on a whim, produced a coin, flipped it in the air, caught it and turned it over on the back of one hand. The others watched, craned their necks to see which side up it had landed: the cross of St George or the Kentish plough. And wondered, in this case, which was heads and which was tails.

But the hand did not lift enough for anyone else to see. Seven pairs of eyes, including those of the old lady who had raised her nodding head, watched silently as the coin was replaced in a pocket and its owner stood up, pushing a stray lock of hair back inside the hood and lifting a holdall from the floor.

'Best be getting on with it then,' were the only words spoken, in a small but determined voice, as the slight figure made its way to the door.

Chapter 25

If Ruth Kemp was overawed by either the architecture or the religious significance of St Paul's cathedral, let alone the desecration of a murder committed in its heart, she gave little sign of either. She continued chain smoking as she examined the bloody mess that had been Michael McGuire sprawled on the marble floor. Behind her, technicians wearing rubber gloves were unrolling a tarpaulin. St Bart's morgue would be receiving another customer. Kemp took a long pull on her cigarette and ground out the stub beneath her heel next to the corpse.

'What is it with you, DI Stark? Got the idea I have too much free time on my hands or something?'

Stark gave her a look that said this time he was not in the mood for laconic world-weariness.

'At least there's not much doubt about cause of death with this one,' Kemp said, taking the hint. 'Skull smashed on impact. Brains splattered all over the floor. Looks to me like a fall from a great height.' She stared up into the cracked dome. 'A fall from grace?' she added, in a deadpan voice that suggested she wasn't so much wisecracking as following Stark's dangerous train of thought. Stark gave her a look, and Kemp raised her hands in a defensive gesture that said, I don't need to know.

'At least there's no doubt about this one's identity,' Kemp added, handing over the grubby laminated ID card she had extracted from the dead man's thin wallet.

'Michael McGuire, St Paul's churchwarden. Been in the

job for more than fifteen years, according to his colleague.' She nodded at the woman in thick glasses who now sat on a seat next to her desk, sobbing into a grubby handkerchief.

Kemp had got more out of the woman in two minutes than Stark had in the more than half an hour that had passed between his call to the pathologist and her arrival. Stark had questioned the dozen tourists and other visitors, all of whom insisted they had noticed nothing other than the scream and the horrible impact of the body on the floor. Nobody even admitted noticing a man emerge from the stairwell door and rush out of the cathedral. They had been too shocked, they insisted. Each and every one.

Neither EDR citizens nor foreign tourists were keen to be involved in an investigation by the Metropolitan People's Police. Only some had more choice than others. Stark took their details, including visa numbers in the case of the tourists, most of whom would be out of the country by midnight. They breathed an audible sigh of relief as Stark let them go, vanishing through the wicket gate without so much as a glimpse back at the bloody mess on the cathedral floor.

From the phone in the cathedral office, he called Forensics, told them to search for traces of fibres or anything else up in the Whispering Gallery. Not that he had much hope they would find anything. Or even look very hard. The only witness was Stark himself. Two men were dead, both murdered, both linked to an American reporter who had thrust his way into Stark's life and done his best to turn it upside down. Harry Stark had been presented with an agenda. A personal agenda. Only he had no idea what the next item might be.

Stark had never had time for the grey-faced men of the Department of Social Security. There were questions better not asked about some of the interrogation methods in the cellars of the Barbican. But 'persuasion' was one thing. Murder was something else. And if the Department did something, usually they did it in secret. They didn't hang their wares out for everyone to see. A gesture intended to intimidate? Most people were intimidated enough just by the sight of a black Bevan. But the missing newspapers suggested not everything the American said had been a lie. And the McGuire man had been trying to tell him something. Something important enough to get him killed?

Chapter 26

At his desk in New Scotland Yard, Detective Sergeant Dick Lavery scratched his head and let his eyes wander out across the river to the great chimney of Bankside power station belching out black smoke in the distance.

He was not a man who involved himself much in politics. He believed, even more than his boss, that being a policeman was about the simple business of keeping the peace, nicking thieves and solving crimes. Ordinary, everyday crimes, not 'political crimes' whatever those might be. He knew, just as everyone his age knew, there were things you didn't say, not because they were right or wrong, but because that wasn't the way the world worked.

There were tramlines. And as long as you ran along them, life ran smoothly enough. Try to deviate, to follow a route the tramlines didn't run along and you crashed. Simple as that. Your career got derailed. Fast. He had heard people say it was different up North, or in America. But Dick Lavery had never been up North, and nor had anyone in his family. And as for America, well that was another continent, an ocean away. About as accessible as Mars.

And in any case he was by no means sure things were as different as all that. He knew all about the McCarthy business in America back in the 1950s. He had learned about that in school. America had its 'dissidents' too: people who believed in the socialist system. What had happened to them? They had been hounded. People who admitted to being communists could end up in jail, and if not, then certainly out of work. In fact, anyone could be suspected of 'left-wing' leanings, even the rich and famous, the big stars of Hollywood. People famous all over the world could be hauled up in front of a committee, little better than a kangaroo court, accused of 'un-American activities'.

Those who were found 'guilty' could expect never to work again. Was it that different really? Even those who talked – and Lavery did not know many – about them having a 'freer' system up North admitted that the McCarthy period – named for the American senator who had spearheaded the witch-hunt – had been a 'mistake'. But there were people on this side who admitted 'Uncle Joe had made a few mistakes' too. No, Lavery knew only one thing about that sort of stuff: it was a kettle of worms and one he was not going to lift the lid on, if he could possibly avoid it.

Which was why he was in such a despondent mood as he gazed at the chimney of the power station. As far as he was concerned, Winston Churchill was a bogeyman from another generation. Definitely not someone you expected to be involved in a present-day investigation. It was like interviewing a witness in a murder inquiry only to find out it was the ghost in *Hamlet*. Lavery was quite proud of himself for that little Shakespearean analogy. He hadn't read much of the great man, but *Hamlet* had been a set text at school. A great play about the sort of corruption and evil doing that went on in monarchies, if he remembered right. Also a lesson that putting your head above the parapet only made it more likely to get shot off. There were certain things it just didn't pay to find out. That was what he felt about the current case. It was one for the Department of Social Security and the sooner they took it off the hands of ordinary decent policemen the better.

Why his boss had all of a sudden taken it into his head to go tearing off to a museum when he had a murder to deal with, even one that really shouldn't be on their plate at all, was beyond him. Museums were about history. Winston Churchill belonged to history. And as far as Dick Lavery was concerned, history was the past. And the longer it stayed there the better.

It was precisely at that moment he was rudely dragged into the present. By the shrill ring of the telephone on his boss's desk. Lavery hauled his increasingly corpulent frame out of his chair and answered it: 'DI Stark's phone.'

The voice on the other end was instantly recognisable. 'Is the DI there?'

'Due back any moment, sir. Detective Sergeant Lavery here.' Lavery had only rarely had occasion to converse with Colonel Marchmain of the Department of Social Security, but that had been enough to convince him the best answers to give the man were always those closest to what you guessed he might want to hear.

For a microsecond Marchmain sounded nonplussed.

'I see,' he said. 'Well, Lavery, can you give him a message. An important one. I think he'll find it good news.'

'Yes, sir. Of course, sir.'

'It's about the incident. At the cathedral.'

'Incident, sir?'

'Yes. I see you aren't aware yet. There's been a death. Most unfortunate business. DI Stark was there, by coincidence I believe. Dare say that's what's detained him. Though, as you say, I would expect him back by now.'

Lavery kept quiet. Another death? Another murder? The more he heard about the events of the last forty-eight hours, the less he wanted to hear.

'Anyway, as I say good news. Although I suppose that's a rather cynical way of putting it. But I'm sure you appreciate, Detective Sergeant, and I'm sure your boss will appreciate even more that, with your hands full with a murder case, the last thing you need is an extra complication.'

'Indeed, sir,' said Lavery who had not the faintest idea what the colonel was talking about.

'Anyway just tell Stark, DI Stark, I mean, that the case was brought to my attention very quickly. Given the man's position in the church, de facto curator of a national monument and all.'

'Yes sir,' said Lavery, his confusion growing.

'Name of McGuire. Michael McGuire. I had my people do some quick background research on the man.'

'Yes, sir.' Lavery hoped to God he would never be in a position to discover the DoSS had done 'quick background research' on him. It almost certainly meant they had a file going back years.

'Turns out he was a homosexual, you can tell Stark. A right bugger in fact.' Lavery could hear a snigger in his voice, the sort of conspiratorial innuendo that was intended to make clear this was 'lads' talk'. 'Seems he was rogering another of the clergy and was about to be outed, have his pants pulled down in public by some foreign press busybody. You know how the party looks at that sort of thing. It was going to mean immediate loss of his job and public disgrace. More than the bugger could cope with. His death, therefore, is clearly a case of suicide. Tell Stark he can forget all about it. Got that?'

'Yes sir. A suicide. Forget all about it.'

'Good man.'

Lavery put down the black plastic receiver, wishing to hell he could forget he had ever picked it up.

Chapter 27

The spring storm clouds were rolling over as Stark pushed open the door of the Corner House restaurant on The Strand. He had decided to walk back to the office. He had too much on his mind and walking was something he had done ever since his teens when he needed to clear his head. So far, however, he had not succeeded. And he was hungry. He had swallowed no more than a cup of coffee at breakfast and most of that he had puked over the balustrade.

A Corner House would not normally have been his first choice but it had the advantage of being there, and being open. The chain had altered little since being introduced as a wartime austerity measure to provide cheap, filling sustenance and the residual morale-boosting illusion of 'eating out'. He ordered a sausage roll and washed down the doughy pastry and gristle with a cup of weak milky tea. It was not much better than the office canteen, but not much worse either. They probably had the same bulk suppliers from the same government stockpile as they had had in his father's day.

His father's day – all of a sudden the cliché no longer had the same meaning. There was a certain seductive magic in the dream of a truly egalitarian society, but Stark was beginning to wonder if his father too had realised the dream had long since been stifled by a drab monotone mundanity and the blatant abuse of privilege. He cleared away his teacup and walked out, around the corner and into Stalingrad Square. Once named for a different battle in a different war, between old empires, now it bore the name of the great turning point in the Great Peoples' War. The few buildings around it, scarred and mutilated, still housed the ghosts of their previous imperial incarnations, the great chiselled letters that spelt CANADA and SOUTH AFRICA still visible through the pockmarks left by shell and shrapnel.

Stark had seen pictures of the statue of the old one-eyed, one-armed admiral which used to dominate the square but he was so used to Motherland on her plinth that he could no longer imagine it; any more than he could imagine the square crowded with taxis and buses. Today this was nothing more than a turning circle at the end of the Strand, dominated by the neoclassical bulk of the Soviet Embassy that ran along the northern side and had allegedly once been the National Gallery. The Wall ran just behind it, as was so often the case. It had a habit of running behind things, as if scurrying away from prying eyes.

Only at the edge of the Square had the Wall itself been incorporated into the landscape, running like a white-washed garden fence across what had once been the busy entry to the gentlemen's clubland of Pall Mall, now a few ruins on the little visited eastern edge of West London. Around the grandiose isolated monument that was Admiralty Arch, the Wall looped out again, though it was only a few feet high here to allow a view of the uniformed sentries of the English People's Army who proudly guarded the Anti-Capitalist Protection Barrier. Work was almost completed on the tribune erected in front of it, the porticoes of the gallery adorned with pictures of the 'four great thinkers': Marx, Lenin, Stalin and Attlee.

The American's depiction of traffic once again streaming through the Arch in both directions was beyond Stark's

powers of imagination. For his entire life the Arch had represented not so much a gateway as a closed door. Beyond
it, he knew, an old royal road led through parkland to what
had once been a royal palace, but that – like the very idea
of royalty itself – seemed something out of another, ancient
world.

Stark had no Latin, but a defence lawyer had told him the
shrapnel-scarred letters, still just about visible, carved above
the gateway described its dedication to Victoria, Queen
and Empress, by her son Edward VII. There was an irony
that a monument to monarchy now provided a reviewing
point for the Socialist Labour Party leadership to take their
annual salute, their rostrum mounted so that they showed
their rear ends to the ideological enemy.

Stark turned left down Whitehall. It was impossible to
imagine that the great slabs of government offices on the left
had once had alter egos on the right. Now there were just a
few nondescript flat blocks, thrown up in the early sixties
to house party officials, and of course to hide the Wall that
once again ran behind them. The most miraculous survival
on Whitehall was the seventeenth-century Banqueting Hall,
where King Charles I had been forced to march through the
window onto a hastily erected scaffold. A memorial plaque
informed visitors that this was where the first, sadly short-
lived, English Republic had been born. It was a matter of
pride to the Central Committee to remind their French and
Russian comrades that the English had killed a king more
than a century before it became fashionable in Paris or
Petersburg.

On the other hand, there was nothing whatsoever to indicate where, beneath the great plot of devastation beyond the
Wall across the street, somewhere under the earth, lay the

remnants of the bunker where the last great drama of the old empire had been acted out. They said the old ogre's body had been burnt after he cheated the hangman; that there was no last resting place for the truly wicked.

Out of curiosity, Stark did something he had never done before. He crossed the street to where the Wall itself ran along the scarred edge of the pavement, where once the walls of government buildings had stood. Signs at fifty-metre intervals proclaimed, 'Warning: State Border'. Yet there was a distinct anonymity to the Wall on this side: a stained concrete structure, little more than two metres high. A tall man might almost stand on tiptoes and look over it, if he was foolish enough to dare. The actual Wall, the one Stark had only seen on Northern television, the one the non-communist world was familiar with, three metres high, graffiti-daubed and topped with concrete curves like giant barrels with a circumference too great to grant human hands a purchase, was at least ten metres away, across a strip of sand laced with barbed wire and constantly patrolled by armed men and dogs. All to stop, so Attlee had said, innocent southern Englanders being seduced by empty greed into becoming wage slaves of the capitalist multinationals.

Stark had never once thought about crossing the frontier. But he knew more than a few of his fellow citizens, lured more – as Attlee had warned – by the television advertisement-driven images of the consumer lifestyle than by any political philosophy, had done so illegally, or more frequently died in the attempt. The Wall was a draconian – Northern propaganda said 'inhuman' – measure to prevent the haemorrhage of a state and a system. It was not an argument Stark had ever been encouraged to have. Not with himself or anyone else. Until now.

Up ahead of him, on the other side, the battered tower of Big Ben, pockmarked with the craters of howitzer shells, poked its head over like some sinister scarred night watchman. Just in front of Harry a few hardboard hoarding panels, probably surplus material from the stands and backdrops erected for the parade, leaned against the Wall partly obscuring one of the 'State Border' signs. Instinctively, the policeman who believed in orderliness over anything else taking command, he pushed them along to reveal it. Only when the sign was completely visible did he notice the red paint next to it, in the unmistakable shape of an elbow.

With the trepidation born of anticipating the unthinkable he pushed the hardboard panel to one side. And immediately recoiled, stunned by what confronted him. Larger than life in the red paint of the Republic. Winston bloody Churchill himself. Trilby on his head, right hand raised in the trademark V-sign that had become synonymous with savagery. The same image that had been on the note in the murder victim's pocket. The same image painted on the wall of Bankside power station.

No, not quite the same. The left hand held a pistol pointed at his head. But beneath it was a question mark.

Filled with an overwhelming sense of both shock and awe, Stark, in a reflex action, put out his hand to touch it. The paint was still wet.

Chapter 28

For the second time that day DS Lavery jumped to his feet at the sight of his boss entering a room. But instead of the turret office they shared in New Scotland Yard, it was the snug bar of the Red Lion on Whitehall. Lavery was wondering how to tell Stark that whatever it was he had accidentally or otherwise walked into this afternoon, the DoSS was determined he should forget it. The Harry Stark he knew was not a man to forget things to order, especially if he thought it was a murder. Especially one he had witnessed himself.

One look at Stark confirmed his fears. The detective had seen more than one corpse in his career; right now he looked as if he had seen a ghost.

'A beer, now please, and a chaser,' Stark gabbled out at the barman, who was used to not asking questions of policemen in a hurry. Within seconds there was a pint of Red Barrel and a double vodka on the bar. Stark took a large swallow of the beer and downed the vodka in one. Lavery sensed his job was getting harder by the minute.

'Sir,' he said. Stark turned, noticing him for the first time. His expression suggested surprise to find his sergeant here rather than at the office. It was only 5 p.m. He had no way of knowing his sergeant had decided he needed a large dose of Dutch courage. To Lavery's surprise and intense gratification, however, Stark actually seemed glad to see him. But it was the sergeant who found his voice first: 'I've ... I've got something to tell you.'

There was a noticeable stammer to his voice. Stark picked up on it.

'I know,' he said. 'I know,' and put a hand on Lavery's sleeve. 'I've just seen it. Unbelievable. Right under our very noses.'

'Sir?' Lavery wanted to be sure they were talking about the same thing.

'What the hell is going on, Lavery?'

The sergeant shook his head. The one thing he was sure of was that on that score he had absolutely no idea.

'For half a century nobody mentions the old bastard. The initials WC reduced to a toilet joke. A bogeyman dead and buried. Then all of a sudden he's everywhere. The Yanks are making a film about him, asking God knows what sort of awkward questions that don't want asking. We find a corpse with its head half-off and a stencil drawing of the bogeyman in its pocket. Then a larger than life-size image, almost identical, appears on Bankside power station. And now there's one on the bloody Wall itself!'

'What wall? Oh … *that* wall? You don't mean?'

Stark nodded, looking at Lavery as if his sergeant had suddenly lost his wits.

'Right across the bloody road.' He nodded backwards towards the saloon bar doors. 'Half covered up with a couple of plywood hoardings. Isn't that what we're talking about?'

'Yes. I mean, no. It's …'

'What? You haven't seen it? I thought …'

'No. I mean, no. I mean I got a phone call. From the Department. Him. That colonel. You know the one, with the posh voice. Marchmain. About something that happened this afternoon. You told me you were going to the museum. But he said something about St Paul's Cathedral. What happened?'

Stark narrowed his eyes, looking at Lavery as if he were trying to read the man's mind. Or remember what was supposed to be on his own.

'What did he say? What did he tell you?'

'Nothing. I mean, nothing much. There was an incident? A ...' he hesitated over the word, 'a suicide. Right?'

Stark pulled back and opened his eyes wide.

'What?' He held his breath a second. 'A suicide. That's what ... You're telling me Marchmain rang you up and told you it was suicide?'

'Yessir. I didn't even know what he was talking ...'

'Never mind. Never mind.'

'He said forget about it, sir. I mean, he said you were to forget about it.'

Stark closed his eyes.

'I'll bet he did. I'll bet he did.'

'It wasn't though, was it, sir? Suicide, I mean?'

Stark almost laughed.

'No, Lavery. It was most certainly not suicide.'

'Who was he? Why? How? The colonel mentioned a name. Michael Mac something or other. Said he was, you know, a homo. One of them. Said that was why ... why he done it.'

Stark shook his head. 'Is that what he said? Michael McGuire. He was a churchwarden, Lavery, and as for his particular sexual orientation, I neither know nor care. But that is not the reason he met his end. He was killed because he was trying to tell me something.'

Lavery looked more confused than ever.

'About ... about the murder. The other murder, I mean.'

Stark shrugged.

'Maybe. I don't know. Maybe I never will. It was just then

149

that …' His mind flashed back, a sudden queasiness washing over him as he remembered sitting there next to that precipitous beckoning void, and then seeing the man opposite him lifted up and plunged into it. He tried to conjure up the man's last words, what it was he had been saying when … Had something he said been equivalent to pulling a trigger against his own head?

There had been some mention of 'underground', 'the Underground'? The Tube? Or the American's shadowy conspiracy?

'What was it, sir? Maybe something …'

'Something about "another man", and "love", maybe he was right, the old DoSSer …'

Lavery suppressed a look of shock. The common street nickname was frowned upon in work circles, even though everybody used it at home.

'Something about "love … the church …", he mentioned a bride and then said "Christ", though the second time I think it was more an imprecation than a theological reference.'

'A bride?'

Stark shrugged. 'Doesn't make sense to me either. Though it is something they say, though, isn't it?'

'It is?'

'About the Church, with a capital 'C' being the bride of Christ.'

'Oh, yes. I have heard that. Not much of a churchgoer myself. I thought there for a minute …'

'What?'

'No nothing, it's just …'

'What? Come on, Lavery, spit it out.'

'It's just, just that I thought of something else. I mean, if it was true …'

'If what was true?'

'What he said. That colonel. I mean if this bloke, Mac ...'

'McGuire.'

'If he was, you know, a bit ...'

Stark closed his eyes and nodded.

'It's just that it's a bit of a coincidence, that's all.'

'What is, man? For God's sake.'

'Well he might not have meant the Bride of Christ. He might have meant St Bride's Church. Just down the road like. I mean, it's well known the priest there, old Arthur Rye like, I mean he's as bent as a nine-bob note.'

Stark's eyes opened wide. He turned and stared his sergeant directly in the eyes.

'Come on, Lavery. What the hell are we doing sitting here?!'

Chapter 29

The slight unassuming figure of Canon Arthur Rye, sitting upright on his hard-backed chair gazing up at the slow trickle of raindrops from the corrugated iron roof above his head, was deep in meditation. An innocent passer-by might have thought him rapt in profound contemplation of the divine. In fact, he was trying to think of a birthday present for his lover of ten years' standing.

What Michael would most appreciate, he knew, although he disapproved of the habit – apart from anything else it made the man's mouth taste like an ashtray – was American cigarettes, Lucky Strike or Marlboro, though anything would be better than the 'bloody Balkan baccy' he complained about relentlessly.

But American cigarettes were hard to come by, unless you were in possession of hard currency. Arthur Rye had never even seen the hallowed grail of hard currency addicts, a US dollar. B-Pounds were a different matter; enough of them found their way into the coffers of the Church of England, thanks to its officially tolerated links to the sister church across the border (tolerated specifically because they brought money south). But they did not find their way into the stipends of middle- and lower-ranking clergy. Even those whose churches were in ruins.

The only access Canon Rye had to that sort of money was through the generosity of a rare visitor from the North or Westminster paying in hard cash at the official rate for one of the postcards of the church as it had once been and with luck would one day be again, though privately he thought a miracle would be needed, given the far greater draw of St Paul's just a few hundred metres away.

It really had been a miracle that the Luftwaffe bomb, which gutted Sir Christopher Wren's beautiful baroque interior, had struck on the night of Sunday, 29 December 1940 rather than four days earlier when it would have been full. But perhaps the greatest miracle of all was that it had left standing the soaring, tiered seventy-metre spire, with its diminishing octagonal archways stacked one above the other. On its completion in 1701, it had inspired a local baker to imitate it in a wedding cake, setting a style that spread across the world.

Once, in a flight of unimaginably foolish fantasy Arthur Rye had looked up at the great spire, imagining he and Michael might one day have a wedding cake. Now, used to the bitter taste of reality familiar to those whose sexual orientation was a crime, he no longer saw a wedding cake in white Portland stone, just the defacing black streaks left by tongues of fire. At least the Church understood the quality of mercy, especially to its own.

He got to his feet, dismissing the problem of the birthday present for the moment, and began mechanically sorting through the collection of material on sale at his little desk: the postcards with their before and after images of the church's destruction and the badly-reproduced roneotyped history of the site, going back to its sixth-century foundations. He shook his head. They were barely legible, some of them, roneoed on to pale green recycled paper. But other than for government publications, printing materials of any sort were scarce, good paper and inks hard to come by. He was deeply grateful that the church had access to them. For more reasons than one.

He stretched and looked up once again at the sky. The thick grey clouds that had overcome the early overoptimistic glimpse of sunshine and loomed ominously overhead ever since had settled down now like a sodden blanket. There would be a downpour at any minute, unless this soul-eroding half-hearted spatter of dirty heavy raindrops continued indefinitely. Which was always a depressing possibility. The only thing that seemed certain was that there would be few, if any, more casual customers for church memorabilia. It was time to shut up shop. The only passers-by after nightfall were regulars.

Except that the two men looking at him from the far end of what had once been the chancel were definitely not regulars. For a start, one of them was dressed too well. Not well enough to be a Northerner – his clothing was definitely from the Comecon zone (the canon had an eye for well-cut clothes, at least good enough to know when someone's weren't). He was wearing a beige raincoat, not the classic trench favoured by the DoSS but the old-fashioned, short type that had been popular in the sixties. The canon wondered if he might have inherited it.

The two were walking towards him now, as if they'd only just noticed him. That at least suggested he wasn't a DoSSer. In any case it wasn't their 'time of the month'. There was a certain unwritten code that covered dealings with the DoSS these days, an uneasy 'live and let live' that might or might not reflect the recent changes in the Kremlin even if they were not reciprocated in the Mansion House. The canon felt certain that if he was about to receive an unscheduled visit from the DoSS, he would have had advance warning.

In any case that was not his biggest worry. There was something about this pair, the way the taller man carried himself that suggested he wielded authority, and the way the shorter one deferred to him, that suggested a partnership of unequals. Like a pair of plainclothes policemen. That was the possibility that worried Arthur Rye most. The DoSS interest lay only in the activities they almost certainly suspected were carried out in his crypt. But he was all too conscious of the fact that they – or almost anyone else with a grudge against him – could pass on information to the Metropolitan People's Police that could see him end up in Brixton Prison on the same charge that had confined Oscar Wilde to Reading Gaol. In Arthur Harkness's strait-laced workers' and farmers' republic, a longing for political freedom was not the only 'love that dare not speak its name'.

He bit his tongue for even having the thought. There was no one amongst the regulars who'd blab, was there? The last thing anyone wanted to do was to attract undue attention. Particularly now. Even amongst one or two of those hard cases. He did nobody any harm. And Michael, for God's sake, wouldn't hurt a fly. Even still, you could never be too careful. Six months in Pentonville Prison would leave the canon a physical and psychological wreck; but it would kill Michael. He continued packing away his bits and pieces in the fervent hope they might just go away. They didn't.

The canon turned around, reluctantly. The kiosk was raised up on bricks above the mud and rubble of the church's ruined nave, and he found himself almost at eye level with the taller of the two. The man facing him was tall, with dark hair, a square jaw, in his mid-thirties or thereabouts and good-looking in a butch sort of way. Except that his eyes seemed somehow too soft for his face. And there was something eerily familiar about him.

Which only partly explained the tremor in his voice when

he turned and said with as unforced a smile as he could manage: 'I was just closing down. Is there some way I can be of help to you gentlemen?'

It was the shorter, stockier one that answered: 'Yes. Did you know a certain Michael McGuire?'

'Why, yes of course,' the canon answered, trying his level best to keep his voice neutral in tone. Never incriminate yourself if you don't have to was a lesson he had learned hard. 'He's the churchwarden at St Paul's.' And then he tripped over the tense like a man stumbling into darkness. 'Did … did you say "did"?'

The short man nodded and was about to open his mouth, when his obvious superior intervened.

'I'm afraid there's been an … incident.'

As one man Stark and Lavery rushed forward to help as the slight figure in the dog collar and dark tweed jacket collapsed to the ground. Harry Stark had seen grown men cry before; but never one whose world he had so obviously pulled from beneath him.

Chapter 30

'Wh … what happened?'

Stark turned to Lavery. They had rehearsed this bit, in advance: Lavery would tell him the bare facts. Stark would confirm with whatever detail seemed appropriate. But now that it came to it, looking at the broken man in front of them, trying desperately to summon up the strength to confront such a terrible truth, he felt he had to do it himself. As gently as possible.

'I'm afraid he fell to his death. From the Whispering Gallery.'

'But how? And how do you know this? Who are you anyway?'

'I was there. I was a witness.'

'But how …? It's not possible. Not simply to fall.'

'The Department of Social Security has declared it was suicide.'

Stark was not happy about the line, but he had to test the man's response. Had the Department lied to him? How honest would this man be?

'Suicide! That's ridiculous. He would never. Why?'

'They said he was afraid. About his relationship. With you.'

Both policemen felt acutely embarrassed. Neither believed it was the truth about what actually happened. One knew for a certainty it was not.

Yet for a moment it looked as if their words had beaten the man in front of them from his knees to the floor, as if they had piled not just grief but guilt on top of tragedy.

And then suddenly something changed, something wholly intangible. Arthur Rye lifted his head and got to his feet and stared at a point in space between both of them with red eyes.

'No,' he said. 'It's a lie. Michael was not a strong man. But he would have rather been a martyr than a coward. That is not what happened. Is that who you are? DoSSers? Did you kill him, or have you locked him up, shut him away in some dark cell, using ... using "whatever", some sort of pretext?'

Stark could see from the man's eyes that his defiance was a cloak for hope. But he had already said enough to get himself locked up for months, if not years, had he and Lavery really been from the DoSS.

'Tell me the truth,' the priest challenged him, more anger in his voice than grief, until he asked the question that mattered: 'Is he really dead?'

Stark nodded slowly. And said: 'I'm afraid so. I saw the body.'

The canon's head fell to his chest. Then he looked up and said: 'He didn't jump, did he?'

'No. He was pushed.'

The canon closed his eyes and put his head in his hands. Stark turned to Lavery and said, 'Dick, let me have a quiet chat with the canon here for a minute, will you? Why don't you nip out onto the street there and have a fag. I'm sure you could do with one.' He took from his pocket the packet of Marlboro the American had given him and offered one first to the canon. Rye shook his head, obviously suppressing another flood of tears. 'I don't,' he said. 'But Michael did. They were his favourite.'

Stark handed the pack to Lavery. 'Make sure we're not disturbed, will you?'

The sergeant took the pack and vanished down the alley-way that led out onto Fleet Street.

Stark turned back to the churchman and watched as he lifted red eyes to look at him squarely. He could almost sense the anger welling up in the sparse, emotionally drained figure of the man in front of him. 'I knew it,' Rye said at length. 'I knew something like this would happen one day. But why, why now?'

There was something in the way the man looked up at Stark that made him think he already knew the answer. He dug into his pocket and produced the piece of paper found in the pocket of the corpse hanging under Blackfriars Bridge.

'Does this mean anything to you?'

He watched as Rye took the paper and unfolded it, and noticed the slight intake of breath when his eyes fell on the image printed on it.

'How did you come by this? How did you come to be there when …' he let the words trail off. 'Who the hell are you anyway?'

It was a question Stark had been waiting for. He had pre-pared his response, as far as he could. In truth he was not at all sure how to play this, how much to say, how much not to say, and not at all sure what he was looking for, and what he hoped or feared to find.

'My name,' he said, 'is Harry Stark. I wanted to speak to Mr McGuire because somebody told me he could help me find out something important about my family. About the death of my father, nearly twenty years ago.'

The canon was shaking his head as if all this was an irrelevance.

'I don't see how … What did you say your name was?'

'Stark. Harry Stark. My father's name was John. John Stark.'

'John Stark?' The canon repeated, as if the name rang a distant bell. A distant bell in an empty long-unused chapel. Then he looked up at Stark again, scrutinising his facial features.

'Your father,' he said. 'What did he do?'

It was another moment Stark had anticipated, and for the moment he was grateful he had been as economical as he had been with details about himself.

'He was a policeman. In the Metropolitan People's Police. Major John Stark.'

The canon put his hand to his forehead and ran his fingers through what remained of his thinning hair, then looked Stark in the eyes and produced a line Stark was more used to saying than hearing.

'Young man, you'd better come with me.'

Chapter 31

The man lingering in the doorway of the little newsagents on the corner of Fleet Street and Ludgate Circus lit up a cigarette and looked on with mild envy at the dumpy plain-clothes policeman opposite.

The policeman was holding a packet of Marlboro and tapping it with obvious satisfaction to produce a second cigarette, having only moments before ground out the stub of his first one beneath his heel. He rubbed the cigarette under his nose, clearly savouring the aroma of the tobacco before lighting up.

Nonetheless the man in the doorway opposite was impressed. Either pay in the People's Police had risen substantially recently or he was looking at a detective sergeant with rather better contacts than usual. It was not that he didn't have access to such foreign luxuries himself – he could use the special shop in the Barbican – but he was not allowed to enjoy them on the job. That would have been a dead giveaway.

He had been put on this particular job barely half an hour ago, alerted by one of the two cars which had tailed the pair of policemen from New Scotland Yard on the Embankment. He had no idea why precious Department resources were being used to tail two detectives from the Metropolitan People's Police, but then it was his job to obey orders not question them. He had followed a senior member of the Party Central Committee in the past, reporting his every contact and movement. He had no idea in what way his own activities had contributed but he was not in the least suspected when several weeks later the man had resigned 'for health reasons'.

The portly figure opposite was walking up and down every couple of minutes, clearly waiting for his colleague who had not emerged from the alleyway that led up to the steeple and ruined nave of old St Bride's church. He was obviously not happy in the drizzle which was slowly but surely getting heavier and took frequent covetous glances towards the door of the The Olde Bell public house just a few metres away. There was little doubt that was where he would rather be.

And that meant he was not only waiting for his colleague but supposed to be watching his back. In which case he should have spotted the obvious figure lurking in the doorway opposite pretending to shelter from the rain. Clearly counter-surveillance techniques in the MetPP were not what they ought to be. Even so, this was not a 'show and silence' operation, the type in which persons under observation were deliberately allowed to become aware of the fact in order to intimidate them. The man in the doorway dropped the stub of his own cigarette to the ground and stamped on it – he hated bloody Bulgarian baccy anyhow – and with a grumbling, resigned look up at the glowering rainclouds walked into the street.

Just for the hell of it, he crossed the road, right in front of the plainclothes policeman. He was almost tempted to walk up St Bride's Passage to see if he would try to stop him. Or better still, go up to him and ask for a light. Just to see what would happen. Probably be told to 'move along, sir', he thought with a smile. Instead he made do with a cheery, 'Evening mate, nasty night, innit?' as he passed, and was rewarded with a frown but one that showed no indication of suspicion. Just to rub it in, he turned in the door of the Bell.

He had already spotted his replacement coming down Ludgate Hill and knew that by the time he was inside the warmth of the public house, there would be someone else keeping an eye on the poor little plod. He passed straight through the pub and out the back door into the part of St Bride's Passage that curved left by the side of the ruin into the side street below, and out onto New Bridge Street where there was a public call box. He closed the heavy red door behind him – how useful it had been that the old imperial colour had necessitated no rebranding, just the crown moulding chiselling from above the doors – and dialled the unique number that would put him straight through to the Barbican.

Chapter 32

There was a moment's silence, in which Stark could feel the cold water creeping down his neck and hear the swish of tyres on busy Fleet Street just a few metres away. Raindrops spattered on the remnants of what must once have been a chequerboard marble floor protruding from the mud.

'Come with me,' the churchman said again, quietly this time as if he were offering Stark a passageway into another world. Stark watched him cross to a piece of wall behind the wooden information stall where an old wooden curtain hung. He pulled the curtain aside to reveal not some fresco or memorial plaque as Stark had suspected, but a steep staircase descending into the bowels of the earth. He beckoned Stark to follow.

'Where are we going?'

The churchman turned and with a wry, inestimably sad attempt at a smile said: 'Where else but into the realm of the dead?'

Despite a creeping feeling of apprehension, Stark knew he had no alternative but to follow. From a niche in the wall the canon removed a large, rubber-handled torch and turned it on, casting a yellow pool of light on the dark stone stairway that turned on itself back under the main body of the ruined church. 'Watch your step,' he said.

In front of them was a blackened wooden door. The churchman turned a heavy, rattling iron handle and it swung gently open.

'They say that every cloud has a silver lining. Even the very darkest. This is ours – the entry to the crypts.'

'How long has this been here?'

Stark had no idea that such a thing existed underneath the ruins of a church in the heart of London.

'It was only rediscovered in the aftermath of the bombing. It would appear that when Sir Christopher built his St Bride's in the seventeenth century he built over the remains of the six previous churches on the sites. There were land shortages in London even back then. To save space, bodies from overcrowded churchyards were often disinterred and reinterred as bones. It was commonplace and not as macabre as it sounds. There are the remains of over 7,000 human beings down here, but after a cholera epidemic in the nineteenth century crypt burials in the City of London were banned and they were all sealed. It took a 200 kilo bomb to reopen this one.'

Stark didn't know what he expected. Something macabre. Stacked skulls and crossed bones. Whole skeletons dangling from hooks. Instead he saw a plain, stone-walled chamber, gently lit by a single hanging light bulb and two candles on a table dressed as a simple altar.

'This is where we worship,' the canon said, ushering him in. Who were 'we', Stark wondered. How many Christians came here, to this cellar, rather than attend one of the admittedly dwindling number of still functioning churches in better repair? To the left and right were openings into unlit passageways.

'That is where the bones are stored. Our catacombs, you might call them, though they are hardly on a scale with those in Paris. Nonetheless, this place is something of an underground warren. There are still parts that are inaccessible, or at the very least unsafe. But come along, there is someone here I think you need to meet.'

'Someone here? Who?'

'Come with me.'

Stark followed the canon gingerly along the passageway to the left. The torchlight revealed that here indeed were the bones Stark had been anticipating: neat piles of them, all identical.

'The mediaeval monks were very methodical, you see. They matched all the bones and stored like with like. I suppose they might have thought it would make reassembly simpler on the Day of Judgement, although I can just as easily imagine it causing some confusion. But then not for the Creator, I suppose. All the skulls are in a separate chamber. A regular little Golgotha.'

Stark shivered.

They turned a corner and found themselves in another chamber, almost as big as the first, and also lit by a solitary bulb, with what appeared to be – and almost certainly was – row upon row of femurs lining one wall. The wall opposite was lined with camp beds.

'People live here?' said Stark.

'Not exactly. Let's just say the church has always provided sanctuary to those in occasional need of it. And some have more occasion than others. This gentleman here is one of those. Isn't that so, Mr Ransom?'

For the first time Stark noticed that there was someone else in their presence: a small, slight figure sitting hunched against the wall on one of the beds in the semi-darkness just beyond the yellow pool of light cast by the solitary bulb. He might as well have been a bundle of discarded rags and didn't move even when his name was mentioned.

'Mr Ransom,' the clergyman repeated. 'I've brought you a visitor.'

The small head turned and in the half-light Stark could just make out a wizened face with eyes screwed tight shut.

'Who is it?' the little man barked out in a surprisingly shrill, angry voice. 'You know I don't like strangers. It's not your pooftah pal again, is it?'

The canon flinched visibly.

'No,' he said. 'Mic … he won't be coming here anymore.'

'Coming somewhere else I suppose then,' the old man said, with a gruff chortle.

Stark, taken aback, glanced at the clergyman beside him and noticed the reddened cheeks and pursed lips.

The canon shook his head. 'It's okay. He gets like this. It's understandable.'

Stark looked sceptical.

'No really, you see …' he shone the torch fully onto the face of the old man who ~~stood~~ ^{SAT} there totally unblinking. Stark immediately realised why.

'Oh my God, what happened to him?'

Stark had bent down to the old man's level with the intention of looking him in the eyes only to recoil with horror. The canon put his hand upon his arm.

'It's all right. He doesn't feel any pain. Not any more.'

'But how …? What …?'

'It was an accident. Or so they said.'

'Who?' though he already knew.

'The Department of Social Security, who else? They took him prisoner about five years ago, accused him of organising the riots in Bristol.'

'What riots? I've never heard of any …'

'No. You wouldn't have. They tried to get him to talk, reveal some links to mysterious figures they believed were trying to destabilise the regime. He said he knew nobody, had seen nothing. So they took him at his word – they sewed his eyelids up. Except that somebody wasn't very careful with the needle. Twice.'

Stark swallowed hard. He felt bitter bile rise in his throat. 'It's unbelievable.'

'Yes, but then that's what they say about Christianity too. I know which I prefer.'

Stark gulped. 'He's lived here ever since?'

'More or less. Somebody has to look after him. And he has friends, people with a long association with this church. That's why I brought you to see him. There's just a chance he might be able to tell you something about your father.'

'Tell whoever it is to get out of here,' the old man said. 'I ain't playing some fucking question and answer machines for some geezer I don't even know. Pretty boy, is he?'

The churchman turned his torch away and looked down at the ground. Stark could hear the hurt in his voice and knew the man was only waiting for him to be gone to give full vent to his grief.

'But if he doesn't want to, there's nothing to be done. I'm sorry. Perhaps you'd better leave. Mr Stark.'

It was not what he wanted to hear. But then he no longer knew exactly what he did want to hear.

'Wait a minute.' The old man's voice had risen slightly, though the initial anger in it had not quite returned.

'What did you say his father's name was?'

It was the detective who answered.

'Stark. Major John Stark. He was …' hesitantly, he didn't know what effect the words would have, 'he was a policeman.'

There was silence. A silence that seemed so long to Stark he wondered if the old man had not heard him, or had maybe even fallen asleep. Then suddenly, in a version of that rasping voice that was subtly different, the old man said: 'Come here. Down here. In front of me, let me feel your face.'

Stark knelt down before him, trying his best not to look into the scarred, mucus-lined scabs of flesh that covered the misshapen eyeballs. Ransom put his hands out and Stark guided them onto his own face, only too glad of the excuse to close his own eyes. The hands crawled across his face, feeling the breadth and curve of his forehead, the lobes of his ears and particularly the shape of his aquiline nose, the nose that he hated but shared with his father. Stark found it a disconcerting experience, but not entirely unpleasant.

Then all of a sudden, the old man drew his hands back and made the sign of the cross over his sunken chest. Stark thought he could see traces of moisture seep out from the corners of his mutilated eyes.

'It can't be. But maybe it is. It has to be. Bless my all too mortal soul. Little Harry Stark. Your father was a hero, son. A hero of the Underground. He hated the fucking commies.'

Chapter 33

Lieutenant George Henry of Second Regiment, Order of Lenin, English Democratic Border Control Service glanced at his watch and sighed as he watched through binoculars the growing queue of cars snake past the American checkpoint fifty metres away on the other side of the Wall.

He had come on duty at 1400, which meant there was more than another seven to go before he could relinquish his post, and leave the night shift to secure the borders of socialism during the hours of darkness.

He was not looking forward to the next couple of days. All leave had been cancelled as the state was expecting record numbers of dignitaries to mark the fortieth anniversary of the English Democratic Republic's inception. That meant there would, more than likely, be more tourists than normal from 'Westminster' and 'up North'.

The foreigners, the Yanks in particular, made a fuss about being obliged to change a minimum of £20 a day at the official 1:1 rate between 'British pounds' and the English pounds of the Democratic Republic. Henry knew as well as anyone you could get four or five times that on the black market, but he resented the way the foreigners who earned vastly more than he and his comrades sneered at the notes they were handed and called them 'Mickey Mouse money'. Mickey Mouse was, after all, one of theirs.

He could see the American marine on duty in the little glass shed peering back at him through binoculars of his own. The big sign on the edge of the street facing him said

'You are now entering the American Sector'. He supposed on the other side it said 'You are now leaving the American Sector'. They still called it that, a sector, refusing to recognise, even forty years on, that this was an established international boundary.

He knew, like everyone else knew, that on the other side they called the Oxford Street/Tottenham Court Road border crossing 'Checkpoint Charlie'. That too was a leftover from the tense few days that followed the 1949 ceasefire, when the lines were drawn but the frontiers not officially established. 'Checkpoint Alpha' was the entrance to the transit road which crossed into the territory of the Democratic Republic just south of Birmingham, 'Checkpoint Bravo' the spot where the Oxford Road crossed the old Grand Union Canal to enter the enclave the party called 'Westminster', but many ordinary folk, not least on the other side, still called West London, and sometimes bizarrely just 'London'. Some people never learned.

The tall man in the raincoat with the glasses, the breezy easy smile and the little wheelie bag bouncing along behind him as he stepped off the pavement walking towards the EDR frontier looked a classic of the kind. He presented his passport to the guard at the pedestrian entrance to the border control zone and then proceeded, still beaming broadly, to the Immigration and Customs Control shed where it would be checked thoroughly and his visa issued. Lieutenant Henry waited a few seconds before, as he expected, the telephone on his desk rang. He put down his binoculars, picked up the receiver and gave a curt response to the duty passport officer. A minute or two later the door of his office opened and a female corporal entered, saluted and handed him the tall man's documents. As he had anticipated, he was American.

Lieutenant Henry examined them carefully, made a few notes, then told the corporal to photocopy them and bring them back to him. He lifted the second telephone on his desk, the red one, and made a call to his superior. Not the Regimental colonel, his real superior.

High in his office in the Barbican like a spider at the edge of a well-spun web, Colonel Charles Marchmain sat picturing in his mind the flies fumbling their way towards its sticky centre. It was an analogy he savoured. If things went as he anticipated it would be a right royal feast at the end.

Stark was at St Bride's and had made contact. The precipitous disposal of Michael McGuire had not been exactly what he intended. There were always over-enthusiastic idiots who took things too far. People who thought they could presume to anticipate orders rather than simply obey them. He would deal with that later. In the end it hadn't really mattered. It had probably proved a catalyst. Stark had made the connection anyhow. What mattered was where it went from here. The game was afoot. And moving fast.

The watching detail in Fleet Street's report made clear that Stark and his chubby little sidekick had put two and two together after all, and made the right answer. But the sergeant had been left on the street, which meant Stark was aware there was an uncomfortable personal dimension to this case. So far, so good. It now remained to see how far it got them. And him.

His musings were interrupted by a trilling ring of the third phone from left on his ample desk, the one directly connected to the crossing points between the capital city and 'Westminster'. Benjamin T. Fairweather, it seemed, had arrived at precisely 5.21 p.m., and this time had requested an extended visa, 'in order to cover the official celebrations for the fortieth anniversary of the English Democratic Republic'.

Marchmain ordered that he should be granted a seventy-two-hour visa. Single entry and exit. He had no intention of allowing the man to flit back and forth. What did he think this was: a free country?

Chapter 34

Harry Stark left St Bride's churchyard by the alleyway that led down past the ancient Olde Bell public house, grateful for the falling dusk to conceal the tears that to his irritation uncontrollably welled in his eyes.

He walked out onto New Bridge Street almost bundling into a man with a foul-smelling cigarette hanging out of his mouth leaving a phone box.

'Sorry guv,' the cigarette-smoking man said, before apparently remembering he had another call to make.

It was only then that Stark remembered Lavery. He turned left and left again into Fleet Street and saw his sergeant still pacing up and down outside the other end of the L-shaped alley. He started when he spotted Stark approaching from a different direction as if he thought his boss was playing tricks on him, and bustled up: 'How'd it go, boss?'

Stark pulled up his coat collar as if against the rain, but in reality to stop Lavery noticing the lines on his face. He did his best to shrug dismissively.

'He's taken it bad. Obviously. Whether it gets you and me anywhere for the moment, I'm not sure. Anyhow, I'm beat for today. See you tomorrow, Dick.'

Lavery looked fazed a moment and Stark realised his sergeant had been expecting they'd talk things over with a beer or two in The Olde Bell. He put on a smile and said, 'Have one for me, mate. Bit wrecked after today. I need some fresh air. Catch up tomorrow, eh? Oh, and don't worry if I'm a bit late.'

Stark didn't really notice his sergeant's reaction, or whether or not he made for The Olde Bell, though knowing Lavery he couldn't imagine anything else. He needed a drink all right. But not here. Not in this company. He needed air. It took one hell of a deep breath to accept that everything he had ever believed might have been a lie. And if that was true of his own family, how much more might it be true of the world at large? He was going to find out. Maybe.

'Can you come back?' the canon had said. 'Tomorrow, very early in the morning. Around dawn. There will be others here. There will be a small congregation.'

'For a religious service?' Stark wondered if the man was inviting him to some sort of requiem for his late lover.

The canon gave the ghost of a smile: 'Not exactly. But then again, the Good Book does say, "Where two or three are gathered together in my name, there am I".' Stark had heard the quotation before. He had never been sure what it meant. He was even less sure now.

He knew one thing. He had found his – rather the American's – 'Underground'. A blind and bitter old man and a grieving homosexual cleric. It was not exactly the stuff of revolution. Stark had no idea how much, if any, belief he could place in the American's optimism about the 'wind of change' wafting in from Moscow, whether or not there really was a growing readiness – in the Kremlin if not yet the Mansion House – to face up to communism's economic failures and casual cruelties. You didn't change a way of life overnight. Even if his father had embraced some sort of alternative, where had it got him?

But that was also the problem: if it really had got him a bullet in the back of the head, his son wanted to know. More than that, he wanted it exposed. He wanted other people to know. The people who venerated the old man's memory. Most of all, Harry Stark wanted his mother and sister to know. Even if the truth hurt, it was always better to know it. Wasn't it? He thought about the argument in the pub the other night. The American film about Churchill. The Churchill drawings – no, stencils, that's what they were – in the dead man's pocket, on Bankside power station. On the Wall itself. Was that about the same thing: truth and lies. Mistakes and mythology? His head hurt.

He looked at his watch and took stock of where he was. He had walked miles without noticing it, on autopilot. At least it was an autopilot that still had a compass. He was south of the river. Almost home. How much had his mother known? Everything? Nothing? Or something in between. He had no idea. Would the truth – whatever it was – be too little too late or too much too soon? Either way he would be back at St Bride's before dawn. He had told them he was indeed his father's son. He had told them they could trust him. And could they? And could he trust them?

He was still trying to configure the questions, never mind find answers, when out of nowhere a figure appeared in front of him, blocking his way. A tall figure, looming over him. And laughing.

'How's it going, Harry?'

The shock on Stark's face only added to the obvious delight on that of Benjamin T. Fairweather at turning the tables so neatly as he stepped out of the same doorway from which Stark had ambushed him barely twenty-four hours earlier

Never in his life had Harry Stark been so suddenly seized by two conflicting impulses. The first – and strongest – was to smash his fist into the American's face; the second, which occurred virtually simultaneously, was to hug him.

Instead he stood back and took him in with his eyes. He was older than Stark had thought, tall and well built despite a certain ungainliness, as if he had been an American football player and never quite got used to walking without the helmet and body armour. The smile on his face was trying hard to exude friendliness and not just the smugness that clearly his little prank of hiding in the doorway had inspired. But if Stark was any judge, the warmth in his eyes was genuine. He was wearing the thick-framed spectacles from the photograph in his press card. He held out his hand. Stark took it. As he had noticed before, the squeeze was firm, manly but not aggressive.

It was a strange world, Stark thought; this awkward big Bostonian had been his own unwanted messenger from the gods, an archangel out of nowhere who had delivered a world-altering revelation. The last thing he wanted to feel towards him was gratitude. Nor could he afford to alienate him. Without Ben Fairweather he might have gone on living with a legend that was rapidly turning into a lie.

'Sorry I startled you. My turn to play Injun Ambush, I guess. I've brought you this,' Fairweather said. 'I thought you might need a bit more convincing that I wasn't just making things up.'

Stark began slowly to shake his head. He wasn't going to be strung along, as if the American alone had pirate gold in his pocket with which he could drip-feed him. Stark had seen the hoard and the curse that lay on it. He stood there in stony silence, while the American delved into his jacket pocket and once again produced the expensive wallet, with yet another newspaper cutting. Or rather another photocopy. He unfolded it and handed it to Stark, who glanced down at it, then took it for a brief moment and handed it back.

It was from the *Telegraph*, marked 'final West London edition', the same date as the piece the American had shown him from the *New York Times*, the same subject. From what Stark could tell the two pieces might as well have been written by the same reporter – so much for the vaunted variety to be found in the so-called 'free' media. There were a few minor differences in wording, but the story was the same: the alleged execution by the Department of Social Security of a 'rogue' major in the Metropolitan People's Police. A Major by the name of John Stark.

'It just occurred to me,' the American said, 'that the record might not be complete over here.'

Stark handed the piece of paper back to him with a grudging admission: 'It wasn't.'

'I thought not.'

'So, here we are then.'

'Where?'

'Here. We're still here. Both of us. Me more than you.'

'It doesn't have to be that way.'

'Doesn't it? I rather think it does. What do you want me to say? Thank you? For fucking up my world?'

'You know, Harry, if there's a God in heaven and perhaps more importantly, a new mood in the Kremlin, and you're the man I think you are, well, then we'll carry this off.'

Those were big 'ifs', Stark thought. Even if he had any idea what it was they might 'carry off'. Or whether he wanted to.

'Don't think you can do this alone, Harry. I'm here to help you. It makes sense for both of us. I've moved over here, this side of the Wall. I checked into the Savoy for a few days. Here are the numbers.'

He wrote on a card and handed it across. Stark took it, saw the embossed *New York Times* crest, the name Benjamin T.

Fairweather, and a list of telephone and fax numbers. Across them the American had scrawled another, the number for The Savoy Hotel, and 'Room 405'.

Stark looked at him sceptically but slipped the card into his inside jacket pocket. The American held out his hand. Stark looked down at it for a second, then walked off.

'Harry?'

He turned.

'Fucking up your world wasn't my intention, you know.'

Stark gave him a lopsided grin.

'No?'

'No. The world happened to be fucked up. I just made you look at it. Shake?'

Stark met Fairweather in the eye and for a moment what he saw there was a genuine desire to please, to be liked. He took two steps towards him and stretched out his own hand. The American took it and squeezed it with a grip that was only slightly too strong, and said: 'Keep me in the loop, Harry. This means a lot to me.'

'It means a lot to me too.'

Chapter 35

'I hate him.'

'No, you don't.'

'Yes, I do. I hate him and everything he stands for. I hate the whole fucking sanctimonious set-up.'

'You don't mean that. Not really.'

A pause. A sulk. Kate Stark bit her lower lip and pouted. The two of them were standing on a street corner in Bermondsey, shivering. There was a cold wind blowing in from the Thames.

'How would you know? You don't have to live with him.'

A moment of hesitation. As if it were something Lizzie Goldsmith had actually thought about.

'No. I don't.'

'Or her. Or the fucking framed photographs. The medals wrapped in tissue paper. The middle-aged prats who smile at me in the street, who pop round to pay their respects to "Widow Stark" and treat me like some twelve-year-old kid and still cop a feel of my arse on the way out.'

'Now, that I do understand.'

'And I bet you don't like it either.'

'It comes with the territory, darling, and believe me that's something that isn't going to change overnight.'

'It's not fair.'

'The world isn't fair. That's what it's all about: us, them; men, women; communism, capitalism. In the end everything's a trade-off. One man's freedom ends where another's begins.'

'Or woman's.'

'Yeah. Right. In theory.'

'You don't believe that. In women's equality?'

'Of course I believe in it. I just don't see it happening any time soon. Remember, we were the first to declare it. Over here. On our side of the Wall. And what good did that do? Ever seen a woman in the Mansion House? Or the Kremlin, come to that.'

'Yeah, but that's what you'd expect. They put it into practice first, though, didn't they? Over there, in Britain, or whatever they call it, I mean, they've had a woman prime minister.'

'And a fat lot of good she did. Spent half her time up Ronnie Reagan's arse and the rest giving reactionary speeches about the supposed benefits to civilisation of the British empire, about her devotion to her "oppressed fellow subjects" – that's you and me, kid, and by the way don't you love that "subjects" word, as if anybody anywhere still owed jackshit loyalty to some old gaggle of German aristocrats wasting away their days on the Bahamas?'

'That's not what I mean.'

'It's not what I mean either. But it's what it is. It's what happened. You might not want to live with the status quo, but you at least have to start by acknowledging it.'

'It doesn't mean you have to stick up for my stupid brother who's spent half a lifetime at least trying to live up to the legend of a father who died when he was barely out of his teens.'

'He was your father too.'

'Yeah, but I never knew him, did I? I'm just told to worship the graven images.'

'I know. It can't be easy.'

'It's not. That's why I'm doing what I'm doing.'

'And you're doing a good job. A great job. You know, you could end up making the difference.'

'I could?'

'You could.'

'He had a Yank in the other night.'

'Did he now?'

'Me mum couldn't believe it. Thought he'd turned traitor. Consorting with the enemy an' all that.'

'I can imagine. What'd you do?'

'Me? I wasn't there. I suppose I'd have thought he'd nicked him. Probably was something like that in the end. Mum said he'd taken him back to the frontier. At midnight like. Some visa thing, probably.'

'Probably.'

'Don't explain why he brought him home in the first place though, does it?'

'No, it doesn't.'

'I sort of wish I'd got in earlier. I mean, it's just that … I've never met one, like. A real live American.'

'I have. Believe me, kid. They're not all they're cracked up to be. Ask my gran.'

'Yeah, I did. She's been helping me. With my project. For the parade.'

'You're going ahead with that? With all it entails?'

'I am. And nothing anyone could say will stop me.'

'I know. I wish I could think of something that would. But I can't. And even if I could, I'm not sure I'd want to.'

'Thanks, that means a lot.'

'Good luck. You'll need it.'

Chapter 36

Harry Stark breathed a sigh of relief when he saw Lizzie behind the bar. She smiled and nodded to indicate she would be right with him. Harry held up his hand as if holding a pint glass and she smiled again to show that she understood what was required was a pint of the usual.

The usual customers were at the bar, in their usual places. And from what Harry could hear their conversation hadn't moved on from the last time he was here, and with no Del in sight this time to shut them up.

'It can hardly be a coincidence, can it? The Yanks bring out a film trying to change history, trying to make old Winnie the Pooh smell of roses. And then somebody goes and paints a picture of him on Bankside!'

So it had got out. How could it not have? Was there anyone who didn't watch the BBC for the news? Even in the upper echelons of the Socialist Labour Party itself, Harry wondered. After all, if they didn't watch 'the other side', how would they know what to censor out, the old popular saw went.

He found himself trying to recollect what if anything his father had said about Churchill. He always said he had no time for the 'Tories', but did he ever mention Churchill spe-cifically? Stark couldn't remember him doing so. But then he wouldn't have done, would he? In those days particularly it was a name used to frighten children. The 'recent past' was something best not talked about. Even now, it was hard enough: you could see it in old people's faces. Old faces with ancient worry lines etched into them. Best to let the past take care of itself. Thinking too hard gave you headaches. Sometimes literally.

It didn't appear to be stopping young Ken Atkinson who seemed to have taken the new whispered message of *glasnost* from Moscow more literally than anyone else Stark had come across, at least on this side of the channel.

'All I know,' he was saying, 'is that it's a new take on the story. Artistic licence maybe, and maybe there is politics in it, but it makes for a good finale. After all, they never did find the remains, did they? Not for sure.'

'Pah, humbug.' Davy Hindsmith had obviously not changed his point of view either. 'Revisionism. That's what it is. They try to make out he didn't kill himself at all, show him sitting down writing a last will and testament handing over the "mantle of civilisation" to the Yanks, all that guff about "Greece to Rome" and the "destiny of the English-speaking peoples", an' then going out and taking on a Stalin tank single-handed, crushed beneath the treads – as you might be, mind – with just 'is fingers clutching a smoking gun at the end. Balderdash, the lot of it!'

'A powerful image, though, you have to admit.'

'Powerful propaganda, I'll admit that,' said Hindsmith, his voice rising, 'powerful and bloody dangerous.'

It was, Stark admitted too, a potent image. The only thing he couldn't see was the point of it. Particularly now, with a new leadership in the Kremlin, all the talk was of a return to the age of détente, a thaw in the cold war. Surely this was not time to raise the ghosts of old ogres, let alone attempt to cast them in a new, more favourable light.

It turned out Hindsmith had an answer to that too:

'You know why they're doing it too, don't you. All this

bloody nonsense coming out of Moscow about *glasnost* and so forth. It's a sign of weakness, that's what it is. At least that's as sure as hell what the Americans'll see it as. Open the door a chink and they'll blow it off its hinges. You can bet your bottom Yankee dollar they'll be encouraging all sorts of trouble in Warsaw, Prague and Paris, and this is their attempt to do it here. Get people over here to see Churchill as some sort of betrayed hero. Next thing you know they'll be claiming they "won the cold war". That's what *glasnost*'ll get you.'

Stark decided he was best out of it. He lifted his pint and moved to one of the corner seats in the snug bar, the little alcove for regular quiet drinkers. It was empty but that was what he wanted. Under the circumstances, the words 'Mind if I join you?' were the last he wanted to hear, until he looked up from his pint and realised it was Lizzie who was speaking:

'Del's come in. Shut that lot at the bar up again. Said I could go early. And I thought you might be in need of a bit of company. You're not half looking under the weather.'

'Am I?' he hadn't meant to smile, but it was amazing how she provoked the reaction. 'Sorry, I don't mean to.'

She sat down beside him, plonking a large gin and tonic alongside his pint.

'Don't be sorry. I just meant you look like you've got the weight of the world on your shoulders.'

'Do I? Sorry.'

'Tut, tut, sorry again. Is it work?'

'Hmm? I suppose. Sometimes one thing leads to another. As if a case has come looking for you. You have to get to the bottom of it. No matter how deep you have to dig.'

'Can you talk about it? I mean, only if it would help.'

'You heard about the body? The one found hanging under Blackfriars Bridge.'

Lizzie froze. 'Yes. Of course. It was on the BBC. Nearly had his head cut off. You want to stay out of things like that.' Stark gave her a sideways look. 'No, I don't suppose you can, can you. Not in your job. Have you got a lead of some sort? Do you know who did it?'

'You could say that.'

'Really? You're getting close?' There was an edge to her voice that caused Stark to wonder, just for a second, if she might care for him.

'You might say that. Then again, you might not want to. Not in public anyhow.'

'You're not suggesting …'

'I'm not suggesting anything at the minute. Anyway I've got other stuff on my mind.'

'Another case?'

Stark gave a bitter little laugh. 'You might say that too. More like a cold case.' He paused for a moment, and then said: 'How well did you know your father? Really, I mean.'

'You don't know?'

'What?'

Lizzie took a deep breath. By the time she finished speaking, in a low, muttered voice, her eyes scarcely looking up from the table, Stark learned Lizzie Goldsmith had been fourteen before she discovered that the father she idolised dealt in drugs and pimped prostitutes for the Soviet base down at Woolwich. She only found out when he propositioned one of her schoolmates. She had made a scene and the old man had hit her, hit her little sister, little more than a toddler at the time and stomped out, never to be seen again. Her mother had never forgiven her.

'Anyhow,' she said. 'It doesn't matter. It's my gran who's the real hero in our house, holds the family together. Always has done.'

Stark gave her a questioning look. Her face brightened.

'A tough nut, the old lady. Came over here as a little kid way back in the thirties, from the Ukraine. Jewish, see. Like me. Married a local boy. No shortage of eligible Jewish lads in the old East End. Done well for herself, she did. Fluent Russian, German, English. Got a job in the war office. Secretarial just, but to the higher-ups. But that's another story.'

'Not like the one they were on about?' said Stark with a wry laugh, almost dismissively waving a hand at the gaggle at the bar.

'Sort of,' she said with a strange, lopsided smile. 'Nothing's exactly what you read in the history books, is it?'

'You can say that again.' Without meaning it, and with a flood of unanticipated relief, it flooded out of him. Only leaving out the details about St Bride's, Harry Stark gushed out the story of how he had come to doubt the legend of his own father's lifetime.

'The thing is,' he said at last, 'I don't even know if it's true. Or how I'd tell my mother if it is. Or Kate. She hardly talks to me as it is these days. I have no idea how she'd react if she were told the father she never knew was an imposter involved with some shady underground?'

Lizzie was silent for a minute and then said. 'You never know, she might not think that was all that bad.'

'You think so?' Stark smiled and looked back at her. 'What I want to do,' he said, staring at the backs of his hands laid flat on the table between their drinks, as if they belonged to somebody else, 'is to make a difference.'

'Sure, Harry, don't we all? Don't we all?' She put her hand

on one of his, her long fingers cold from the ice in her gin and tonic glass, and Stark let them rest there, afraid to say anything that might cause her to move them. But in the end, of course, she did.

He lifted his beer and raised his glass to her, and she raised hers to him, and they clinked them and Stark said, 'I'll drink to that,' all too conscious of the stupid grin on his face.

'To what?' she said.

'To not doing something silly,' he said, and they caught one another's eye and both burst into laughter at the unacknowledged innuendo.

Some time and several drinks later, it might have been an hour, or maybe less, but it was certainly gone 11 p.m. and Del had rung the bell and called closing time and was noisily putting upturned seats on tables in the public bar, Stark and Lizzie left the snug almost surreptitiously, but not before the landlord could eye their unsteady gait and open the door for them with a good-humoured 'Mind how you go,' before going back to his die-hards at the bar with a markedly less gentle, 'Let's have your glasses now. It's long gone time.'

Arm-in-arm, supporting each other, the inebriation providing the perfect excuse for physical contact, they stumbled steadily to the end of the street. That was where their ways parted. Stark stopped first, bringing Lizzie up short with an amused, 'Whoops!' She put her hand to her chest as if to relieve a moment of indigestion. Stark put his arm around her to steady her and silently cursed the English Democratic Republic's accommodation crisis.

If he'd had a flat of his own he might have asked her back, but there'd be his mother who'd fuss like an old hen if he brought a 'young lady' home, and then be censorious afterwards when she found out it was just some common barmaid. Anyway, what was he thinking? She had just been nice to him, nothing more. It was time to say goodnight, or he thought it was until Lizzie turned to him, smiled that smile and, lurching with a giggle against the wall, said softly, 'C'mon then, Harry, you'd better walk me home.'

He did. Down dark, dirty, blissfully empty streets, towards the river and the ancient warehouses that nestled in the shadow of Tower Bridge.

In the distance the neon radiance from Westminster cast its artificial glow into the night sky obliterating everything else, but above their heads the weak glimmer from Bermondsey's under-powered streetlights allowed them still to glimpse, if not the stars, at least two glittering pinpoints, Jupiter and Venus. Stark put his arm around her and held her close. She giggled and laid her head against his shoulder.

'This is it, Harry. This is where I live.'

He looked up. Devon Mansions was one of the old nineteenth-century blocks erected by wealthy philanthropists to house London's poor, six stories high in crumbling yellow London brick. More than a few had survived the bombs and bullets to become models for the 'new' socialist housing that in most cases had still to be built.

She pulled him into a doorway. 'I'm on the third floor,' she said, and Stark's heart raced.

She put her arms around his head, and slid her tongue between his teeth. She pulled him towards her and he felt her soft breasts press against him and the urgency in her kiss as she ran her fingers through hair that he suddenly wished he had washed that morning. He breathed deep, inhaling her perfume, and his: gin and beer and an acrid forenote of pungent sweat. He thought he had never smelled anything more arousing in his life. And his body testified to it. He let his hands run down her back, clutching her taut buttocks through the cheap raincoat and pulling her hard against him. She moaned softly, sank her teeth into the lobe of his ear and then pulled back and said: 'You can't come up.'

Stark felt the words land on him like a lead weight in his pocket.

'I'm sorry, Harry,' she whispered. 'But we have the world's nosiest communal caretaker. It's not just the party he reports to, but every twisted-tongued old gossip for miles around. And anyway, you forget – I have a little sister too.'

He nodded, groaning inwardly, and fighting the hormones that were forcing their attention on him physically.

'And I have to be up before dawn.'

'Hmm, an early riser, eh. So I see.' She put a hand down and felt him through the front of his trousers, licked her lips and kissed him gently on the mouth. Stark moaned aloud.

'Who knows, eh? Another time.'

'Sure,' said Stark. 'Another time.'

'I didn't intend this, Harry. But I don't regret it either.'

'Nor do I.'

She kissed him again, and turned into the dark outside stairwell. 'Good night, Harry Stark,' she called softly from the darkness. 'Look after yourself. Don't do anything I wouldn't do.'

She might as well have told him not to fly.

Chapter 37

The good sentinel never sleeps. Nor does an old one worried about his job and his pension, thought Colonel Charles Marchmain as he put down the telephone.

It was a long time since he had taken a call from an IA, an 'Informal Agent', in person. These days he had a whole battery of staff to funnel and filter the vast array of information that such a continuously surprising number of upstanding citizens thought the authorities ought to know about their friends and neighbours.

But this was different. He had placed the surveillance of Detective Inspector Harry Stark and the American Benjamin T. Fairweather in a special category, a category all of its own. All operational intelligence was to be directed to him personally and immediately, all verbal contacts relevant to the case rerouted directly to him when possible.

If there were questions to be asked he wanted it done straight away rather than rerouted through the Informal's usual handler. There was a risk involved, of making the Informal feel too important, of attaching a level of interest to the party under observation that could lead the IA to give himself away and thereby negate any future use. But in this case it was a risk Marchmain had unilaterally decided was worth taking.

They said there was a new mood in Moscow, a new broom in the Kremlin. Marchmain was not sure if it was true – he was old enough to have heard rumours like that before and seen the consequences, or lack of them, right back as far as Khrushchev's day – but he knew one thing: if there was any 'sweeping out' to be done, it was not going to include him. He was a survivor, and survival meant staying ahead of the game, rewriting the rules when necessary and cheating if you had to. It was a rough game; Marchmain had seen enough blood to know. And spilled enough himself.

So when the call had come through from the Rose public house in Bermondsey around 11.20 p.m., just after closing time, the young man's usual handler had noted as he asked his contact if he would mind holding a second while he was put through to a 'senior officer', and pressed the buttons that patched the call directly through to Marchmain's tenth-floor Barbican flat.

The colonel, as always, had been briefed. Kevin Atkinson was an ambitious young actor, just a bit-part player in a television soap at the moment but grateful that the unchallenging role was slowly winning him street recognition and hoping that he would sooner rather than later gain promotion into the heady ranks of the National Shakespeare Company. That meant membership of the Arts Academy, a job for life, access to the same exclusive shops as Department staff themselves, and, most important, opportunities for foreign travel.

To get there, however, he would have to attain party perfection on topics such as 'Popular Wisdom: the role of the proletariat in the history plays', 'The Malvolio model: Shakespeare's debunking of the dynastic class system' and 'Shrew Syndrome: gender politics in Elizabethan England'. But most importantly he would need a clean bill of political health from the Department, and that implied voluntarily assisting its work. He had been taught to be controversially outspoken in public: there was no better way to get someone else to incriminate themselves.

Nonetheless, he needed to learn a thing or two about respect, Marchmain thought, when the young man's nasal tones inquired: 'Who am I speaking to, please?'

'The right person. Please go ahead.'

'Ah, yes, well, it was just about DI Stark. I know he's just someone whose welfare is important to ...' he could almost feel the man searching for the word '... security ... the state.'

'Yes indeed,' Marchmain sighed inwardly, tired already of the weary clichés used by Informals to justify themselves to themselves.

'Well, it's probably nothing ...' Marchmain sighed to himself again – everything was nothing and nothing was everything, that was up to him, not some Informal whose insight into human psychology came from soap opera scripts. 'Go on,' he said.

'It's just that he got a bit squiffy tonight, a bit tight, if you know what I mean.'

'Yes. And?'

'Well, he seemed to be getting on well with the barmaid, Lizzie Goldsmith, very well, if you know what I mean.'

Marchmain was silent. He wondered what the man was trying to say. It was true that the sex life of anyone the Department was interested in was, by definition, a matter of interest, but usually those who reported relatively routine liaisons had an interest of their own. He wondered if the aspiring great actor saw himself in a Casanova role and felt jilted.

'It's just that, her father, I mean you probably know, he used to have connections with the fraternal forces, out at Woolwich barracks. I thought, I don't know what I thought really.' There was, entertainingly, just a note of embarrassment now creeping into his voice.

That Goldsmith, thought Marchmain, the old pimp. Of course. He had quite forgotten. Amazing really, some of these Informals were wasted in civilian life. That said, he couldn't really see any significance in the fact, but it was another little item for the dossier.

'You did the right thing,' he said quickly. 'Was there any suggestion of sexual congress?' The formal language was calculated to make it easier to talk about, as if they were talking to a doctor instead of gossiping about saucy details from their friends' and neighbours' sex lives.

'Oh, I don't know. I mean, not in the pub obviously, but they left together. I wouldn't be surprised. She's a barmaid, and you know, good-looking, dark eyes, alluring but in the end she's still ... well, let's just say she's not quite the sort of girl I'd expect a Detective Inspector to be interested in.'

Marchmain shook his head. Would Britain ever shake itself free of the class system. He thanked Atkinson politely and told him to be in touch as usual if there was anything else that struck him. Like Harry Stark's fist, if the detective ever found out, he thought as he put the phone down.

So Stark was doing a line with the little barmaid, eh? Well, why not? Sooner or later sex always raised its ugly head. Or maybe not that ugly: from what Atkinson had implied she was quite a looker, and that from a man who earned his living alongside actresses. Oh well, maybe she too could play a role in this little drama. If Stark was forming an attachment to her, it could prove useful. The Department had a healthy respect for personal relationships: there was nothing like having a few extra hostages to fortune.

Chapter 38

Sometimes, Harry Stark thought ruefully, the blind leading the blind makes sense. He could see hardly anything and despite the sleep dust in them at such an ungodly hour of the morning he at least had eyes, unlike the wizened old man who held his hand, helped him find his way down the uneven steps without the need of the priest's torch. They negotiated a second set of stairs that led from the crypt beneath St Bride's down to a lower level. The only light came from somewhere beneath them, a dull glimmer.

'We're below the level of the eighth-century Saxon church now,' Ransom said. 'Can't be certain, but this probably dates from Roman times.'

The space they had entered was wider and had lighting, of a sort: dangling forty-watt bulbs. At one end there was a small table draped with an altar cloth. A makeshift place of prayer. Against the side wall a wooden trestle table held two antiquated Roneo copying machines. Stark could not help staring at items that seemed so out of place in the cellar of a catacomb.

'Actually, we have a licence for these,' Rye explained. 'This is where we produce the leaflets about the church's history I sell for the restoration fund upstairs.'

Stark picked up a leaflet from a small pile next to one of the machines. It was entitled 'St Bride's, the Cathedral of Fleet Street'. The quality and grain of the paper were identical to that of the note found in the dead man's pocket. He had come across printed material like this before: copies of texts the authorities didn't want given a wider distribution. Chunks of poetry, short stories, even whole novels by dissidents or Northern propagandists. They existed even in Moscow where they were known as *samizdat*, Russian for self-published. He had found something similar underneath Katy's bed: a satirical anti-socialist novel called *1984* by a satirical product of the old empire who went by the pseudonym George Orwell.

In the EDR, for reasons Stark had never been certain of, they were known as 'winkies'.

'You've come across the product of our presses before,' said Ransom. 'Pity they can't do 'em in Braille.'

'A nod's as good as a winkie to a blind horse,' said Stark.

'What?' said Rye.

'That's what people say when they come across this sort of thing. That's what they're called, isn't it, "winkies"?'

For the first time since Stark had met him something remotely akin to mirth came through in the canon's voice. 'I'd never thought of that. How very apt. I always thought it was homage to our spiritual mentor.'

'Come again?'

'Winkyn de Worde. The first real English printer. Assistant to William Caxton who brought the first proper printing press to England. He was the man who really sparked the print revolution. From a cellar somewhere around here. You could say he was the man who founded Fleet Street. In the old sense, I mean, before it became just the *Guardian* and *New Times*.'

'Are you telling me this is where this thing,' he produced the folded leaflet with the Churchill image, 'was turned out. An image of an arch-imperialist aristocrat masquerading as some icon of free speech?'

There was a sudden frostiness in the canon's reply: 'I'm not telling you anything, Mr Stark. That is something for others to decide. One way or the other. Come.'

Stark followed him further along a half-lit passage, until they came into a low room, barely two metres high but some six metres square that had been cleared of bones or whatever else it had originally been carved out of the London clay for. Another half a dozen passageways led off it in various directions, dark spaces of various dimensions, like wormholes leading down into the London clay.

'Storage, some of them,' the canon explained. 'Others, tunnels of various sorts. Some filled with bones, unsorted bones, maybe from as far back as Roman times. This would have been a good site for a graveyard, just outside the city walls. Others may have been used by smugglers, leading down to boats on the Thames, long before the embankment was built. But this space serves our purpose.'

The 'room' itself was lit by a single bulb which was fixed to the ceiling near the door and cast long shadows. There were three rows of seating: a number of chairs and several benches, some with backs, sections of pews rescued from the church. It reminded Stark of old carvings of 'hides' where religious dissidents in the sixteenth century gathered together in secret to profess a faith different from that prescribed by their ruler. Maybe the situation wasn't that different.

'Please sit down for a moment,' the canon said, gesturing towards a seat in the front row.

Stark did as he was told. The old man Ransom sat beside him, still touching Stark's arm with his hand, not so much to compensate for his blindness, Stark thought, but to reassure himself of his presence. He felt a sense of unwanted obligation weighing heavily on him: like a promise to repay a debt he had never incurred.

One by one a few others began to drift in. Stark couldn't tell how many. He understood it would be inappropriate to turn round and look. He had been invited in, as a guest. But he was also at their mercy. He had considered informing Lavery where he was going and then at the last minute decided against. If something went wrong, the sergeant would guess soon enough where to start looking. And he did not expect anything to go wrong. He had not come unarmed.

'You've all heard what Mr Ransom has told us about this young man's father, who he was and what he did for the movement.' Canon Rye was standing at the front of the little room as if he was preparing to say mass.

There was a rumbled murmur of assent. Stark understood that the old blind man had some sort of venerable status in the group but, for obvious reasons perhaps, his approval was not considered sufficient in itself. These were men of an altogether different complexion. And a very different generation,

A man seated just behind Stark said: 'I'm not sure about this. It's a funny moment for somebody just to turn up on your doorstep, Canon, immediately after what happened to Michael'. The canon looked away and dropped his head. Stark saw him wipe away a tear. 'And anyway, I've heard stuff. About his father. There's stories and then there's stories.'

'That'll do,' said a big man in the corner, speaking with a broad Dorset accent. 'But you'll just cause more problems than you might solve.'

The man reddened. He was not to give up.

'Has anyone even searched him this morning. He might

be carrying a wire for the DoSSers.' A couple of men from the sides moved towards Stark as if preparing to pat him down. Which would not reveal a hidden microphone but would certainly uncover a police issue revolver.

'Wait a minute,' said Stark. 'I've come here on my own. You know who I am. Maybe more than I know myself.' He wasn't sure how sincere he sounded. He wasn't sure how sincere he was. But he wanted to avoid being frisked if at all possible. The two lads stopped in their tracks, partly distracted by someone else entering the room at the far end.

The man seated behind Stark hadn't noticed and wasn't going to be put off his stride.

'We might – and I say "might" know *who* you are – but we don't know *what* you are. I say we wait until Malcolm gets here.'

'I'm here,' the new arrival said. Loudly. 'And I know what he is.'

Stark recognised the voice, but only vaguely. He turned round to see a large, middle-aged man in a leather bomber jacket. The face too seemed oddly familiar: thick spectacles, floppy greasy hair, and flabby age-spotted hands. He was staring at Stark as if he were the incarnation of Satan. One of the tough kids moved towards him.

A scream sounded above them. A clatter of boots on the stone stairs and then Harry Stark's head exploded and his world was engulfed in darkness.

Chapter 39

Fleet Street, even in the hour before dawn, could be a busy place. Not as busy as it had once been when it had been home to both editorial offices and printing works for a dozen newspapers feeding the appetite of the world's most voracious consumers of news, analysis and tittle-tattle. Back in the 1930s the rags had rolled off giant presses through-out the night before being transported by fleets of lorries to the railway stations where consecutive editions were loaded onto the relevant night trains departing for Aberdeen, Edin-burgh or Liverpool and Hull, the packet boats for the conti-nent and eventually the far-flung reaches of empire.

Fleet Street remained the centre of newspaper production for the English Democratic Republic. But its fiefdom was greatly diminished. As was the size and quantity of news sheets it produced. Two great buildings, patched up from their wartime wounds, still dominated the street, though their owners had changed. The great stone edifice that had once housed the *Daily Telegraph* was now home to *New Times*, the official organ of the ruling party.

Since partition the *Telegraph*, the archetypal paper of the old Right, had been produced in distant Manchester, as was its former neighbour the *Daily Express* with its deliberately provocative 'chained crusader' masthead. The old *Express* building, in its day an ultra-modern art deco temple of glint-ing black glass and steel with great glistening silver warrior statues in the atrium, had been refurbished as the new home for the *Guardian*, an old left-wing newspaper that itself ironically had relocated south from Manchester and was now the house journal of the DoSS. It also produced *The Watchtower*, a monthly magazine for frontier guards.

As befitting the serious duties performed by its audience, the *Guardian* rarely descended to the trivial. But it did pay homage to the human side of its readership with occasional articles on everyday fashion, with the unstated understanding that 'everyday' included 'operational'. It would have been interesting to know to what extent the authors of such articles would have approved, had they been present in their office at such an hour and looked out of their window, of the taste on display. There appeared to be a marked preference for short leather jackets amongst the men gathering in ones and twos outside the closed pub, or the municipal tea kiosk that served print workers and lorry drivers a stewed milky version of the national beverage in reusable plastic cups.

Later there would also be a display of navy blue trench-coats although these were mostly not yet on parade, their owners still being seated in the number of parked cars, unusual for that time of the morning, or indeed any time of the day on the southern side of the street near the junction with Ludgate Circus, almost directly opposite the *New Times* building and along New Bridge Street.

There were four men in each. All of them were wearing watches, so they did not need to look up Ludgate Hill towards St Paul's to see the clock on the front of Sir Christoper Wren's battered masterpiece which in any case had long since relinquished its time-keeping functions. The minute hands on the men's identical service-issue Sekondas ticked relentlessly towards 5.30 a.m.

At 5.28 a long black Bevan had swung into the street and slid to a halt precisely next to Bride Lane in the lee of the wedding cake pinnacle that was all that remained above ground of St Bride's. But it was not what remained above ground that interested its occupants, or their gathering army.

At precisely 5.30 the rear door of the Bevan was opened from within and a tall figure in the trademark navy trench-coat got out, looked up at the imperceptibly lightening dish-water sky, adjusted a wide-brimmed black hat on his head and gave an abrupt decisive nod of his head.

The charred wooden door was reduced to splinters in seconds. The crunch of heavy shoulders assisted by the leverage of iron bars saw to that. The noise of its breaking merged into the thunder of boots on stone steps and the scuffing of leather sleeves on stone walls. Powerful torch beams cast hard white light on sepulchral walls scraped out centuries before by monks with iron spoons. Neat piles of ancient bones, cranium and clavicule alike, were shattered with iron bars by men for whom such mortal remains held neither terror nor awe. This jetsam of departed souls was smashed not deliberately but out of the habit of destruction and long familiarity with the powerful intimidation inspired by a display of wanton violence. The blows were not systematic but randomly struck by those who followed as the vanguard ploughed bellowing into the labyrinth.

If there was any apprehension in the minds of those who led the charge there was nothing to demonstrate it. These were men used to following orders not questioning them, men who delighted in force because it was something they dispensed, who were blind to the concept of danger because it was something others encountered in their presence. Except that in this instance the others were missing.

The camp beds against the wall were tipped up and turned

over. Bottles of precious ink were wantonly smashed, and two ancient Roneo copying machines hurled to the ground and set upon with lead-lined wooden truncheons, reduced in seconds to battered scrap. At the end of a long corridor of skulls a small room laid out like a Sunday school class-room, though none present could remember such things, was reduced to a repository for broken furniture.

And then, all fury spent, they looked at one another. A few, in response to barked commands, investigated side passages that led to dead ends or fallen rubble or broken bones. The hubbub diminished, the adrenalin eked away to be replaced by the frustration of unexhausted anger, con-tained only by the strictures of discipline and training as heels clicked together and left hands snapped to foreheads with the automatic stiff-lipped 'Sir'.

Striding amongst the debris the man in the trenchcoat and the hat, which he had deliberately disdained to remove on entering so-called hallowed ground, pursed his own lips pensively and ran his eyes over the scene like a pirate captain who has seized control of a prize ship only to discover her an abandoned rotting hulk. The men who had carried out his will stood to attention in his presence, fearing that somehow they might be held to account for having attacked a mirage.

'So,' he said, as if he were consciously choosing the words of the English monarch who attempted to stop the march of fate and in so doing met his death at the executioner's axe – and given Marchmain's enthusiasm for the history of the first republic he might well have been, 'I see the birds have flown.'

'All except one,' said the leather jacket behind him.

Marchmain turned and saw the creature held by the scruff of the neck by his lieutenant. But the thing he held did not

so much resemble a bird with the means to fly as a fledg-
ling sparrow, thrown out of the nest by an invading cuckoo:
featherless, crippled and blind. Except that this creature was
nearer the end of its life than the beginning. Much nearer,
in fact.

'Take him away,' snapped Marchmain.

Chapter 40

Long after you are dead and the worms have eaten your brains, boys will play football with your skull, Harry Stark had been told by a particularly cruel history teacher at school. Now it had already happened and his soul was condemned to live through the experience.

The space between his ears vibrated like timpani in a Wagner opera, his cranium ached as if the bone had been surgically removed; nerve endings burned where his eyes should be. If they were still there, there was little to prove it. The world was a featureless void. Except, he realised with a curse, banging his shin on something hard and angular, that it wasn't empty. It also stank, of damp and something sickly sweet, almost chemical, vaguely familiar. There was a metallic tang in his mouth.

He tried to sit up but his feet were trussed, his hands tied behind his back. He rolled on to his side and realised he was lying on rough, cold ground – probably stone or concrete. There was something metallic, like a box or a bench, on the floor next to him, a little out from the wall. That was what he had banged his shin on.

The darkness was real. Either that or something really had happened to his eyesight. He choked on bile at the thought of Ransom with his eyelids sewn together. He could hear water, running water. Not close, and not like a tap or a pipe. Maybe he was close to the river. There was something else too: a faint hum and every so often a louder, but still distant rumbling, and then near at hand, barely distinguishable but unmistakable: voices.

With difficulty, in a motion like a crippled crab, using his elbows and knees, with his toes for leverage, he inched himself painfully along the hard surface of the floor towards the sound. It was coming from his left, a few metres away, the other side of a door maybe, though if it was it let no chink of light escape. He could make out two voices. Then it stopped.

He froze. Had they heard him? Did he want them to? Whoever it was had to know he was there. Had to have brought him there. Wherever there was. He tried to reconstruct what had happened and failed. There had been shouting, footsteps, A raid? A DoSS raid? Had to be. And that explained where he was too. In a DoSS cell, some tomb deep under the Barbican he shouldn't wonder.

And then the voices started up again and he realised he was wrong.

'I still say we shouldn't have left Ransom.' It was the broad West Country accent of the man who had spoken in the room below the crypt. The second voice was also male, but sounded older, more educated, yet still strangely familiar although the context seemed wrong.

'He refused to come. What were we going to do? Knock him unconscious too and carry him? It would have killed him.'

'He'll talk.'

'He won't. He'll tell them whatever he wants to and nothing more, but they've done all they ever could to him and he's too frail to take any more. He'll die.'

'Almost certainly. I'm quite sure he intends to.'

'I still don't like it. And in that case, why'd we bring *him*?'

Stark caught his breath. There was no doubt who they were talking about.

'Because like you said – today's the day of the parade, there's only hours to go and all of a sudden we get a visit from a copper, whatever his supposed pedigree. And then *this* happens. We need to know what he knows. And who he's told. Before the others get here.'

'*If* he knows anything …'

There was a grunt that sounded like acknowledgement.

'If he's a spook, we have to know, if only to know how much they know. We were damn near caught like rats in a trap this morning.'

'It is still possible he might be on the level.'

'But how likely? We've been caught before by being too trusting. We can't afford to take risks. Not now. We'll find out when he wakes up.'

'What do you want me to do.'

'Give him a bit of a slap. Nothing too hard, for the moment at least. See what he says.'

'And if he says nothing?'

There was a perceptible pause. Then, the same voice continued: 'I know what I'd do.'

'What?'

Another pause. Whatever he would do was obviously being demonstrated rather than enunciated. Then: 'Don't be stupid. Apart from anything else, it's far too risky.'

Another pause. Then the other voice again: 'There's always a risk involved in this sort of business. The question is, whose risk? Look what happened with the American.'

'That was different.'

Stark's mind whirled. They'd had to leave the old man somewhere but taken Stark with them, unconscious and trussed. And now they were going to beat him, interrogate him ... or worse. What did they know about Fairweather? Or were they referring to the other American? The dead one?

He had to get out of there. If he was going to talk to these people again it would be on his own terms. Or not at all. He wondered how much time he had and decided it was not long enough. The only advantage was that they thought he was still unconscious. That meant they had drugged him – chloroform, that was what the smell was. And it explained the taste in his mouth.

'Should I go and look at him?'

His heart stopped.

'Leave it a while yet. That stuff should have him out for another half an hour at least. Let him sweat a bit, then go in and kick him gently in the balls. I'll see you later.'

Stark breathed again. Silence. Where the hell was he? No longer in the crypt, that at least was certain. It reassured him slightly to know that he was not surrounded by human bones. Although he might have found something to help him escape. He had a vision of himself working on his ropes with an ancient human jawbone.

His bindings were not so tight as to be painful; they had relied on the chloroform to keep him quiet. And the lump on his head. He wondered if he had sustained brain damage. A cerebral haemorrhage could kill him two days or two weeks from now. But he had to live that long first.

He had to get his hands free, and then untie his feet. His feet! He was wearing the size 10 black leather brogues that had belonged to his father. He had waited years to grow into them and never quite managed it. In so many ways. They were still one size too big for him. Which just might be his salvation.

Painfully rubbing his ankles together, slowly he pulled

his heel out of the left shoe, then, more slowly because he had done the laces more tightly, the other. Perspiration was dripping off him. His gamble was that without his shoes he would be able to pull at least one foot through the rope that bound his legs.

Arching his back he tried and failed, failed again and then finally succeeded in getting his hands, tied behind his back, to the ropes at his feet. There was no way he could untie them in this position but at least it gave him more leverage. With a wrench that felt as if he had dislocated his spine, to add to his other injuries, he eventually managed to get his right heel inside the loop, and then slowly, minus his sock, through it. The relief was a minor transport of ecstasy. With one foot free, he could pull the other through, although not quite as easily as he had imagined. The rope remained caught around his ankle until he managed to use the other foot to keep it taut. At last, he could stand.

That meant he could walk, even if he did still have his hands tied behind his back. Crushing down the leather at the heel, he crammed his feet minus one sock back into his shoes. He held his breath. How much noise had he made? There was no sound from behind the door. Was it the only way out? Were his captors still there? If they were not – and it had been silent for several minutes at least – then maybe he could get out that way.

Walking sideways, he edged along the wall feeling his way with his fingers behind him: cold, stone, no, not stone, too smooth, not brick either, there was no pointing, concrete probably. The darkness was complete. Did that mean he was still underground. Buried somewhere in the bowels of the earth beneath St Bride's. But then wouldn't the wall be rough stone not smooth concrete?

Then, almost beside him, came an unexpectedly loud, squeaking, scraping noise. He froze. Immediately to his left he could feel cold metal. He was next to the door, yet not a chink of light emanated. The sound again. Not so extreme. Someone pushing back a metal chair from a table, scraping on a stone floor. Then a cough. And again silence. Just one of them, waiting for the other to come back, before they would make their decision. Then from the other direction, somewhere in the distance, came the same noise he had heard before: a long, low rumbling that rose and then fell again.

Still feeling his way along the wall, he edged past the door. There was a round metal handle in the middle. Maybe there was another door. Barely two metres further the wall turned at right angles. Stark felt his way along it. Five, maybe, six metres long, then another right-angled turn. Then he bumped into something, hard, round, metal. Stark found what he had been praying for: a second door. With an identical, round handle.

Here too no light leaked through. But was it locked? And if not, what or who would he find on the other side. He leaned his ear against the cold metal, but could hear nothing beyond the faint hum that he had almost come to ignore as part of the background. At the same time he heard the scraping of chair on floor again from beyond the door on the other side. Any minute now, Stark realised, they could come to get him.

He had no alternative. With his back to the door – just about the worst position possible for opening one – he turned the handle and edged it open, expecting at any moment a shout of discovery, a flood of light. Instead a rumble from the distant throat of a snoring giant turned into an ear-splitting rattling roar and a whistle of wind behind his back throwing him forward onto the concrete floor. He got up and in the low lighting beyond realised immediately why the background noise had seemed so familiar. He was underground alright. In *The Underground,* a service facility for the Tube.

For a second his dilated pupils were confused by even the glimmer of light from the vestigial illumination in the train tunnel. The door opened on to a ledge recessed into the tunnel wall for about three metres before descending at either end some sixty centimetres to the tunnel floor. He had found an escape route. Of a sort. Which direction hardly mattered; either way had to lead to a station. What worried him was whether a train could pass him. He doubted it. And then there was the high voltage power rails. To touch them accidentally meant certain death. He listened for the sound of an approaching train. Nothing. How frequently did they run? He had no idea which line he was on. Some ran more frequently than others.

He was not even sure what time of day it was. With his hands tied behind his back, his watch was useless. In rush hour there could be trains hurtling through the tunnels every three minutes on average. But fewer later in the day. How long had he been out? If he was lucky there could be more than ten minutes between trains. Not enough to make the distance between stations. But in one direction he could see another recessed ledge in the wall. Another service facility. That decided it.

Making his way as quickly as he could – he dared not run in case he stumbled or fell without the use of his hands to steady him. He doubted if there was more than ten centimetres clearance between a passing train and the wall. Anyone who tried to flatten themselves against the wall would find the experience a mite too literal for comfort.

He had heard that if caught in the path of an approaching train, it was best to lie down flat in between the tracks but he doubted that was a safe prospect in the tunnel where both inner rails carried the voltage. Even if the clearance was sufficient to allow a man to lie beneath it, he would have to remain perfectly still to avoid touching either.

He tried counting off the seconds but realised there was no point. If a train came, it came. And then he saw it, dimly, ahead of him, a faint glimmer of expanded light as the tunnel straightened out. He breathed a sigh of relief. A station. It had to be. He could make out now where the tunnel opened out to the platform, and in the distance the dark hole where it narrowed down and once again became a tight circular tube. The platform was barely fifty metres away, closer than he had dared hope at first, but not quite close enough for total comfort. It was not as well lit as normal, even considering the recent brownouts, and seemed empty. Odd. It had been barely daybreak when he had arrived at St Bride's. How long had he been out? It couldn't be longer than a few hours at most. But he would worry about that later. He was almost safe. Relief flooded through him. A moment too soon.

Even as he relaxed, the rumbling began again, unmistakably behind him and rapidly rising in volume, a harsh, metallic sound accompanied by a high-pitched zinging from the rails. Stark cursed, picked up his feet and ran, his tied hands flapping behind him as uselessly as the rope that dangled from them as he rocked dangerously from side to side. Any second he could topple over and fall onto the tracks to be either electrocuted instantaneously or seconds later sliced in two by the speeding train. Why wasn't the damn thing slowing down? They were approaching a station, after all. Why had they turned the goddamn station lights down?

The only illumination he could see was a baleful little green light near the end of the tunnel, which he realised with an extra frisson of horror was a 'go' signal. He wanted to look behind but didn't dare. The platform was still metres away. To make matters worse there were no steps; he would have to climb up on to it.

The noise was deafening now. Stark felt a blind panicky urge to leap out into the middle of the tracks waving his arms. He knew it was the sort of urge that inspired men to suicide. And then he saw it, just this side of the platform, four metres in from the end of the tunnel, right underneath the glowing signal that illuminated it in ghostly green like a sarcophagus cut into the Victorian brickwork: a niche barely big enough to hold a man. A refuge, they called them. Now he knew why.

Stark hurled himself into it and flattened his back against the wall, blood pounding in his veins and his chest heaving. Not a microsecond too soon, as he watched the red-painted front of the driver's compartment hurtle towards him out of the dark and screech thunderously past his face, only centimetres away.

His heart palpitated, his ribcage rose and fell with snatched short intakes of breath as the speed of the train's passage sucked the air behind it. His heaving lungs ached but it was his brain that was reeling as it registered what he had seen. The commuters inside. Not their faces. Their clothes. And the adverts, glimpsed too fast to register anything but the very fact of their existence. The colours, the light, the intensity of the bright, constant neon, clear and white not yellow and flickering.

And the train itself: its front had not been grimy red but shining silver and bright blue, as it flashed in front of his eyes.

And above all his final view of it as it sped past the platform without stopping, the defacing scrawl, as unimaginable in itself as the other world inside, of orange spray-paint graffiti in metre-high lettering across its rear end: LICK MY ARSE.

Stark hauled himself up onto a platform bathed in the right sort of lighting for the world he had found himself in, a twilight world. His hands were still tied behind his back. Otherwise he would have put his head in them. And laughed. Or maybe cried.

He shouldn't have been surprised, he told himself. It wasn't as if he hadn't known places like this existed. It was just that it was easier for him, as it was for everybody else, for the state and the party, to simply forget about them.

But there was no arguing with the big letters picked out in blue enamel on the white tiled wall in front of Harry Stark's face, between signs warning of air raids that had long since ceased and behind them faded posters advertising shows that were already a poignant memory when the last passengers had alighted here: LEICESTER SQUARE.

Chapter 41

Harry Stark raised his eyes to the curved tiled ceiling of Leicester Square Underground station. It was as if it was still all there, a vanished world above his head. As if he could walk to the end of the platform and take an escalator up into theatre land, a world of bright lights and self-indulgent fantasies, the heart of a bustling cosmopolitan metropolis instead of a wasteland of scrub grass growing over barren foundations and a concrete wall that marked the end of the world.

The white space on the big map on his office wall was like the uncharted ocean on ancient mariners' charts with florid script proclaiming 'here be dragons'. Now he had seen one of the dragons close up, a great blue and silver worm snaking underground beneath the streets of the city unbeknown to the people above. He was not on the other side of the wall. What had once been Leicester Square was still, nominally, in the capital of the EDR, except that it lay next to the 'dead zone', the so-called no-man's-land between the two walls that formed the Anti-Capitalist Protection Barrier.

Stark walked along the platform, wondering at the ancient adverts, the wartime public information posters, relics of a world that had already long vanished by the time the 'barrier' had been built. His father had known this world, had seen its passing and learned not to mourn it but to welcome the new. And then the new had let him down.

Once upon a time, he now dimly remembered hearing, the Westminster trains that passed through a station in the 'other half' of the city had slowed down as they passed through, even opened the doors on the off chance that any 'fellow Londoner' might have found their way into the closed station and made a dash for a 'freedom train'. Armed border guards patrolled the platforms. Then a more convenient solution had been found: the station entrances had been concreted over, the signs that marked them removed. The memory, and with it the face, of this 'other' Underground had been erased.

They have forgotten us, thought Stark, as surely – if not more so – as we have forgotten them. The difference is that they can afford to. He was as sure at that moment as he had ever been that those who dreamed of reunification were living in a fool's paradise; or a fool's hell.

He was so lost in his reverie that when once again rattling thunder announced the arrival of another train he threw himself backwards in startled shock, jarring his shoulder. He looked to see what he had bumped into and found a pair of ancient vending machines fixed to the wall. One advertised a 'full pint and a half of milk in every bar' of Cadbury's Dairy Milk Chocolate, the other once dispensed maps of the Tube, a very different Tube from the one Stark knew. Both had been vandalised, long ago, perhaps even during the war when Londoners had sheltered down here. But for all his police training, this was one piece of attempted larceny Stark was grateful for.

The tray that would once have delivered a chocolate bar had been prised out by a jemmy, and now jutted out from the machine in a mess of twisted and jagged metal. A jagged edge that Stark had painfully fallen against, but was, in the circumstances, just what he needed. Turning his back to the machine he lifted his hands as high as he could behind his back and slid the ropes that bound them over the tray. It was difficult. Particularly because he could not see what he was doing. The idea was to press the ropes down on the metal edge and saw, but every so often his position slipped and the metal tore his wrists causing him to swear loudly. But he could feel the strands gradually tearing and ripping until he could pull his hands a good ten centimetres apart and saw easily through the remainder.

Stark sighed with unexpected bliss – like a man freed from prison – when the last strand parted and he was able to bring his hands, albeit bleeding and aching, in front of him. He discarded the ropes on the platform floor. All he had to do now – all, he almost laughed! – was find a way out. At that point he realised that although he knew where he was in theory, he had no practicable idea how to get back above ground.

He was tired, he suddenly realised, and hungry and thirsty. More in hope than anticipation, he turned the ratchet on the chocolate machine. In vain, not that it would have been at its best after forty years. But that did not stop Stark thumping the machine in exasperation. To his surprise, however, similar abuse of the second machine produced results, in the form of a yellowing Tube map that fell to the ground at his feet. He picked it up: a souvenir, he thought wryly, as he opened it out to reveal a map of the London Underground that resembled nothing he had ever seen – a great sprawl of a network, nearly four times the size of the Tube he was familiar with since childhood. There was a similar map he now noticed, further along the platform wall, but there was something magical in holding a copy in his hands.

The black lettering of the sign on the wall indicated Leicester Square was on the Northern Line. The Northern

Line that Stark knew, and travelled on regularly, was a three-pronged affair centred on Old Street: one spur ran north and west via the Angel to Highgate, another north and east to Finsbury Park and a third, the one Stark was most familiar with, south of the river via London Bridge to the Elephant and Castle. Once, he now saw, the southern spur extended onwards and onwards out into the distant south-west suburbs of Wimbledon and Morden.

The only question now was how the hell would he get out. It made no sense to retrace his steps to his dungeon, even if he had wanted to. He looked at the watch on his wrist, which he could now see clearly for the first time. It showed 9.15. In the morning? It had to be. It had been 6.30 a.m. when he had turned up at St Bride's. He had no idea how he had been moved from the room beneath the crypt to a disused service facility on a Tube line that was supposed to be inaccessible. But there was no way he could make any further progress through the tunnels. The trains were clearly running. And they would be on rush-hour timetables.

Even as the thought crossed his mind a third of the blue and silver dragons sped through the platform, this one more covered in graffiti than either of the others: meaningless brightly coloured lettering that Stark could have taken for decoration had it not been so totally anarchic. One bit of proof, he mused, that some of what we are told about the evils of the society on the other side is not wholly invented.

Even so, it reinforced his belief that to go back into the tunnels was madness. Could there still be an exit here? He knew roughly the area above ground where Leicester Square had once been. It was only yesterday that he had driven past it with the American. But there was nothing there even to indicate where once a Tube station entrance might have been. The labourers who had eradicated it had done their work as thoroughly as the men with the airbrush who had taken Trotsky out of the history books.

A map of the network, even one that his own government would have considered seditious, was not going to help him escape from it. At least not obviously. An exploration of the passageways marked 'Way out' was a surreal excursion into darkened halls that were all at once strange, alien and eerily familiar. The low-level lighting on the platforms leaked out into the concourse but where there should once have been escalators up, there was a wall of breeze blocks. There was no way out here. Not now. Not ever. Staring at this manifestation of the Wall that extended even underground, Stark found it hard to believe there ever had been.

The only alternative indicated was signs to the Piccadilly Line. The Piccadilly, Stark knew, was the old name for what in his city was now called the Holborn Line, for the obvious reason that it no longer went as far as what had once been Piccadilly Circus. The corridor that led towards it was unblocked but it could hardly do any good; the Piccadilly lay deeper. The signs pointed to old wooden escalators leading down, though it had been decades since they had ever worked. Almost certainly passengers from the lower line had had to pass through this same upper concourse to the exit.

There was a remote possibility that there was a separate exit, but even if there was, it had undoubtedly been blocked too. Still, he had nothing to lose. There was something irresistible about exploring this surreal underground world. The light diminished with every step and as it faded, one by one, the wooden-framed advertisements that lined the escalator walls dimmed into obscurity. Stark strained his eyes to make out decades-old adverts: brands he still recognised from television – Coca-Cola, Schweppes, Ford – mingled with others – Robinson's Barley Water, Rowntree's Fruit Pastilles – which Stark assumed had either gone bankrupt or perhaps, because of their geographic location, become People's Own Enterprises.

Here and there, like totems from some historic Roman war, public information posters conveyed warnings from an ancient era: the officers, army, navy and air force, with their Brylcreemed hair wafting cigarettes and swapping boastful banter around the smug seductive blonde in an armchair: Careless Talk Costs Lives, the motto warned. It was the slogan his mother still remembered, the one that half a century later was still too close for comfort. Stark descended into darkness.

As he reached the bottom of the escalator, a faint glow returned, a pale bluish light similar to that on the platform above. It was like being underwater, in some cold northern sea, except that the light on the white rectangular tiles of the concourse wall made it look more like the bowels of some vast but disused municipal swimming baths. Stark took the corridor that led to the right, signed 'Piccadilly Line, Westbound,' with beneath it a list of stations that existed only in his imagination: Piccadilly Circus, Hyde Park Corner, Knightsbridge.

The blue light emanated from a series of low wattage bulbs on the platform ceiling. The emergency level power supply provided for safety purposes on the Northern Line platform had to be on the same circuit as that down here. At the platform's western end, rather than the gaping black hole of a tunnel, another wall of concrete blocks crossed the track, as high as the ceiling. This was it, then, the definitive end of the line.

And then he saw it. The concrete barrier closed the western exit only. Obviously trains on the renamed Holborn Line no longer came this far, even though the surface above was still on the 'right' side of the Wall, because as he had surmised there was no way up that didn't intersect with the concourse for the Northern Line platforms. In any case the land above was derelict, the Wall and the watchtowers too brutally evident for the state to encourage its citizens to come and gape.

But the eastern tunnel was unblocked. That had to mean that if he followed it, not only would there be no danger of a train passing, but he ought theoretically to be able to get to Covent Garden station. To his fellow citizens Covent Garden was the end of the line, one stop beyond Holborn, which had been maintained for the dowdy old opera house with its never-ending regurgitations of Mussorgsky and Brecht and for the old fruit and vegetable market.

The market still struggled on, even though there were few among the deliverymen from the collective farms of Kent and Sussex who recalled the days when bananas were a regular sight. Stark frequented it rarely, only when his mother asked him to pick up some apples or pears in season. But he would be glad to see it now.

Gingerly, he climbed down from the platform onto the track once again and, taking care to tread on the sleepers – he was in less of a hurry now and with both hands free was less afraid of losing his balance – headed into the darkness of the tunnel. The chief question on his mind was whether the electrified lines here would still be live or whether the power would only stretch as far as the next station. At some stage in the extraordinary operation of dividing the city the power supply to the Tube had obviously been rearranged.

How on earth that might have been done, he had no idea, but it would have eased his mind considerably to know what it meant in terms of the rail close to his feet.

And then ahead of him, brought into unexpectedly sudden view by some quirk of tunneller's topography, was the station platform, crowded with early-morning passengers. And there, advancing rapidly towards him was a train. Stark held his breath and then exhaled with relief as the familiar red-fronted, dirty but undefaced carriage with an equally familiar cranking rattle, shuddered to a halt. He thought for a moment he saw a look of open-mouthed incomprehension on the face of the man in the driver's compartment at the vision of someone striding out of the unbreachable abyss.

Then the driver did what ninety per cent of his compatriots would do under the circumstances. He turned away and climbed out of his cab. He was at the end of his line. He had seen something he shouldn't have; therefore, he pretended he hadn't.

Stark sighed; he was home.

Chapter 42

In the Mansion House office of the General Secretary of the Socialist Labour Party, Arthur Harkness adjusted his heavy black-framed glasses in the gilt-framed mirror that had once reflected the images of Lords Mayor of London. He swept back his silver-grey hair with one hand, adjusted his tie, wine-red as always, set off by the bleached white of his well-pressed shirt, and the sedate, sober black of his suit.

His father may have been a miner in the Welsh valleys used to grime and dust but the son, even in late middle age, was a man who cared about his appearance. Appearances mattered. What the people saw was what determined their attitude. Look too much like one of them and God knew what might happen.

He allowed himself a slight, internal, smile at the unconscious reference to the deity. He had not been brought up a strict Methodist. Upbringing left its marks, the relentless tedium of Sunday school as much as the ingrained cynicism that came with seeing generation after generation of good men ground to dust and an early grave by long hours down mine shafts in conditions little better than those of the pack donkeys that were their closest companions.

All for the benefit of the toffee-nosed swaggering gentry, stuck-up sons of earls and dukes who owed their fortunes to ancestors who'd been no more than protection racketeers licensed by mafia bosses who called themselves kings. Them and the new ones, barons who boasted they'd picked themselves up by their boot strings when all they'd done was climb over the corpses of the poor and greedy conned into deserting their rural idyll with the promise of fool's gold to be earned in factories. Or in the mine shafts.

Harkness knew the weaknesses of the common people, and knew it was his job to protect them from themselves, from their baser instincts. That was the job of any true Bolshevik: to guide the masses on the path of fairness for all, to take them on that journey to an egalitarian socialism, no matter how hard it might sometimes seem, no matter what sacrifices for some – and occasionally for all – it might entail.

He had been doing that job for nearly half a century now, at first as a young organiser in a communist party that existed on the fringes of legality, then, perforce, in the armed forces, in the reluctant service of the capitalists against the greater evil of fascism, and then, when the plutocrats turned traitor and showed their real colours, as a deserter in the underground, working for the betrayed ally right up to the glorious moment when the Red Flag had flown over Whitehall. He had been there to see it and the tears had flooded his eyes.

Then the Mansion House, scarred but remarkably little damaged by the inferno that had swept around it, had still been home to the Lord Mayor of London, an absurd pseudo-noble title bestowed in rotation on one after another of the plutocrats who dominated what they called the City, and through it the financial markets and commodities of half the world. Now it was his home; his official home at any rate, for Harkness liked to pride himself on being a modest man and still kept a suitable property outside the capital, a simple farmhouse on the Kent Weald, even if the demands of his security people – excessive in his own opinion – required the isolation of some 100 hectares surrounding, in which only chosen members of the politburo were allowed to reside. Such were the constraints, however, of public service.

It was not as if he had been simply anointed in power. Over the first fifteen years of the Republic he had worked his way up through the cadres, played a leading role in the (admittedly) sleight-of-hand manoeuvring that had seen the old Labour Party first infiltrated by and then merged with the communists to become, in accord with the new geopolitics, the natural party of government. Arthur Harkness had been an enthusiastic apologist of the Anti-Capitalist Protection Barrier. Sad though he was that his own home county remained under the old regime's new incarnation, he was – like all good politicians, he often reflected – at heart a pragmatist. Perhaps one day the dream of global revolution would be a reality, but in the meantime there was what the German comrades called *Realpolitik*, and he was damn good at it. So good, in fact, that he was about to celebrate twenty-five years as leader of his party and therefore, by definition, of his country.

He had served well, he liked to think, and indeed so he had been repeatedly told, not only by his own faithful, but by the fraternal allies whose might guaranteed the security of the socialist system. It was unthinkable that they should fail him, even more unthinkable than that he should ever fail them. That was not the way of the world. And Arthur Harkness was determined that the way of the world should be preserved. He rankled at those pathetic greed-driven commentators from up North who said he had made the Mansion House a bastion of 'die-hard communist conservatism'. Had they read no books? Did they know no politics? Communism and conservatism were antipathetic in eternity. Some things didn't change and that was a principle he would fight to the last to defend, and no fickle faint heart who might have wafted to temporary power in the Kremlin was going to alter it. Maybe they had forgotten what had happened to Khrushchev; and he had been lucky.

No, as he stared in the mirror, he could hold up his head with pride. The handful of dissenters and would-be unionists were as irrelevant as royalists, and almost as foolish. The Department of Social Security did what it said on its charter: it kept society secure. Today was his young nation's finest hour. Forty, he told himself, was an age of maturity for a man, and so it might be for a state. He liked that idea and indeed had let it leak out to others in the politburo so that he felt it might not even be surprising to see something of the sort even crop up on placards in the crowd – the people liked that sort of thing: ideas that percolated down from the top.

'Life begins at 40'. So it would be for the English Democratic Republic. Those who had said the partition would never last had long since come to accept it; even the Northerners had learned to live with it. It was already five years since he had paid a state visit to Durham, toured the Northern capital like any other foreign dignitary, even looked in – briefly of course – on his old home village, which had been tarted up for his arrival he had noted, and he had been treated with full honours. There had been protesters of course, but only a few, and he had noted with satisfaction how efficiently the Northern police had kept them out of his sight. His own men could hardly have done better, he had said publicly, though he had thought privately that in a well-mannered – and well-run – state, the slightest hint of popular displeasure at a visiting foreign dignitary should have been ruthlessly suppressed.

As they would be today if there was any nonsense. It was Harkness's turn to host a visiting dignitary. And not just any dignitary but arguably the most important man in the world, the General Secretary of the Communist Party of the Soviet Union. Certainly the most important man in Arthur Harkness's world. After himself, of course. The only trouble was that the current man in the job seemed to have forgotten what the job was. All this talk of *glasnost*, transparency, led to the risk of forgetting that the minds of men were blank sheets: anyone could write on them. And more often than not they wrote the wrong things. What was it the old bastard Churchill himself had said? 'History will be kind to me, because I intend to write it.' Thank God he hadn't got the chance. And now the Americans were making a film to glorify the old bugger, to exhume some symbol that might stir *his*, Arthur Harkness's, people, into some pipedream of so-called reunification.

The danger was it might work. Already there had been that absurd piece of graffiti on Bankside power station. And he had heard rumours of another, though he was not sure where. He had a horrible feeling from the expressions of the craven yes-men who surrounded him that they were scared to tell him. Anyway he hoped they were gone now. Or heads would roll. Any rumbling of dissent, and attempt to exploit the appearance – and surely it was superficial appearance only – of 'new thinking' in Moscow, was to be crushed relentlessly. He had put his best man on the job. Charles Marchmain knew what he was doing.

There was a knock on the door. 'Enter,' he called.

'Comrade General Secretary,' the junior official who timorously entered said. Harkness liked it when they used his title as party leader. It was, after all, the office to which the honour was due, not the man. Besides, it emphasised that the party and state were one. 'The guest delegation is ready for the preliminary talks.'

Harkness nodded a gruff acknowledgement. He saw no reason for these particular talks. It was a formality, of course, part of the routine of such visits, that the fraternal leaders would talk in private before the public celebrations. But what was there to say, beyond 'congratulations', and it was not as if he found this new man convivial. 'Businesslike' might be the way some people had chosen to describe him, but as far as Harkness was concerned they had no business to transact.

Trade, economic, military relations were all as they always had been. And internal affairs were not on the agenda. Not like they had been in Paris or Amsterdam in 1968 when control had been lost, things had got out of hand and fraternal assistance was urgently required to ensure the stability necessary for continuing progress towards the socialist ideal. It was unimaginable that anything like that could happen here, in England. Arthur Harkness ran a tight ship. And he intended to keep it that way. There were six hours still to go before they stood on the rostrum together to take the salute. He did not intend to spend all of it in needless talks, nor indeed any of it being browbeaten.

'Tell them to wait,' he replied.

Chapter 43

Stark stood on the fast emptying platform of Covent Garden Underground station and took a long look at the mouth of the tunnel he had emerged from. He could no longer think of the world beyond the Wall as 'over there'. It was beneath his feet.

It was as if he was Alice in Wonderland, suddenly thrown back up through the rabbit hole into the real world. Only the piece of paper in his hand proved that it had not all been a dream: a map of the London Underground as nobody had known it for four decades. On it, with a stub of pencil, he drew two little square boxes on the Northern Line south of Leicester Square. That was where he had been: how he had got there was another matter altogether. He shoved it into his jacket pocket.

Almost nobody had looked at the figure who climbed onto the end of the platform. Perhaps they had taken him for a maintenance worker. Perhaps, like the train driver, they just didn't want to know. Today was Republic Day, the fortieth, a day for celebration. Compulsory celebration. Certainly not a day to be asking questions. He let himself melt into the flow towards the escalators and up into an unexpected flood of sunshine. Even heaven was smiling on the Socialist Paradise.

He was grateful for the anonymity of the crowds. Not least, he reflected with a certain irony, because they shielded him from the ubiquitous uniformed police. There were uniformed constables on every corner and God only knew how many 'colleagues' from the Department in plainclothes among the crowds. Not to mention the unseen ranks of 'informals'. The knees of Stark's trousers were torn, his clothes were covered in dust and grime and there were thin smears of dried blood on his wrists. The last thing he wanted was to attract attention from police who would be looking to weed out beggars from the crowds of citizens dressed in their Sunday best.

The side streets leading down to the Strand were lined with battered buses that had brought factory workers in from Dagenham for the parade. They unloaded here and let the 'volunteers' walk or take the Tube. It added to the appearance of spontaneity, though nobody – not even the Northern television crews – was fooled. Stark passed lines of grumpy middle-aged men trudging along trailing their 'home-made' placards behind them: 'No More War', in black letters on red, 'The EDR – a bulwark of peace and socialism', '40 years of progress', '40: for a mature socialist society'.

Almost all of them had been shipped in wholesale by their factory managers eager to prove provincial party loyalty to the regime, thereby securing another year's untrammelled rule over fiefdoms as far flung as Yeovil and Yarmouth. The workers themselves by and large were philosophical about the wasted holiday, treating it at least as a day out in the big city.

Several carried the national flag, the socialist red rose imposed over the red-on-white cross of St George. Stark had heard it had been old Harkness himself, despite being a Welshman by birth, who had thought up the idea of holding the national holiday on 23 April, the traditional birthday of Shakespeare, 'the first people's playwright', and St George's Day. Religion be damned, St George was also conveniently the patron saint of Russia.

It was when he reached the Strand itself, already closed to traffic for the parade, that he saw a placard that took his breath. For a moment he thought the world had gone mad. Here was a factory worker from Dagenham carrying a picture of Churchill. But it was not the same as the stencil on Bankside or the one he had seen on the Wall. This was a crude caricature – a baby face with a cigar and bowler hat and a glass of champagne, the classic capitalist. Across it was scratched a big bold letter 'X' and below the words 'You can't teach an old dog new tricks'. The party had finally decided on its response to Hollywood's *Bulldog Breed* movie.

Stark found a phone box, rummaged in his pocket for change and found a ten pence piece. He could have called the emergency police number but that would have raised even more flags. Particularly on a day like today. Lavery picked up: 'Where the hell have you been, boss? I would have sent out the search parties if I'd had anybody to send. Virtually the whole force is on duty …'

'Never mind,' said Stark. 'I'm okay. But I've got a lead.'

'I'm not sure, boss, not today. We haven't got the manpower.'

'Don't need manpower, Lavery. Not for this one. It's something I've got to look into. On my own. Understand?'

The line was silent.

'Look, Dick. You know how it is. Sometimes things just come up. Stuff you have to do on your own.' Stark wondered if Lavery would assume he was having an affair. Fat chance. 'Just trust me, mate. Tell them I've phoned in sick. On my deathbed, if you have to.'

'If you're sure about this, boss.'

'I'm sure.' He put the phone down. He was anything but sure.

The doormen outside the Savoy Hotel were never going to turn a blind eye to someone in Stark's state of dress entering what was one of the Republic's prime hotels for foreigners. No sooner had Stark turned into the short drive that separated the entrance proper from the Strand than two men in nondescript grey suits blocked his way.

'Sorry, sir,' the first said, with distinct verbal inverted commas around the 'sir'. 'Residents only.'

Reluctantly, though he had known there would be no alternative, Stark reached into his jacket pocket and withdrew his warrant card. Luckily his underground captors had not taken it, as they had his weapon.

The man in the suit took it, examined it closely, then handed it to his colleague, who merely shrugged, handed it back and waved Stark through. Stark was aware of them shaking their heads as they stared at his ripped and dirty trousers. The official doorman standing in front of the revolving door in a top hat that had seen better days gave him an astonished look and glanced back and forth at his colleagues. Stark went through the same procedure and entered the grand if faded foyer of the English Democratic Republic's most famous hotel.

Ignoring the stares from hotel employees and foreign guests alike Stark marched across the fraying Persian rugs laid out on the chipped marble floor to the lift. When at last, with a grinding of gears, the ancient mechanism delivered the lift to the ground floor, Stark entered, pulled the iron cage gate across behind him and pressed the button for the fourth floor. He hoped Ben Fairweather had not gone out early for the parade. He was about to get a visitor.

Chapter 44

'What's happening, Harry? Where are we going?'

'On an excursion. I'm taking you to see the people you wanted to meet.'

'You mean you've done it? You've made contact? You're a genius, Harry Stark. I knew you could do it. So come on, tell me. Where are we going.'

Stark stopped in his tracks, turned and looked at the American with a weary eye. 'Look, you'll find out when we get there. If we get there. Just be on the level with these people. And with me, okay?'

'Okay? Of course, okay. But what do you mean, "if"?'

Stark ignored him. They were hurrying along the Strand, towards the Aldwych and Fleet Street. Maybe it was dangerous, maybe not. But there was only one way to get these people who knew more about Harry Stark's father than he did himself to trust him, and that was to take them the American, the man who promised he would publicise their cause on the other side of the Wall. The man who would take the same risk his colleague had paid for with his life.

The problem was that Stark had no precise idea how to find them again. Going back down the tunnels via Covent Garden was simply not an option. Walking the Tube lines on foot was simply far too dangerous. Even if it had been night rather than the middle of the day on a public holiday. The only solution was to go back to where he had started, follow his nose and see where he ended up. He was sure of only one thing. They would be meeting again today. They had said as much. They and 'the others'.

Except that he was not sure retracing his steps would be easy. Or possible. A hint of what had happened was immediately obvious the minute they entered the churchyard behind The Olde Bell public house. The little lean-to stall where the canon had sold his roneoed history sheets was nothing more than a pile of shattered timber. The curtain behind that led to the stairwell down to the crypt had been ripped off its rail and lay sodden and dirty on the ground. Stark and Fairweather exchanged glances.

There was no one in evidence. Down the narrow entry that separated the remains of the belfry from Fleet Street they could see only the backs of people apparently turned out early to get a spot to watch the parade. Stark led the way down the stairs. The heavy door that had survived the Blitz had been smashed through the centre; the splintered remnants still hanging from the ancient iron hinges. There was still light in the staircase, but the glimmer that came from below had been extinguished.

'Shit, the light's gone.'

'It's cool, use this,' said the American, and took from his breast pocket a little torch barely thicker than a pen. Stark had seen them on TV. Fairweather flicked a switch and a clear bright beam of light came on.

Stark held out his hand. Fairweather pulled his back.

'I'm not going to pinch it. I know what we're looking for.' Up to a point, he added silently. With a show of good-natured reluctance, the American handed it over.

They descended the second set of stairs only to find that the little room that had served as a makeshift chapel was now littered with bones, old bones, ripped from the neat piles that had lined the walls. The old Roneo machines lay smashed on the ground, scraps of torn paper lay everywhere. He picked one up. It was a 'winkie', another image of Churchill giving his V salute, torn to shreds. But there was only one thing on Stark's mind: the old man, Ransom. The one who had vouched for him. Was that why they had left him behind? The draped table that had served as an altar lay overturned in the corner, its altar cloth thrown to the ground and ominously stained with something that might have been blood. Ransom's blood.

'Holy shit,' said Fairweather. 'If this is where the Underground gathered, it looks like your friends have paid them a visit.'

'No friends of mine,' said Stark, instinctively. But nor were the other lot, he reflected silently. Sometimes knowing who your friends were was no easy matter.

'This was a mistake, a stupid blunder. I think most of those who came here were low level – only the priest came here every day, and the old man who lived here …'

The words died in his mouth. Without a second look at the stained altar cloth he led the way along the narrow corridors. The light bulb in the second chamber had been smashed too. The debris revealed in the pool of light from the pen torch was sombre. The chairs lay scattered on the floor, several of them broken. The violence against inanimate objects was excessive, the violence of men frustrated that they had nothing human to beat; except for the evidence of the bloodied altar cloth.

'Halt. Is there someone there? Show yourself. Department of Social Security.' The shout came from upstairs. Stark could have kicked himself. Of course they would have left someone to watch.

Fuck, thought Stark. 'Fuck,' said the American. But it was Stark who had the greater sinking feeling in his gut. He could show himself to the DoSS, say he was on police business, although explaining away the presence of an American journalist in the circumstances could be more complicated. And in any case, his refusal to explain himself would quickly be overridden; he had no enthusiasm for a 'private inquiry' in the basement of the Barbican. Especially if, as the American claimed, that was where his father had met his end. It had to be a possibility that Stark's unquestioning acceptance of the official story of the old man's heroics on the side of socialism had been his safety blanket.

Stark stared in confusion at the various holes in the walls around them. Different sizes at different heights, leading in different directions. The DoSS couldn't have searched them all either. Maybe they contented themselves with beating Ransom to a pulp. But one of them had to be the way the others had used. Carrying Stark's limp body along with them. At least four were big enough for a man to get along at a crouch. At a crawl, it would have been possible to get through almost any.

Stark could hear footsteps on the stairs, a stern shout:

'Show yourself. Social Security. This area is out of bounds.'

Stark flicked the beam of light around in panic. He discounted the crawl passages. Too hard to have taken an unconscious body along one of those. That left four, two on the left, two on the right. What was it the canon had said about tunnels that might have led down to the Thames? Tunnels from Roman days adapted by later smugglers. Downhill, that was the key. It had to be. That implied the passages on the right. Out of pure contrariness he chose the second, dragging the American after him and extinguishing the torch. If it led nowhere maybe at least they could hide until the DoSSer had gone, and hope he could convince himself he had just imagined he heard a noise.

For the moment the passage seemed to continue looping round to the left. At least that meant they might be out of sight if someone shone a torch down the passage. The ground was sandy, which suggested indeed that it at one time had led down to the river shore. It also had the advantage of muffling any noise their feet made. In any case the DoSSer was making his own noise. Stark could hear him shouting loudly, imagined him flashing a torch down each passage in turn. A flicker of light behind them confirmed his scenario and also gave him a glimpse of the American crouched behind him with a look of sheer terror on his face.

'Anyone there?' the distant voice boomed. 'These passageways have been condemned.' Stark put a finger to his lips. The look of panic on Fairweather's face was getting worse. Then the light vanished. Stark waited for minutes that seemed like hours until he was as sure as he was going to be that no one was either coming after them or still shining torches down the passageways. He turned on the pen torch at ground level, taking care to point it forwards and grateful that its beam was so narrow. He flicked it up towards the roof of the passage for a second, so the American could see his face and silently mouthed, 'Come on.'

He felt a tug on his jacket, and heard one word, whispered quietly but with determination: 'No.'

Reluctantly Stark let the little beam turn on his companion's face and saw the man rolling his eyes and making frantic gestures with his hands at the walls around them. He understood. Fairweather was claustrophobic. He did the only thing he could. He turned out the torch and continued some five or six metres ahead on his own in the dark. Then he stopped, turned the torch back on, and shone it at Fairweather. The American was frozen to the spot. Stark pointed back, mimicked a gun at his head and then beckoned him, holding up the torch, so Fairweather understood: it was staying with him. As if on cue, for the first time in minutes there was a shout in the distance behind them. With what looked like tears in his eyes, the American hugged himself and came shuffling towards Stark.

When he got close Stark pulled Ben Fairweather to him and bent down flashing the torch beam along the ground. In front of them the tunnel divided in two. One led off to their left. The other sloped down, and at an oblique angle, so that it was impossible to tell how far it went without getting into it. Stark pointed at the ground. The sloping tunnel had a clear furrow down the middle of its sandy floor. Something had recently been dragged along here. Or someone.

As far as Stark could see the tunnel was good, or at any rate not a dead end. The walls were damp, green in places with mould, but seemed solid and secure, almost as if they were made of cut ashlar rather than dug out of the earth. Only the smell was getting worse. The dry dusty atmosphere of the crypt had given way to a distinct dankness. The slime on the walls was growing more luxuriant with every metre and in places almost seemed to glow with an eerie fluorescence. But worst of all was the smell. Dry mustiness had long since yielded to acrid, salty bitterness overlaid with something putrid. The tunnel no longer sloped downward. It had levelled out but was now so low and narrow they had to bend almost double and it was impossible to turn around. Ahead there was a dull, distant roar, constant rather than the occasional rattle of trains. More importantly, there was no sound behind them. Either their pursuer had not found their escape route, or had thought better of it. Stark was not complaining. Yet. He felt a tug from behind.

'How ... how far does it go? I can't take much more of this. It's like the walls are closing in.' The American's voice was a sensible whisper, but Stark could clearly hear the anxiety in it, although it was nearly impossible now even to get his head at an angle where he could turn around and see the man's face. He could not imagine what it would be like if they had to go back.

'Wait here, just a second,' he said. 'I'll go a bit further and see if I can get an idea how far it goes.' Or if it gets any tighter, he didn't add. But he knew it couldn't; he had been dragged through here, chloroformed, unconscious. It certainly explained the state of his clothing and the obvious reason why taking the old man Ransom with them would have been impossible. There was no way this tunnel could get any smaller; unless, of course, he was totally wrong and this was not the escape route at all but an ancient ditch that went nowhere.

'No, it's ... it's okay. I can ...' The American was doing his best.

'Trust me. Just a few seconds.' Stark understood. Ben Fairweather was having a crisis: he didn't want to go on, but he also didn't want to be left alone, in the dark, even for a few seconds. He probably couldn't even imagine crawling out backwards. But he had had an idea. The depth he imagined they were at now, coupled with the smell could, he felt certain, mean only one thing. The passageway they were in, whatever its origins, had to lead somewhere, and Stark had suddenly decided he knew where.

He crawled ahead as fast as he could, his elbows now

complaining almost as much as his already suffering knees. Apart from looking like a tramp, he must stink like one too. And then, all of a sudden, the narrow crawl tunnel ahead of him vanished. Barely two metres away, the torch beam shone clear into a cavernous darkness.

'Come on,' he called back, smiling as he imagined the terrified American journalist's relief – was this the glamorous life of a cold war correspondent he had imagined back amidst the skyscrapers of New York? – 'We're out.'

Chapter 45

'Out' was a relative term.

'Welcome,' said Stark as he helped the American to his feet, 'to one of the wonders of the nineteenth-century world – the London sewers.' Not words that were uttered often, Stark imagined, and rarely – if ever – accompanied by such a huge sigh of relief. The narrow crouch way had come out less than half a metre above a great arched highway lined in dirty yellow brick that stretched in a straight line in either direction, with a rushing if less than fragrant river running in a deep-cut channel down the middle.

'This is amazing.' Fairweather stood and stared at the vista opened up by the torchlight. 'How old did you say this was.'

'About 130 years,' said Stark. 'I'm not sure exactly but I think most of it was built in the 1860s, after the great cholera epidemic, although what they told us in school was that they only built a proper sewage system when the stink from the Thames got so bad the members of parliament had to evacuate the Palace of Westminster.'

Fairweather gave him a look that said, 'that's what the sort of teacher you have over here would tell you'. Maybe it was, Stark had never given it a second thought. Until now. And even now it wasn't the reason for the sewer's construction that concerned him, it was its use as a conduit for human beings, as well as their waste products, underneath the streets of London.

'We turn right,' he said. 'This is the way they must have come.' Lugging me, unconscious, with them, he thought.

'You're sure about this?'

'Stands to reason. The main sewer follows the river. That's why they built the Victory Embankment – the Victoria Embankment,' he corrected himself and for the first time in his life thought of it as a correction. 'Where the city used to slide down towards the riverbank, they shored it up and built huge ramparts which contained the sewer and – somewhere' – he gestured vaguely with one arm – 'the District Line Tube from Blackfriars to Charing Cross. But if what I remember is correct,' he stopped in mid-flow and began searching his pockets, 'shit, I've lost the map – the old Northern Line, the one that Westminster trains still use, must cut across it at right angles. That means there has to be another Charing Cross station down there, another ghost station, only one stop away from the phantom Leicester Square. If we've come south from the church crypt, downhill towards the river, as we have to have done, then if we turn right, eventually we will come to where the sewer goes between them, as it has to. That's where we'll find the link. It has to be. It makes sense,' he said, adding only as an afterthought, 'if any of this does.'

The American shrugged: 'Lead on, Macduff.'

Stark strode out, watching his feet on the slippery wet brickwork, and letting the torch beam play up and down the rows of brickwork and the vaulted ceiling. The tunnel was over three metres tall and nearly five across. It was like being an archaeologist in your own city. The more Stark discovered about the complexity of the world underground, the more he was forced to scorn the vainglory of the men who had so thoughtlessly sliced in half a city that was an organic entity. How many maps had they pored over, how many decisions met with calculated clinical cynicism, to snip an artery here, a vein there?

Above ground the Wall seemed ancient and unbreachable, perhaps because it was there, visible, day-by-day and
given time, one got used to anything; even the greatest and
most cruel absurdities could come, with time and habit, to
seem eternal and immutable. Yet there was something eating
away at Stark's self-confidence. He had told Fairweather he
was absolutely certain of their bearings, but for a reason he
could not put his finger on, that confidence was being whit-
tled away with every step. He looked round at the figure following him and, realising that the time had perhaps come
to show a bit more fellow feeling, smiled and used the man's
first name: 'You all right?'

Fairweather's skewed spectacles cast strange shadows on
his face, ghostly white, in the torchlight; his nose was wrinkled against the pervading stench. He looked not so much
sceptical as uncertain that any of it was a good idea. Stark
had a twinge of sympathy, but not over much; it was the
American, after all, who had got him into this in the first
place. He had booked the ride; if it was making him queasy
he had only himself to blame.

It was only then that he realised what was wrong. If his
assumptions had been correct – which surely they had to
be – then turning right along the sewer had been the only
option. 'Right' had to be west, the direction they needed to
follow if they were to get to Charing Cross. But the water
– to give it the euphemism – they were walking next to
was flowing the wrong way: with them, rather than against
them. Sewers, like rivers, drained downhill, at least until
they came to pumping stations. And downhill, following
the river, meant east, towards the distant Thames estuary
and the North Sea. It didn't make sense, any of it. Until
almost immediately they came to something else that didn't

243

make sense: a T-junction, where the sewer they walked along poured itself into another tunnel that crossed at right angles.

Stark stopped dead, looked left, looked right, like a schoolchild preparing to cross the road, then back at the American two paces behind him. Fairweather was watching him with an expression that if it had not been overlayed with such obvious consternation, Stark might almost have called 'smug'.

'Okay, Sherlock, which way now?' he said.

For a moment Stark was genuinely nonplussed. He had been so certain. It had seemed so obvious, so easy. Apart from the stink, it could almost have been a Sunday afternoon stroll. Compared to the tiny tunnel they had crawled through, the sewer was a king's highway and he knew the route. Or rather, he had thought he did.

Now he was not so sure. There was a marked difference between the two tunnels. The one they had been walking along had a wide pavement at each side of the central trench; the one that it opened into was more egg-shaped in cross-section. If it had been as full-flowing as the stream they had just walked along, it would have been impossible to move along it without wading over ankle-height – hardly a pleasant thought – but it wasn't, at least not consistently. The fast stream that fed it flowed in its new channel off to the left. Obviously that way was downhill, following the course of the Thames.

And then Stark realised instantly where they were. The tunnel from St Bride's had led them not immediately into the Victorian sewers, but into a much older, more natural water system, although one long since tamed by man. The pavements they had been walking along were the long-since canalised and eventually covered-over banks of the Fleet River. The Fleet flowed down towards the Thames entering it at almost right angles, or had done before the embankment had been built and the sewer intercepted it. And besides, there was daylight.

On the opposite wall of the tunnel, a few metres downstream from where they stood and at least a metre off the sewer floor, was a wide opening. All of a sudden it made sense: the buried Fleet emptied into the main sewer but the outlet opposite was an overflow that in times of flood or heavy rain would allow the ancient river – and sewage – to spill out again directly into the Thames.

Stark turned to Fairweather but the American was already with him, staring out from their subterranean labyrinth to where the dull light of a grey spring day fell across the river. Noting the intensity of his gaze, Stark followed it, and realised that what they were looking at was not just visual confirmation of their underground orientation. Barely 100 metres away was a span of metal that could only be the underside of Blackfriars Bridge. If he had been standing in this position two dawns earlier, he might have seen a corpse wrapped in blood-soaked sacking hanging from it.

'Okay,' said Fairweather. 'I guess there's no doubt about where we are now. Though we could maybe get out of here through there …' There was almost, but not quite, a note of optimism in his voice.

'It wouldn't do us any good though. Not if we want to find the people we're after. Besides, even getting swamped by sewage is probably less dangerous than taking a dip in the Thames these days.'

They turned right into the new stream. It was a decidedly less pleasant experience, the tunnel was loosely egg-shaped and the sewage regularly lapped at their feet. At one moment it seemed as if the fetid waters were coming alive. Stark sprang out of the way as an army of rats routed by their passage rushed by.

One thing still worried him: how would they know when they were at the point where the sewer crossed over the Tube? He needn't have worried. The American saw it first.

'Harry, up there, on the wall, to the right. About a hundred yards ahead.'

Stark instinctively found the right spot with his beam. Funny, how the Americans and Northerners used the same old measuring systems. He wondered, briefly, if both – or either – still called it 'imperial'. But why not? It was the Americans' empire now.

'I hadn't expected it to be that obvious.'

It could scarcely have been more so. A proper door, albeit half-height and set about two metres from the sewer pavement. Reaching it would not be a problem either: there was a set of narrow brick steps with an iron handrail. It was obviously in regular use; the door swung open easily.

Beyond was a full-height narrow corridor that extended half a dozen metres to where a spiral metal staircase descended, as if down a vertical bore hole around a wire-caged central shaft. The shaft contained a lift, or what had once been one; all that remained were cables, dangling in an empty space, descending into the darkness.

'The Victorians built this?' Fairweather was either sceptical or impressed.

'No. The materials are all wrong. These walls are concrete, not brick. This is twentieth century.' Stark looked up. The staircase and lift shaft continued upwards, but in the torchlight it was easy to see that not far above them the stairs were increasingly clogged with debris. 'It must be something left over from the war. That's all I can think. Blocked at street level, probably.'

'Do we know where street level is? Here?'

Stark was nowhere near as confident as he had been. 'I'm assuming we're near Charing Cross. That somehow this leads to the room I woke up in, between there and ...' the unfamiliar words stuck for a moment, 'between there and Leicester Square.'

'You think. Don't you know? Jesus Christ, Harry, we could get lost down here.'

'It's okay. So far at least, we know the way back.' But Stark could see from the American's face that that was scant consolation.

Chapter 46

'So now we go down again. Is that it?'

Stark nodded. He could see little alternative.

The steps were rough pre-cast concrete; slabs laid in a spiral pattern. It had all the hallmarks of wartime civil engineering, rough and ready, practicable without being pretty. One thing testified reliably to the staircase being in use: the debris so evident above was signally absent, as if someone had cleared it away to avoid the risk of accident if it had to be used in a hurry. Nonetheless, they moved carefully, without speaking, watching their footsteps in the torchlight. Stark was thankful that the batteries seemed to have been in good condition.

About thirty or so steps beneath where they had encountered the shaft the beam revealed a short corridor going off to the side with, once again, a metal door at the end. Stark tried to work out if it was the same direction as that which led to the sewer but discovered the spiral descent had confused his sense of orientation. He approached it, listening for sounds from the other side. Nothing. He looked at Fairweather who shrugged. He tried the door. It opened. Inwards. Flooding their world with light.

For a moment Stark could only stand and blink. Then he realised he was looking into an empty room, small, square, with a table and four chairs, and a single fluorescent strip light on the ceiling. There was a further door on the other side. He crossed the room and, almost without thinking, opened it. The chamber beyond was dark, with no obvious light switch to hand. Stark turned his torch back on and swung the beam to and fro. It was as strangely familiar as he expected. On the wall opposite hung a rack of fire extinguishers, clunky, heavy old bottles that looked more like antiques than modern equipment. And next to them was another door that Stark had no doubt would lead into a tunnel where trains from another world ran under the streets of his. Nonetheless, just to be sure, he walked across and opened it.

'This is it, all right. This is where I was.'

The American nodded, watching him carefully. Stark had opened the door on the facing wall in the second chamber just a fraction, then closed it again quickly.

'But where are they?'

'I don't know. I thought ...' He didn't know what he'd thought really: that they'd still be here, playing cards and waiting for their escaped prisoner to wander back and say sorry? And yet that, in a way, was precisely what he was trying to do. 'They said they would be meeting later. They talked about the "others coming".'

'Are you sure they said here?'

'No. I just presumed ... I don't know ... I'm not quite sure what we do now ...'

'Aren't you, Harry? There's only one thing to do. We go on down.'

Fairweather was right, of course. The steps in the shaft led further down. Whatever they had been constructed for, it was not this. These two little rooms, with their access to the branch of the Northern Line were incidental. Whatever the shaft had been constructed to give access to lay deeper.

Stark descended first, the torch beam as ever playing on the walls below first, then hovering in front of them on the steps. Most probably they were simply dropping the distance between the Northern Line and the Holborn Line – Piccadilly Line, he corrected himself: like Alice in Wonderland he had gone down a rabbit hole and ended up in another world.

But surely they had gone deeper that that. He had no idea how many steps they had already descended; now he started counting them. They kept going, at least another thirty, maybe forty. Then, all of a sudden, they stopped.

They were at the bottom of the shaft, but not yet as deep as they could go. The wire cage contained a lift car, but not one that had been used for many years. The torchlight revealed an old, rusty concertina gate to the lift, pulled half open. The car within was thick with cobwebs. Straight ahead of the lift door a gently sloping tunnel still faced with concrete led further down into the earth. From deep within the tunnel came the faint glow of another source of lighting. And something far more significant: sound. The sound of human voices. Faint but unmistakable. Arguing.

Stark turned the torch off and pocketed it. Together he and Fairweather, moving as quietly as they could, descended the sloping tunnel. The light grew stronger. Before them they could see what appeared to be a well-lit concrete-walled room, not unlike those above, but with a ceiling of reinforced iron.

'I think I know where we are,' said Stark suddenly, quietly.

'Good, I'm glad.'

'No, I mean, I think I know what this is.'

'A disused Tube, I thought you already said.'

'Yes and no, this is different. It's far deeper, and the ceilings and walls are reinforced. This has to be a Deep Level Shelter.'

'Like an air raid shelter?'

'Sort of, except not for the public. They had to make do with the ordinary Tube tunnels and even then they had to fight to get into them at first. Places like this were constructed for the politicians and the military. During the war there were all sorts of tunnels and shelters underground in the Whitehall area. Most of them would have straddled what's now the border. I imagined they'd all been filled in.'

'Well, it seems this one wasn't. You go first,' whispered Fairweather.

Stark stopped. Exactly how he planned to confront his former captors and convince them they were on the same side was something he had worked out only sketchily at best. The American, according to his own plan, was to figure as an ambassador from 'the other side' and the guarantee of his newspaper's publicity, if that was what they wanted. But these could be dangerous men and might even be armed. They had one gun at least: his. There was no telling how they would react to the presence here, somewhere they assumed was totally safe, of a total stranger. Would they react any differently to a known policeman?

The 'room' was more like a junction box: a concrete-walled interchange with exits at either side. It was empty. The voices were coming from the exit on the left, but still sounded distant. He turned and looked at Fairweather.

'It's better like this,' the American whispered. 'Show them you've come back, of your own free will, without a backup posse. They ought to give you a chance to at least explain yourself, and then you can produce me as proof you're on the level. If they react otherwise, then I can step in, from the wings as it were. As backup.'

Stark nodded uncertainly. It was hardly best police

procedure, but then this was nothing like normal police business. This is the sort of stuff the 'Department' do, he thought, and that was scarcely reassuring.

He edged forward, across the little antechamber towards the exit on the left. It was a tunnel barely three metres long, like the entry or exit of a Tube platform, except that it was lined with concrete rather than tiles. The voices were louder now, and one dominated. Stark recognised it at once as the more aggressive of the two he had overheard earlier discussing his fate. Once again he was struck by something about it, as if he had heard it before, but in a context that was so alien that it got in the way of recognition. And then it came to him, in a flash, along with a vision so absurd that he almost wanted to laugh.

The first time he had heard that voice was not from someone hostile or aggressive, but subservient and wheedling, if a little snide. He could see him now: owlish, pasty-faced, pushing back a heavy oily wodge of hair that kept falling over his thick spectacles. It was the clerk from the Marx-Lenin Reading Room. The clerk at the submissions desk. The one who had been so helpful, if over-interested, in his requests. The one who had seen his warrant card, who knew the one thing Stark had foolishly failed to reveal to these people whose trust he was trying to win: that he was a policeman. Like his father. Except how like his father really was he. He was unsure himself. How could he have expected them to know.

The thought that he had been afraid of this man though seemed absurd, but only for a moment. Physical strength was far from everything. Little men with glasses, who in other circumstances might have lived out their lives as chicken farmers or architects, given the right circumstances and the reins of power, had been responsible for the deaths of millions. He was thinking of Himmler and Beria. But these people were supposed to be on the right side. Weren't they?

Eager to confirm the man's identity, though in his heart he was already convinced, Stark moved to the end of the little tunnel and crouched down. If he could he wanted to see exactly how many of them there were and what their dispositions were before he threw himself onto their – not necessarily so tender – mercy. What he saw took him aback.

Under the circumstances, it ought not to have been a surprise, but somehow it was. He supposed he had been expecting another room. Instead he saw what appeared to be a Tube tunnel, but a Tube tunnel like no other. For a start it too had no tiling, just bare concrete as if the boring machines had only recently gone through and the intermediate work in preparing for passengers had been abruptly abandoned. The platform was there, but bare, with no seats or hoardings against the wall. Instead there were bunks, a long line of them, like crew sleeping quarters on board a ship. Or a submarine. Here and there were items of what looked like military communications equipment, except that it was hardly modern, even by southern English standards: radios with valves, Morse code machines, piled on tables and against walls.

Halfway along the platform a group of people sat, like a casual card school, around a wooden table. Hunched behind one of the bunks Stark could see only a few of them, but there, unmistakable in profile even if it had not been for his voice, was the Reading Room clerk, wagging his finger in the air, as he might do, in other circumstances, at someone talking too loud in the hallowed library.

The Museum Man, as Stark now thought of him, was talking loudly. Talking, it was suddenly clear, about him. 'You're right, of course, it was a mistake. It was probably a mistake to take him in the first place. We should just have left him to the DoSSers. If you're right – and I know, I know, you usually are – then he wasn't a threat. And still isn't. If you're sure you know where he is. So what do you say, Merlin, do we go for it?'

Stark half-smiled to himself. The one thing he was certain of was, whatever information they might think they had, at this precise moment they had no idea where he was. It was good news, however, to hear that whoever the Museum Man was talking to had pronounced him not to be a threat. He gathered himself. It was now or never: time to stand up and be counted, to face these people and find out if they had goals he could share, and if they had evidence he could use to bring killers to book so much the better. One way or another it was time to face his father's legacy.

And then he heard another voice. To his astonishment one that he also recognised. One that he had last heard, also, in a very different context. Only a few short hours before. It couldn't be. Despite himself he stood up, needing the clear view, and suddenly heedless of exposing himself to theirs. But there was no mistake. There, facing him from the other side of the table, sleeves rolled back and for all the world like a general at a military briefing, was …

'Lizzie?'

Chapter 47

'Harry! My God, Harry, you're such a fool. A fool.'

The tunnel echoed with her words. The empty, hollow, gaping tunnel of an underground railway with no trains, in a station with no name, leading nowhere.

'I told you to stay away from this. Why couldn't you just for once do what you're told?'

Stark could say nothing.

The Museum Man interjected: 'This is absurd. We shouldn't even be talking to people like this now. We should …'

'Shut your mouth, Malcolm,' snapped Lizzie. There was no doubt who was in command here. 'I told you not to do this, Harry,' she continued, as if the slack-faced man had never spoken. 'You don't know what you're involved with. I told you, you were better off that way.'

'I can't …' Stark stammered at last, 'I can't believe that you …'

'That's your problem, Harry, you believe too little. And too much.'

He had had a speech prepared, words he had strung together in his head to address the people who had been his father's ideological comrades, the people for whom he had given his life. Harry would do the same. He would risk all in challenging the lawless hegemony of the DoSS. He would appeal to them to believe that the system could be reformed from within. He had no idea whether he believed it himself. Now it seemed a piece of overblown rhetoric hardly suitable for a woman with whom he had been on the brink of intimacy.

Instead, he said simply: 'I don't want to live a lie any more than my father did.' The Museum Man rolled his eyes. Stark ignored him. It was the truth, he now knew it, whether they believed him or not.

'I am my father's son. Maybe I didn't know it, but I do now. And I want justice for the way he died. He deserves it. As does the man who came to meet you, the one we found, the police I mean, hanging beneath Blackfriars Bridge, trussed up like a piece of meat with the top of his head blown off.'

Lizzie had her eyes closed, as if she was shutting out the vision. He was getting through to her. He had to be. He knew her, after all. Or did he? Did he know anything about her at all?

'I've got a contact, an American,' he tried hard not to look behind him, to see if Ben was about to come out and join him, 'a contact in the American media who will publish all of this, your point of view, who will expose the popular resistance to the system. We might not win, but we can't lose, not from the point of view of history.'

Lizzie opened her eyes with a look of immense weariness: 'My God, history! History! You don't understand, Harry. I told you that. And I don't think your American friend would publish the truth even if he knew it. The media on the other side may claim to be totally free, but ask them if even they believe it. Ask their reporters about their proprietors, powerful men with powerful interests. Interests in the status quo, the status quo they created and have nurtured for forty years. It's too late for that, Harry. There's not just a military-industrial complex, there's a media-industrial complex. The same people own them all, the press and the studios. They're still lying now.'

'That film. *Bulldog Breed*. It's a lie, like people have been saying. The history books aren't wrong. He did kill himself.'

'You think so? It doesn't sound like it from this.' She held up a slim volume. 'This is a piece of history, Harry. A piece the world doesn't know about and would have long ago destroyed if it did. Read the last two pages and tell me if it's written by a man about to commit suicide.'

She handed him the little book, an old, dog-eared leather-bound diary. He opened it at the end and read:

The War Room, September 1949

The empire is not dead. Its heart may have been ripped out but the distant limbs are still inviolate. The fight can and will go on.

The King is dying. He was forced into this job by the abdication and has never been in good health. He will not survive this final collapse. But his two daughters, the young princesses, are at his side, already safe and well in distant Canada.

There will be no coronation in Westminster Abbey. Charred stumps, I fear will be all that remain of its great Gothic buttresses and Hawksmoor's elegant towers. Some church in Ottawa will serve the purpose just as well.

A new Elizabethan age will arise, nurtured on the fertile soils not just of Canada, but Australia, India and Africa. One day – however distant – the loyal sons of empire will reclaim the motherland. I only hope that I will live to see it.

I will not let the enemy take me, nor will I take my own life as some have feared. I have made mistakes. I have learnt the hard way that no matter how immovable the object, in the end irresistible force prevails. So be it, for the moment. We must now retreat, to build an irresistible force of our own.

I must for now throw myself, and our cause, onto the mercy of our great ally. I do so in confidence, though not without some trepidation. Had Adolf Hitler not, in an act of loyalty to Japan, declared war on the United States the day after Pearl Harbour, I cannot be wholly convinced that, for all my efforts, Washington would have joined the European war as well. Yet the result has been only to see the Communists' red flag rather than the Nazi Swastika over London.

The landings on the Normandy beaches were a titanic undertaking, far beyond Britain's might alone. But the fighting in northern France and in the Ardennes proved tougher than we had anticipated, the road to Berlin was not the 'Sunday afternoon drive' some of our American allies had imagined. In the meantime the Soviet juggernaut rolling westwards had obtained the proportions of a force of nature.

We watched this steamroller flatten not just the Nazi opposition but the native resistance too, most notably the patriots of Poland for whose sake this country went to war in the first place. When the Poles in Warsaw saw the Red Army on their doorstep in July 1944 and rose against the Nazis, Stalin held back his troops on the far bank of the Vistula until they had been crushed, the better to prepare for the country's subjugation to a new master. One alien totalitarian regime was rapidly replaced by another. It was our first glimpse of the future.

The time had come to think the unthinkable. In July 1941, when I signed the 'mutual assistance' pact with Stalin, I had been moved to reflect that necessity made strange bedfellows and many decent women into whores. I had been in bed with one devil, now it was time for the other.

The Stauffenberg bomb plot against Hitler might never have succeeded without the covert help of our intelligence. But with the dictator gone the men of honour in the German army offered to turn their troops east in the hope of saving their nation, their continent, not to mention their skins. In the end they saved none. Our troops, their former enemies, were welcomed across the Rhine. It was too little, too late. The tide of history had become a red tsunami, particularly after the pro-Communist revolution in France cut the ground from beneath our feet.

The Manhattan Project, designed to deliver us a super-weapon, turned out to be infiltrated with spies, though against our expectations they were not Nazis but communists, includ-ing one, Klaus Fuchs, a German to whom we in Britain had mistakenly given shelter. It was not laboratories in Berlin or Dresden that were hard on the heels of the men at Los Alamos but those in Moscow and Novosibirsk.

Only now, when the Stalin tanks have chewed up the Kent and Sussex countryside and penetrated into the heart of London are our allies ready to test an atomic bomb. But they believe the Soviets are at a similar stage. Last week there was a meeting in Malta between envoys of Washington and Moscow. I was not invited. What it signals I can only specu-late. And hope. And trust. I have remarked before that one can rely on the Americans to do the right thing, after they have tried everything else.

The world is changing fast. I can only pray I may provide leadership to our far-flung dominions to fight for a better future. In this I must place my trust in those who were the first rebels against the British empire, and today are its last hope.

WSC

Stark looked up in astonishment. 'Is this real? I don't believe it and if it's true, what happened?'

Lizzie took a deep sigh, looked behind her to where, Stark

noticed for the first time, a stooped little old lady with her arm in a sling sat, and said: 'Tell him, Gran.'

Chapter 48

The operation had gone like clockwork. Unfortunately these days clockwork wasn't quite enough.

Colonel Charles Marchmain was studying a map of the London Underground, a map with which even he was unfamiliar. A map that showed a network that extended into what was now another city, another country. And this map from the distant past, from another world had been written on. Recently. By someone in a hurry, someone who had disappeared into a tunnel underneath St Bride's. Marchmain had every reason to believe that person was Harry Stark. What he didn't know was the significance of the two square boxes drawn in pencil on a spur of the old Northern Line, a spur nowadays used only by trains from the other side.

Instances of closed stations and through tunnels being used by deserters had fallen to zero since the above-ground entrances had been demolished and their location, or very existence, faded from popular memory. Marchmain showed the map to his oldest officer, a man on the brink of retirement who had been in the Military Police during the war. Did it mean anything to him. The old man had looked at the colonel with some surprise, then delight in being able to provide his superior with important intelligence so late in his professional life: 'I can't be certain, sir. And I don't really understand the significance of the little squares, but I do know what is down there: the old Deep Shelters. Including the one used by General Eisenhower.'

Marchmain's eyes lit up. Was it possible the people Stark

had got involved with, the dissident scum who had escaped his men in the raid on the church, had a hideout he knew nothing about, improbably close to Stalingrad Square? Today of all days he was extremely uncomfortable about that. He had deliberately allowed Stark a slack rein, knowing the risks of the policeman becoming a loose cannon, in the hope that his past would work in Marchmain's favour, giving him an 'in' to the so-called 'underground' that his own men had failed to achieve.

But the possibility could not be ruled out that he had somehow been deluded – or deluded himself – into playing his father's game, or whatever he might have been led to believe that was. Within minutes – a call to the Ministry of Works records office from Social Security was an event seldom enough to warrant immediate attention – Marchmain was perusing ancient plans, drawn up in 1942, for a shelter he had no idea existed. He all but snarled. Whatever was going on down there required attention, and now.

Within less than forty minutes a dozen armed DoSS operatives were assembled on the platform of Covent Garden Underground station. The veteran military policeman aided by a rapidly co-opted member of the London Transport Cooperative led Marchmain and his men down to a passageway behind the main lift shaft to a locked door that had not been opened in decades. The Tube man said he was certain he would be able to find a key somewhere. Marchmain blew the lock away. The door swung back to reveal an antechamber to a lift, descending beneath the main shaft. On the wall was an ancient red trip switch of the sort used for emergency power cut-offs. The colonel nodded to one of his men who flipped it. Against expectations there was a low hum and a light came on in the lift.

Nonetheless, Marchmain led his men, and their muzzled dogs, in single file down the stairs.

Chapter 49

St James's Park, 1949

The old man stood, in his mind's eye, like the last warrior on the field of Armageddon, amidst the smouldering ruins of the empire he had loved and cherished.

The hour had come. He stared out at the wasteland of St James's Park, briefly remembering distant sunny afternoons when he had walked beneath the shade of the trees and fed the ducks. There were no ducks now. No trees either.

The desolation of the parkland was an advantage; the trees would have been obstacles. To the south ran Birdcage Walk. King James I had had an aviary nearby. Now it would help this caged bird fly free. It had been broadened into a make-shift runway, as usable as The Mall leading down to Buckingham Palace had once been but less obvious and as a result less pitted by enemy shelling.

Already the aircraft was waiting, barely fifty yards away. He recognised it at once, a Boeing L-15 Scout two-seater, straight off the production lines, an experimental model specially designed for short take-off and landing.

A fresh peal of artillery thunder shook the ground. Only a core of American forces remained in the metropolis, in the western half of the city, defending all approaches to their own embassy. The rest had pulled north, 'the better to regroup' he had been assured. He could not really complain. It was little more than he was doing himself; but it still somehow left the sour taste of abandonment. Would his 'flight' leave the same taste in the mouths of those he left behind?

If he had seen the small, slight figure who had emerged

timorously, in awe of the destruction around her, from the blackened blast doors he had used just a few moments before, he might even have stopped for a few minutes and tried to explain to her, in the hope that she, in turn, might explain to others.

But he did not. His eyes were on the plane and the man who came to meet him as he stomped towards it. For a moment he flinched. The uniform was unfamiliar. Then he remembered: the new president had renamed the Army Air Corps as the US Air Force. A new name for a new age. Now they had new tailoring to suit. It was typical of the uneven relationship all along: the British forces had barely enough ammunition; the Americans were buying new uniforms.

The empire still had style, though. He put his hand into his greatcoat and found what he was looking for. At times like these a little theatre was called for. As the air force officer came up to him, he pulled out his last Havana cigar, and asked for a light. Something the man would remember. Something to tell his grandchildren.

It was to his immense surprise, therefore, when the pilot produced not a Ronson cigarette lighter but a Colt automatic.

'I'm sorry, sir,' he said with that slow accent that marked him clearly as coming from south of the Mason-Dixon line. 'I regret to tell you there's been a change of plan.'

Chapter 50

'What happened?'

'What do you think? He shot him. Between the eyes. Then put another into the skull to be sure. Went back to his little plane and came back with a jerrycan of petrol. Poured it all over the body and set fire to it. I can still see it today.'

'But how ...?'

'I was there, Detective Inspector Stark. I was his secretary. One of them anyway. I followed him out when he left the War Room. I shouldn't have but I wanted to give him that,' the old lady pointed to the diary in Stark's hand. 'He'd left it on his desk. Probably deliberately I now realise. But I didn't know. I'll have it back, please.'

Stark handed it over, his mouth still gaping in astonishment, turned to Lizzie and said, 'The Americans killed him? Why?'

'Wrong question, Harry,' she replied as if it was the easiest thing in the world. 'Why not? They'd changed the plans. Roosevelt was dead. The new people in Washington didn't feel under the same obligation. How much love do you think America has ever really felt towards England. The relationship might have turned upside down at one stage but in the eyes of most of them we were still the empire they'd rebelled against. Look at their movies even today – the bad guys always have English accents.

'This was their big chance and they weren't going to share it. And certainly not their nuclear weapons. It would be so much easier if there were just two superpowers, not three.

Especially if one of them was governed by an old man hell-bent on revenge. With no Churchill – and no British empire – it would be a hell of a lot easier to divide the world into two new empires.'

'But it was all over. We … they'd lost.'

'No, you were right first time. We'd lost. They won. Both the Russians and the Yanks. Think about it. Think how inconvenient it would have been if the old man had survived. He had no intention of surrendering, of giving up the empire, just because the capital had fallen, no more than the Russians had with Napoleon or the Nazis at the gates of Moscow. He would have had the young princess, Elizabeth,' she blushed slightly at the name, 'crowned in Canada, as Queen and Empress, and used North America as a base to carry on the struggle on a global scale. It could have meant another ten, twenty, thirty even forty years of conflict.'

'But that's what we've had. The cold war.'

'Not cold, Harry, cool. A comfortable temperature. Small wars by proxy in parts of Asia and sub-Saharan Africa nobody cares much about. Afghanistan, Angola, but not Coca-Cola. Weapons testing with human guinea pigs. It's all been light entertainment. The real business was done back then. Think about it. For forty years the world has been neatly divided in two: Europe, mainland Asia and North Africa under Soviet influence. They already had Europe. With Britain out of the picture, the Chinese took Hong Kong back while the rest: India, Singapore, Iraq, Palestine, Transjordan, Egypt, all fell under the sway of Moscow, given 'independence' with communist governments: dictatorship by delegation.

'The western hemisphere, Australia, South Africa, Rhodesia, all the way up to the Sudan all became dependent on American money and muscle, not to mention the whole of the West Indies including Bermuda, the Bahamas, Barbados and Jamaica all joined Cuba and Puerto Rico in the United States' Caribbean co-prosperity zone: a protection racket by proxy.

'It was a carve-up, right from the beginning, a deal done between Washington and Moscow the minute they realised they both had nuclear weapons, and nobody else did. And it's served them very well, until now.'

Stark's mind was reeling. He wondered how much if any of this Fairweather was hearing, wherever he was, or what he would make of it.

'And that's why the Department, the DoSSers killed the American journalist, because they didn't want him reporting it? But he was American. Why would he?'

Lizzie looked at him almost pityingly as if he were a small child with learning difficulties. In a small, quiet but firm voice, she said: 'The DoSSers didn't kill him. We did.'

'I did,' said a deep voice forcefully. Malcolm, the Museum Man, the one with the floppy hair and the flabby hands.

'You. You did *that* to him. Blew half his head off and hung him under a bridge like a bit of meat on a butcher's hook. And you have the nerve to talk about inhumanity.'

'You watch your mouth …' the Museum Man growled.

'Quiet,' barked Lizzie. 'Okay, Harry, your point is valid. Malcolm does get carried away sometimes. There are reasons for it. But it was self-defence. Sort of. He tried to kill my gran. To shut her up and take the diary. To destroy the evidence of what they did. And he would have done it too. The bullet would have gone straight through her heart if Malcolm here hadn't had a premonition and jumped him just as he fired. As it is at her age, she may never have the use of one arm again.'

Stark looked and saw the dark brown stains around the shoulder of the old lady's sling.

'In any case, we wanted to send a message. To the CIA or whoever he was working for. Don't try it again. We thought that if it looked like it was the DoSSers had done it, it would scare off the ordinary plod, that the PP would leave it alone. But oh no, we hadn't counted on Harry bloody "hero" Stark.'

'The young lady's right, Harry. There's no more room for heroics.' The sudden interjection, out of nowhere, startled them all, as much as the old lady's scream that accompanied it.

'Okay guys, don't move, not anybody, not a muscle, and the old lady here's gonna be a-okay.'

To his horror Stark recognised the American accent at the same time as he saw – but barely acknowledged – Benjamin T. Fairweather, his angel Gabriel, the bearer of great tidings, metamorphosed into Lucifer with a drawn handgun held hard against a frightened, wounded, old lady's head.

Chapter 51

'Just move back, all of you, back towards Harry over there. Don't worry, he won't hurt you. He packs a mean rabbit punch, but I don't think he's carrying anything but my penlight torch and he's as surprised as you are. Just look at him.'

Stark's face was ashen. The immensity of the global strategy Lizzie had unveiled slowly sinking in, along the with the realisation that if even half of it was true, he had betrayed his calling not to side with the angels, but with a representative of the devil. In the world she had described, there were no angels. No saints. Only different shades of sinners.

As he stared, stupefied at the American he had trustingly put his faith in, he realised that even the man's voice was different. Before it had struck Stark as conveying an uneasy mixture of braggadocio and self-doubt, now it was cold, calm, self-confident and wholly unfazed by the fact that he was heavily outnumbered. This was not a man who was used to facing hard questions from editors; this was a man who was used to asking hard questions, and using hard means to get whatever answers he required.

It was Malcolm, the Museum Man, who replied, his heavily accented voice now a slow drawl almost languid with venom: 'You fucking scum. Why the hell shouldn't we just blow your brains away now, Yankee.'

'Stop it!' Fairweather snapped. 'Come one step further, and I'll do something we'll all regret.'

'You're going to kill her anyway. Just like your mate tried to. And when you do, you'll meet the same fate he did.'

Calmly, Malcolm produced an ancient-looking pistol and pointed it straight at the American.

'I don't think so,' said Fairweather. 'And nor do you, you know. Does he, Lizzie. Or aren't you running the show any more?'

Lizzie had moved back, not before giving Stark a baleful glare, and was now on the very edge of the platform. Her look was thunder, but she didn't deign to reply.

'You've got it wrong, you see,' continued Fairweather. 'I don't know what happened with my colleague – he always was a bit of a hothead – but I have no intention of doing any harm to this sweet little old lady here. All we – that is me and my compatriots – want to do is to help her regain her memory, make her understand what really happened all those years ago, and not the crazy, mixed-up version that's worked its way into her old grey head in the meantime.

'Winston was half-American. He was our pal. Our big hero. Presidents have had busts of him in the Oval Office since 1949. Now that Russia's teetering, communism's collapsing, we're going to reel you guys back in. Rehabilitate ol' Winnie-the-pooh, give you something to believe in again. So you can live the American dream. Rejoice in the free world. Drink Coca-Cola, eat Big Macs. You know it makes sense. That's the future. Not just for you, for everybody. Get used to it.

'The version of history you guys were getting all so worked up about is just pure pie in the sky. You know that, Miss Lizzie, or should I say Elizabeth – that's who you're named for, isn't it, the princess who should be queen? Hell, even your ol' gran here knows America would never betray Britain. Everyone knows that. And if they don't they soon will. There's a movie about it. The camera never lies. With the right management, this ol' gal here could even be a star. So just back off, Malc, or whatever your name is.'

The Museum Man glanced at Lizzie. She shook her head and he lowered his weapon.

'Now that's what I like to see,' said Fairweather. 'English and Americans all allies again, just like in the good old days. Now just do what you're told and we'll all be fine.

'First thing is – me and Mrs Goldsmith here are leaving, quietly and peaceably, but not by that godforsaken route we had to follow to get here. This is an old Deep Shelter, hell, if I'm not mistaken it might even be the one Eisenhower himself used. You sitting where old Ike used to sit?' Lizzie ignored him. 'Well, I reckon there's another way out of here, a whole lot easier. At the very least the way our friend Harry there got out of your little prison, though I don't fancy train-dodging and I'm not so sure the old lady here's quite up to it.'

The old lady gave a timid whimper. Fairweather was obviously controlling the pressure on her wounded arm. Even so, she piped up in that thin, ethereal voice from another era: 'I know what I saw, sir, and these people know too, and none of your bully boys will make any of us believe differently.'

'Sure thing, ma'am, sure thing. And nobody's going to force you, but I am going to ask you, very firmly, to come with me right now. You'll have every chance to tell the world what you know once we're out of this communist colony.'

'And just how do you plan to achieve that, even if we do show you how to get back above ground?' Lizzie had found her voice at last, and it was cold, chastened and angry.

'Don't you worry about that. We have our ways and means. For very special guests of the United States government, that is. You put in a request one day, and I just might see what I can do for you.'

Lizzie spat on the platform. The American tutted.

'Manners, manners. "Manners maketh the man". Isn't that one of your old English sayings. But then maybe it doesn't apply to women. Leastwise not women like you. But maybe you'd still be so kind as to indicate the exit from this little warren. We'll go quietly ...'

Then all hell broke loose.

It was the dogs they heard first, a sudden outburst of barking and yelping as if a pack of foxhounds had been simultaneously let off the leash, a howling and bellowing that was amplified by the echoing tunnels from which it emerged.

Then the arc lights hit them, a blinding wash of white-blue intensity that instantaneously swamped the subterranean world's glow-worm gloom. And the crackling growl of the megaphones.

'Department of Social Security. Stay right where you are. Do not move. I repeat: this is the Department of Social Security. Do not move.'

Everyone moved: ducked or dived. Throwing himself to the ground Stark caught a fleeting image of Fairweather and the old lady pressed back against the wall, the gun still held to her temple, and what appeared to be the Museum Man in stark silhouette brandishing his pistol.

Then there was an explosion and the light intensity halved, creating a ghastly cartoon world of darting figures and extenuated shadows. Stark scrabbled for the cover of darkness.

Chapter 52

Arthur Harkness stood to attention on the reviewing stand outside the National Gallery, his right arm raised in stiff salute as the first of the floats entered Stalingrad Square.

By his side stood his guest of honour, though the body language of the two men suggested relations were not as warm as the comradely kiss shown on state television had suggested. The 'wind of change' blowing in from Moscow felt decidedly chilly in London.

The crack troops of the New English Army had already passed by, as had the Ernie Bevin Boy Scouts and the Kent Collective Farmers with their tractors and ploughs. Now it was the time for the Socialist Society and Cultural Section, floats displaying achievements of art and design from the best of the capital's colleges.

At the back, on the final float, still halfway down the Strand, Kate Stark's hands were sweating. She knew what she was about to do. Knew what the consequences could be. And she was still determined to do it.

Lizzie had tried to dissuade her. But not too much. She knew that secretly the young woman admired her. And being admired by Lizzie Goldsmith was the best thing that had ever happened to her. Apart from meeting her grandmother, and hearing her story. And reading the pages of the diary of a man she had been brought up to believe was a monster and a coward.

Maybe he had been a monster, in some ways. So many people were. But he was no coward. That was sure. And so few things were sure. That was the point. That was why she had designed the stencils, stolen the materials from the art department at college. Painted the wall of Bankside power station with the image people had tried to forget. And, in a daring stunt that even Lizzie had been shocked by, taken her stencil to the Wall itself, no more than a few hundred metres from her brother the policeman's office.

The fact that her brother was a policeman had of course probably contributed to the ease with which she was allowed to take charge of the float for today's parade. That and the fact her father was a Hero of Socialism. She was a steady pair of hands. Safe. Reliable. She would show them. And she would show Tommy Paine who was a copper's nark. Even if she ended up in jail for doing so.

She had done her research, even if she had not obviously been able to see the photographs. But Lizzie's gran had confirmed they existed, had given her suggestions even. Told her that in any case they used to – probably still did – play tricks with photographs, doctor them to airbrush people out or paint them in.

Well, that's what she had done. Not painted people in but painted people as they were, in situations that had happened. And one that hadn't. She would use art to make a political statement. To shock and to challenge. It was all there, pre-painted on the double-sided three- by four-metre hoarding on the back of the float. The pictures everyone else thought it displayed – a series of working-class characters from Shakespeare – were on paper fixed to cover her own work. Paper she would rip down at the last minute, when she was in front of the reviewing stand. In front of Arthur Harkness himself. And the rest of them.

She would show them.

Chapter 53

Marchmain and his men had emerged in a Tube tunnel unlike any other with a short platform. On the tracks stood a single carriage covered in cobwebs and painted red, white and blue. The sign on the door said in large letter H.M.G ONLY. His Majesty's Government.

They had moved cautiously along the tunnel aware of a low hum and the possibility that the switch they had tripped upstairs to restore power and lighting to the lift shaft might have been a master, in which case the rails could be live too. He doubted it but you could not be too sure.

As soon as he detected voices, the tunnel ahead of them flooded with light and the men from the Department, as designated, raised either their megaphones or their automatic weapons. Marchmain was prepared for trouble, but also knew the shock effect of blinding light and commanding authority. He was not, however, prepared for the lunatic who launched himself out into full target range and with a levelled pistol fired immediately and directly at the source of the light. One of the arc carriers collapsed in a shattering of glass while the other automatically ducked, sending his beam bouncing around the platform ahead like the illumination for some surreal disco.

In the dancing beam the colonel could see people diving in panic for shelter. He ordered his men to fire a volley into the air. He wanted to capture, rather than kill, if at all possible.

The bright beam steadied, its crouching bearer regaining

courage and equilibrium. It picked out an extraordinary vignette. A tall man, holding a small, elderly woman, with a gun held tightly by the side of her head, pointed forward but still too close to her temple to be of comfort to her. The pair had moved towards the platform edge, into full range of Marchmain's armed men. At that moment he recognised Benjamin Fairweather.

'Wait. Hold your fire,' Fairweather called in an unmistakable American accent. 'I think we can negotiate.'

Just what the American thought he could negotiate Col Marchmain was never to know. At that precise moment the little old woman he was clasping tightly lurched to the side with all her weight. There was not much of it, but enough. For a millisecond they teetered on the platform edge, then toppled off, still locked in that unlikely embrace, to fall across the tracks. They must have touched both live rails simultaneously, although one alone would have been fatal. A flash of arcing electricity shot blue and white across the ground and briefly up one wall, accompanied by a sudden smell of cooking that rapidly became the stench of burnt flesh.

Then there was quiet. Marchmain surveyed the deserted platform ahead and cursed. The rats had run off into their hidey-holes. He doubted that they could go far, or fast. Even so, he ordered his men to advance quickly onto the platform to scour the side passages and investigate possible escape routes, using all necessary force to prevent flight, while he himself stepped slowly towards the smoking charred remains that lay across the track, careful not to touch the live rail himself.

It was not a pleasant sight. The voltage had sent their muscles into spasm, drawing their cheeks back in horrible grins, blackening their flesh. Marchmain felt sorry. He would much have preferred to have had a long conversation with the American, at his leisure and in a place of his choosing.

Who the little old lady was, he had no idea.

Chapter 54

From a pool of shadow Harry Stark watched in spellbound horror as the American and the old lady toppled from the platform onto the live rails. It had been no accident. She had pushed them both. He turned his eyes to where Lizzie had been, anticipating her grief. What he saw was her crouching against the wall in the furthest recess of the platform, gesturing frantically at him to come to her. Back along the platform the DoSS agents had lined up several of the others against the wall and were frisking them.

'Come on,' she shouted.

Behind her a steel door was set in the wall. She turned a round airlock-style handle and it swung open.

'Your grandmother … The others …'

'I know. But it wasn't an accident. You saw. She made a decision. She was a brave woman, but she was old and losing blood. A choice between the Americans and the DoSS wouldn't have looked very appealing. Hurry up. There's nothing we can do for anyone right now.'

'Where are we going?'

Stark was already talking to a retreating back. He followed it as best he could into yet another dark tunnel.

'Tell me the truth, Harry. You didn't lead them here?'

'Of course not.'

'You brought the American.'

She couldn't see him, but Stark hung his head, then shook it even though she wasn't looking at him: 'That was stupid.

You have to believe me, I had no idea. No idea about any of it. I'm still not sure I see straight.'

'Who can? It's not a straightforward world. How did the bloody DoSSers get here?'

'No idea. Honestly. I don't even know where we are, other than a crude guess. Was that really true, what the American said, that that was a Deep Level Shelter used by Eisenhower?'

'Probably. It makes sense, given Malcolm's grasp of the layout.'

'The layout?'

'Come on. You'll see. But shut up. We want to hope they stay in the main tunnel, especially as it looks like they've put the power back into the rails all the way.'

They had gone about fifty metres before Stark asked the question he wanted answered.

'All the way to where?'

'All the way to Churchill's bunker. Upon a time, anyway. This is part of a whole mesh of tunnels that they began in the 1930s and rapidly expanded after the outbreak of war. They were working on them right up until 1949, worried as hell that the other side would develop nuclear weapons first.'

'I thought anything like that had been filled in.'

'Most have. Now it runs into rubble and concrete. The whole area where the bunker was located was gone over with a fine-toothed comb in case there was any sign of a corpse. His corpse.'

'But I though it was burnt.'

'It was. But the Russians almost certainly found the remains. With a Colt 45 bullet in the head. Convenient, Churchill's personal weapon was a Colt 45, same gun issued to just about every American officer. Suited the suicide story.'

'So where are *we* going?'

'Wherever Malcolm's gone? He knows more about these tunnels than almost anyone. His job at the Library gives him amazing access to old documents. He almost certainly knows another way out. He told me there were several emergency staircases to the surface. It would help if we had a light.'

'Here,' said Stark. 'Take this.' She turned and he tossed her Fairweather's penlight. She clicked the switch and a thin, high-powered beam darted into the distance, showing a bifurcation in the concrete-walled tunnel.

'Good,' said Lizzie. 'This is where I thought we were. Most of the original government tunnels were like this, pedestrian only. That one leads to the old local telephone exchange underneath Northumberland Avenue and once probably linked through to Downing Street, the Bunker, maybe even the old Houses of Parliament. All the ones that lead under the frontier were blocked off when they built the Wall. You can only get so far in any direction. This one led to the Admiralty. Stops before the Arch of course, but I'm betting Malcolm knows something. Now shut up and don't waste your breath.'

Stark did as he was told. For the next few minutes they ran in silence, the penlight's beam dancing off the walls in front of them until they rounded a corner and its narrow clear beam illuminated a man kneeling at the foot of a fixed ladder.

'Malcolm. Thank God. Is there a way out ...?' Lizzie's question evaporated as she spoke. 'What ... what are you doing?'

From above, dangling down alongside the rungs of the fixed ladder were wires. Wires that Malcolm, the Museum

Man, was busy attaching to some primitive apparatus of chunky batteries that could only be one thing. A homemade detonator.

'I'm going to blow out the candles on their fucking birthday cake, that's what I'm doing.'

'What?'

'Up there,' he flicked his head upwards. 'Strapped to the underside of a manhole cover, an old concealed escape exit that just happens to be in front of the National Gallery where old Arthur and his mates are stood to attention. Fertiliser and sugar, not exactly gelignite, and not enough to take out the podium, but enough to show we're not all slaves prepared to line up and march past our masters.'

'Malcolm, you can't. You know Kate's there.'

Kate. Stark's blood ran cold. His little sister. Of course, the college float. She would be there. He glanced at his watch. Any minute now.

'She's doing it for us.'

Doing what? Stark's gaze flicked from one to the other. Neither paid him any attention.

'It's no good. Not enough. All they understand is force. Even this isn't enough. But it's a start. Why is he here anyway?'

'He's on our side.'

'Like my father was,' said Stark.

Lizzie winced.

'Your father was a …'

'Malcolm, don't.'

'Why the hell not? It's true, isn't it.'

'We don't know. It was never proved.'

'Never proved, my arse. More good men – and women – were arrested in the months after … Your father, Mr Metropolitan PP Stark, was a two-faced bastard. A fucking DoSSer

double agent, that's what he was. I don't know why I don't ...'
He pulled from inside his leather jacket the aged but effective pistol that had shot out the arc lights.

'Don't move. Any of you.'

The voice came from behind them. Marchmain. On his own, apparently. But armed. The bastard had followed them. Stark turned and in the same instant, Malcolm thrust the pistol into his belt and disappeared, pulling himself up the ladder, detonator in one hand.

'Tell him to come back,' said Marchmain, now clearly in view, his service Makarov levelled at them.

'He won't listen,' said Stark. 'You don't understand. There's a bomb.'

'What?'

'A bomb,' said Stark. 'Attached to a manhole cover. We're underneath the square.'

Marchmain's face froze. At that second a dulled but clearly audible blast of music sounded from above: 'There'll always be an England ... ' The national anthem. The parade was reaching its climax.

'I can stop him,' said Lizzie, who grabbed the rungs of the ladder and started climbing.

'Get her back,' said Marchmain. 'I don't want to kill you, Stark. I don't think you're a traitor. I just think you're confused.'

Stark stared up the well of the ladder. Lizzie, lighter and more agile, had caught up with Malcolm and seized hold of his foot. They were about four metres above his head. He heard a gruff expletive, then a shout and a clunk against concrete. At his feet lay Malcolm's ancient pistol. He had pulled it from his belt only to have Lizzie knock it from his hand. Stark dropped to the ground and snatched it.

'What are you waiting for, Stark?' Marchmain shouted. 'You have a weapon now. Use it.'

Stark glanced at the DoSS man for a second in puzzlement and then he understood.

He stared up the length of the ladder. Malcolm had struggled free of Lizzie's grasp and was several rungs above her, the makeshift detonator still clutched in his hand. The image of the dead body under the bridge, its head nearly severed, fleeted through Stark's mind. And then far more vividly, the face of his little sister somewhere up there above them. In harm's way.

'Lizzie, get back. Against the wall.'

She glanced down and understood in an instant.

Stark took the ancient weapon in both hands, braced himself as he had done a thousand times on the Met firing range, aimed up the length of the ladder, to where Lizzie was splayed against the wall a few rungs beneath his target. He hoped and prayed his aim was good enough. And fired.

His aim was not perfect. But it was good enough. Just. A rattle and clunk and the detonator landed on the ground at his feet, splashed with blood. He had hit the Museum Man on his outstretched arm. From above came a cry of anguish and pain, and then a violent curse. Malcolm had lost his grip, and fallen. But not far enough. His uninjured hand had flailed out and caught hold of the first available object. Lizzie's leg. She screamed but didn't try to shake him off, as if torn between self-preservation and saving the life of the man clinging to her. Stark watched in horror, terrified that at any moment she would risk everything by reaching down to give him a hand.

But Malcolm was the heavier by far. Just as she had not been able to hold him back for long, he could not hold on to her. Stark could see his legs dangling in the air, desperate to find purchase on the rungs of the ladder. One of them made it. Just. And then gravity took over. The big man's hand slipped. He reeled back against the opposite wall and then fell.

Stark sprang back, just in time, as the body crashed to the ground in front of him. A thin rivulet of blood ran from one ear. The Museum Man was history.

'Well done, Stark,' said Marchmain. 'Your father would have been proud of you.'

Stark lifted his head and looked Marchmain in the eye. And shot him in it.

Chapter 55

Detective Sergeant Dick Lavery looked at his watch and smiled. He would be off duty in ten minutes. The parade had finished an hour ago. For nearly four hours now he'd been standing in front of the National Gallery, mingling with the rent-a-crowd, keeping an eye out. Just for pickpockets and stuff like that, of course. The Department were on hand for any other sort of trouble.

Not that any had been expected. Just as nobody had expected what actually did happen. Lavery thought all hell would break loose when that business with the float happened right in front of the podium. For a moment it looked like it might. He could see the DoSSers in the crowd moving forward like lightning, and felt an instinctive twinge of sympathy for the young girl who had done the business, even if she must have known what was coming to her. Even she looked stunned by what actually happened. Lavery still found it hard to believe.

Although possibly not quite as hard to believe as what was happening in front of his eyes at this very moment. He thought he had heard a noise, a strange grating noise like scraping metal. Coming from the ground not far away from him. And then the manhole cover had begun to move, screeching as if it hadn't been turned in decades. Gradually, in front of Lavery's bemused eyes, the thing began to lift. But he couldn't stop his jaw dropping in sheer amazement at what emerged from it: the ragged-looking but unmistakable head of his boss, Detective Inspector Harry Stark. Who clambered out and dusted himself down, followed by an equally dishevelled but undoubtedly very attractive dark-haired young lady.

'Sir! Boss! What the f … Pardon my French, miss!'

Stark gave a brief smile as he threw an arm round his shoulders.

'I was expecting a welcome committee. But this is as good as it gets. You know we've been hanging on the top rung of a ladder down there for an hour waiting for the fuss to die down.'

'Harry, come here. Look at this. Look what your amazing little sister did.' Lizzie was standing staring up at the one remaining float on the square, parked right in front of the National Gallery.

Stark walked across and joined her, staring up in amazement at the float, at the great double-sided hoarding. Only a few days ago he would have been astonished, rendered speechless. Even now he was shocked, awestruck. At the sheer audacity of it.

On each side of the huge hoarding standing on the lorry bed were stencilled images, similar to the Churchill images on Bankside, and the one he had uncovered on the Wall, but painted in to look like photographs, is shades from grey to sepia. Life size. A montage of images with dates written large across each: Stalin seated alongside Roosevelt and Churchill, and the date Tehran 1943, the next Stalin shaking hands with Ribbentrop, Hitler's foreign minister, and the date Moscow 1939. The other side showed Hitler with Molotov, Stalin's foreign minister with the date Berlin 1940, Khruschev with Richard Nixon, the date Moscow 1959, and Churchill with von Stauffenberg, Hitler's assassin, dated Berlin 1944. And finally the image that had become iconic over the past week, Churchill giving the V-sign with a pistol held to his own head and a question mark over it.

There was a caption underneath.

The Lesson of History: √ласность.

Glasnost. At least those years of compulsory Russian had been of use. The idea that his sister, his little sister, was responsible for this filled him with awe. And pride. And sudden fear.

'What happened to her?'

'Her?'

'The girl. Was there a girl on the float?'

'Oh, yes. A girl and a couple of blokes. From the college. I must admit I thought they were in for it. Doing something like this. In front of the old man. As soon as they tore down the paper that covered all this. You could see the lads from the Department bearing down on them. Baying for blood, they were.'

'What stopped them?'

Lavery laughed, shrugged his shoulder and gestured up at the gallery, to the now empty rostrum in front of it.

'He did.'

'Harkness!?'

'Hardly! He looked as if he was about to burst a blood vessel. The other bloke, the Russian. The one with the funny birthmark on his head.'

'You're telling me the General Secretary of the Communist Party of the Soviet Union intervened to stop the DoSS tackling a political provocation.'

Lavery nodded. 'Well, not directly. As such. The DoSS lads were just about to go for it, when he started clapping. You should have seen the look on old Harkness's face.'

'I can imagine. But what happened to the girl?'

'She could hardly believe it either. But she wasn't taking any chances. Done her bit, hadn't she? She and her mates legged it, heading for the pub to celebrate getting away with it, I shouldn't be surprised.'

Stark sighed with unexpected relief.

'But why is this still here?'

'Apparently he wants it for his art collection. I had a word with one of the diplomatic protection boys afterwards. It seems there really is a wind of change blowing. The word is he's also asked for an amnesty for all political prisoners. Harkness is furious, but he can hardly refuse. Without the Kremlin behind him he's nothing. There's talk of rumblings in the Mansion House, a politburo coup against Harkness. History in the making.'

'History?' said Stark, looking up at his sister's artwork and scratching his head. 'Whatever that is.'

Lizzie grabbed his arm and said, 'It's whatever you want it to be, Harry. People don't just live history; they make it.'

'Including my father? I don't even know which side he was on.'

'Yours, Harry. Yours and Katy's. That's the one thing that was never in doubt. He was on your side.'

'If we open a quarrel between the past and the present, we shall find that we have lost the future.' Stark turned to stare at his sergeant. 'Not me, sir,' Lavery said. 'Him. Winston Churchill.'

'Finding the future,' Lizzie said, and stood on tiptoes to kiss Harry Stark on the lips. 'I'll drink to that.'

'Me too,' said Lavery. 'I could murder a pint.'

The End
(or at least its beginning)

Author's Note

Alternative histories are a fetish. You either love them or hate them. I love them and have read and admired many of the genre, from Len Deighton's *SS-GB* to Kingsley Amis's *Russian Hide-and-Seek* and Robert Harris's *Fatherland*. My version is extrapolated very largely from my own experience.

In the early 1980s I lived and worked for Reuters news agency as the sole non-German correspondent in East Berlin and towards the end of that decade returned for *The Sunday Times* to report on the delirious and life-enhancing spectacle of the Berlin Wall's demise. A few weeks before that happened, on the eve of the major parade, attended by Soviet leader Mikhail Gorbachev, to mark the fortieth anniversary of the East German state, major anti-communist demonstrations broke out on the streets of East Berlin. I was caught up in them and like many others was arrested and transported to police cells on the outskirts of the city. As a foreigner I was singled out for interrogation by the Stasi secret police, held overnight and expelled from the country the next morning.

It was only a matter of weeks before I was back. It turned out that Gorbachev had criticised the East German leader Erich Honecker for failing to appreciate the need for reform. Before long he was gone and the chain of events that led to the Wall's collapse set in place. Anyone who would like to know more about those specific events I refer to my memoir *1989: The Berlin Wall: My Part in its Downfall*, also published by Arcadia Books.

Living in divided Berlin, on the 'wrong' side of the Wall, was both daunting and fascinating. In attempting to explain it to others, particularly friends and family back home in Britain, I frequently asked them to imagine what it might be like if the same thing had happened to London. To my surprise it was extremely easy to draw a similar line through our own capital, placing monuments and great buildings in positions that corresponded remarkably to their German equivalents. For example in this book, Admiralty Arch corresponds to the Brandenburg Gate, Trafalgar (Stalingrad) Square to Pariser Platz, the Houses of Parliament to the Reichstag. Similarly my Leicester Square ghost Underground station corresponds to Unter den Linden in Berlin, which was in the East but closed and unmarked above ground, while north-south Western trains passed underneath.

Underground London is a complex and fascinating place. All the tunnels and other structures I have referred to in this book are essentially real, although I have taken some liberties with geography.

My deep shelter between Charing Cross and Leicester Square is based on several that were constructed between 1941 and 1942. The most notable survival is that near Goodge Street (a few hundred metres north of my location) which was commandeered as an emergency headquarters by General Eisenhower, the American head of Allied Forces. It last played a military role in 1956 when it was used as a temporary billet for 8,000 troops bound for the disastrous Suez adventure. Today this is sealed off from the Tube network and run by a private company as an important secure underground storage facility. The original exits at ground level can still be seen in Chenies Street, near Tottenham Court Road

The secret system of government tunnels running under

Whitehall is real and was begun in the 1930s, substantially expanded in the early years of the Second World War, and further during the cold war. Although their existence is widely known, details are highly classified, but the tunnels are reliably believed to connect the Houses of Parliament, No. 10 Downing Street, the Ministry of Defence and several underground telephone exchanges near Trafalgar Square, as well as Churchill's 'bunker', a limited part of which has, since 1983, been open to the public as the Cabinet War Rooms. There is also believed to be a separate spur which runs under the Mall as far as Buckingham Palace so that in a modern crisis the monarch and her prime minister could, if need be, meet without venturing above ground.

During the Kosovo crisis and the war in Iraq, it was discreetly admitted that top-level strategic meetings were held in a modern, reinforced citadel under Whitehall known as COBRA, a glamorous acronym for the more mundane Cabinet Office Briefing Area.

There is indeed a bone-filled crypt underneath St Bride's which dates back to at least the sixth century and probably earlier and was only rediscovered after the bombing raids of 1940. The crypt is open to visitors by appointment and offers a rare glimpse of the city's archaeology. Not all of it has been excavated; however, it does not, as far as has yet been discovered, afford a means of entry to the main sewers.

The Fleet River which features prominently in depictions of London before the end of the eighteenth century (notably Samuel Scott's *Entrance to the Fleet River* painted c.1750 and hanging in London's Guildhall Art gallery) was an important waterway until pollution forced its enclosure and eventual incorporation into the new sewer system.

London's main sewers were substantially laid out by

Joseph Bazalgette between 1859 and 1865 following a cholera outbreak and waste pollution so extreme that members of parliament were in 1858 indeed forced to evacuate their new building because of the stink from the adjacent river. The new sewage system incorporated into the mammoth construction project that saw the Victoria Embankment replace the old river shoreline was considered one of the engineering wonders of the modern world.

Installing the Underground railway at the same time was a stroke of inspiration; unfortunately the District Line to be laid along the Embankment was not far enough advanced, so the whole structure had to be dug up again for its installation some four years later. Some things never change.

Further reading:

1989, The Berlin Wall, (My Part in its Downfall) Peter Millar (Arcadia 2009)

War Plan UK. Duncan Campbell (Burnett) 1982

London Under London. Trench and Hillman (John Murray)

Making of the Metropolis. Stephen Halliday (Breedon) 2003

Dunkle Welten. Arnold und Salm (Ch. Links Verlag)

Subterranean City. Anthony Clayton (Historical Publications)

London Beneath the Pavement. Michael Harrison (Davies)